The DEAD CURE

by
Woody Tanger

BRANDEN PUBLISHING COMPANY
Boston

D1446075

© Copyright 1996
by Woody Tanger

Library of Congress Cataloging-in-Publication Data

Tanger, Woody.
    The dead cure / by Woody Tanger.
        p. cm.
    ISBN 0-8283-2021-7 (pbk. : alk. paper)
    I. Title.
    PS3570.A524D4   1996
    813'.54--dc20   96-13653
                                                        CIP

BRANDEN PUBLISHING COMPANY
17 Station Street
Box 843 Brookline Village
Boston, MA 02147

ACKNOWLEDGEMENTS

I wish to acknowledge with thanks the contributions of many persons who helped make *The Dead Cure* possible. The four physicians who collaborated asked to remain safely behind a curtain of anonymity and I respect and understand their decision.

Special thanks to Captain Mary Kathy Odahl of the United States Air Force whose guidance and wisdom ushered me across so many difficult paths.

Four persons who serve the public in Massachusetts helped me. They are: Mr. Sean Fitzpatrick, Director of the Massachusetts Department of Public Health, Ms. Charlene Zion in the Department of Vital Statistics, Mr. Mark Fairbank in the Boston Medical Examiner's Office, and Ms. Judith McCarney at Boston City Hall.

Without encouragement and enthusiastic support of my entire family, *The Dead Cure* could not have been completed. Much of this book was written at their summer home on Cape Cod whose spectacular views of Nantucket Sound inspired me to keep going.

Finally, I thank my agents, *Ike* Taylor Williams and Elaine Rogers at the Palmer and Dodge Agency in Boston.

***

AUTHOR'S NOTE: The razor thin line between fiction and fact is often unseen. It was necessary to cross into the real world in order to tell this story.

I dedicate this book to those who labor to prevent the day of the "Dead Cure".

CONTENTS

INTRODUCTION

D ying on the 7th Floor is a way of life. There are no reprieves or last minute commutations.

The 7th Floor in Boston's famed Charles River Medical Center has 50 beds and a rotating community of patients whose ultimate fate is certain but whose experimental treatments have headlined medical textbooks. The next Chief of Medicine will not be the first to win a Nobel Prize since John F. Kennedy was President. Since the 7th Floor was inaugurated as a collaborative with Gene World, the Department of Defense, and the Charles, 7th Floor physicians have won worldwide acclaim, fortune and glory. Medical students from across the globe covet a chance to watch Chief of Medicine Dr. Timothy Marks and his Nobel Prize winning wizardry.

In March of 1994, one of the beds was occupied by Mr. Steven Hays, a quiet 40 year old English teacher in the Boston schools. He endured needle biopsies, ultrasonography, computerized axial tomography (CAT scan) and blood chemistry tests. The verdict was unanimous: all tests sentenced him, without chance of appeal, to death from advanced pancreatic cancer. The pancreas is about 6 inches long and shaped like a hand grenade, wider at one end and narrowing at the other. It produces juices that digest food and hormones that regulate how the body uses food. Fewer than 20% of those afflicted survive one year, and only 3% are alive five years after diagnosis. There is no cure.

That same month, a 2nd year resident on the 7th Floor, intoxicated by 48 hours without sleep and endless coffee refills, misread Hays prescribed dosage of oral pancreatic enzymes, bicarbonates and experimental drugs. Six months later in September, Hays was discharged from the Charles disease free.

Since there is no cure, the Charles discharge papers read: MIS-DIAGNOSIS. Steven Hays regained his normal weight and returned to teach school, feeling cured, regardless of what the hospital said.

His physician, 2nd year resident and Harvard Medical School graduate, Dr. Judith Sims, is dead.

The 7th Floor at the Charles is a curious place. It's where those who should die are being cured and those hunting for cures are dying. Welcome to the Dead Cure.

Chapter One:
Funeral in Toledo

The flight from Boston to Toledo for the funeral of Dr. Judith Sims was just under two hours. Dr. Timothy Marks crowded his lanky frame into a coach seat as he reminisced with his wife Sally and the remaining six residents from the 7th Floor.

Dr. Timothy Marks, "Dr. Tim", descended ("ascended" as he preferred to say) from a family of prominent Boston physicians. His father, grandfather and brothers were doctors. Marks married his college sweetheart, Sally, who was devoted to him and their six children. None of his children decided on medicine as a career, and that didn't seem to bother him in the least.

Dr. Timothy Marks looked like the doctor from a Norman Rockwell painting, with just enough gray hair, age, and wrinkles to get you comfortable. His brown eyes peered out from under bushy eyebrows. No one saw him wearing anything except bow ties and a striped blue shirt. Marks' face said, "Relax, it's going to be OK." Bruised black tie shoes testified that he had walked through it all and seen it all. Many people remarked that he had a surgeon's fingers. They were long and thin and matched his athletic build. The Chief of Medicine's age was a mystery, with most guessing he was about 75, although he looked 55. Marks jogged, played tennis, loved summer hiking, and welcomed the chance each winter to bump into younger staff members on New Hampshire ski slopes.

"What are you doing here, Dr. Marks?"

He'd always answer sarcastically, "Same as you, skiing, except I'm going uphill."

Some imagined that he was the walking recreation of movie star Henry Fonda. Marks' commanding presence and deep modulated voice enhanced that image. He never raised his voice. Marks' distinguished and confident *look* remained the same, whether he was in the cafeteria or speaking before a medical convention.

The founder of the 7th Floor offered himself as part doctor, part confessor, and part teacher. Most importantly, he was a hero figure standing atop the moral high ground. He challenged everyone on the 7th Floor to emulate him. Thus, his insatiable desire for public recognition seemed inconsistent with the other parts of his life. Ego was his inside blemish that simmered just below his skin and sometimes broke through in ugly ways. Even the letterhead of the 7th Floor carried his name in type face not much smaller than that of the Charles. Marks' publicity pictures were always available to media through his secretary, in either 5x7 or 6x10, color or black and white--take your pick. Audio or video tapes were also available. He was not a shy man.

His wife Sally trekked in town once a week to join him for the symphony. She picked him up in her car, acknowledging his ongoing love affair with Boston's antique looking subway system-- the *T*. Marks' office was decorated with a huge color map of the entire Boston subway system, including notes at the bottom containing all sorts of subway trivia. It was this trivia that he enjoyed reciting when anyone asked about the map. During a 1977 blizzard, he recalled how his train was stuck overnight and great memories were created with his fellow passengers. By morning everyone had exchanged names and phone numbers. Marks kept the list in his desk for 17 years. The distance from the Charles Hospital to the *T* subway stop was about one mile. Marks proudly walked the distance instead of taking the Hospital's orange shuttle bus. For Marks, the worse the weather, the more fun.

The 7th Floor at the Charles was an obsession inside Marks' head. He worked a full schedule in the Hospital's research department. Marks labored nights and weekends to create a floor dedicated exclusively to experimental research. With no funds from the Charles, he solicited research companies that would underwrite all the Hospital's expenses in exchange for the rights to treatments that were discovered on the 7th Floor.

The charter of the Charles prohibited the conveyance of rights from any cures discovered. Research companies were more interested in the profits from treatments than the all-or-nothing gamble of cures. Marks tapped into his network of war time connections to get the Department of Defense committed as an observer. The Defense Department gained access to his state-of-the-art research at no cost. Some of the treatments would probably have direct military applications. The Defense Department provided military transportation for the Charles. No place in the world would be like this imagined research facility which owned Marks' thoughts by day and dreams by night.

When Marks succeeded, his only problem was to find space. He always thought that it was a good omen that the 7th Floor library was designated as the new location. Now, much of the Charles medical library contains reference to discoveries on the 7th Floor. Marks made the Hospital library move to the 3rd floor--his last stop when showing a senator or governor around the Hospital. As if he had called ahead before the tour, there would be books lying on a table, opened to a chapter detailing some discovery on Dr. Timothy Marks' 7th Floor.

The Great Lakes blurred below and Marks' imagined how distant this was from his last flight with a different team of residents. Ten years ago they had boarded an international flight to Oslo to accept another Nobel Prize. Glory and acclaim surrounded them as they departed Boston's Logan Airport. This time there were no cameras, no reporters, and no comfort anyone could find from the death of Judith Sims. When a 27 year old superstar doctor dies there are no words for consolation. While sun sparkled outside the aircraft, her death made it a rainy day inside.

"Simsy," as most on the 7th Floor called her, looked like she had just acquired her learner's permit. Her blonde hair in pigtails and midwestern green eyes crowned her with the look of an All-American homecoming queen. Marks imagined her riding in a convertible down Main Street, USA with a golden sash over one shoulder while waving to everyone. "Simsy" was more than a petite, cute, pretty blonde. She was a first class intellectual explorer able to traverse thickets of complex medical data. Marks fondly remembered her twin passions. Many lunches in the 7th Floor's special cafeteria were punctuated with endless talk about her beloved *Detroit Tigers* and mastery of *The New York Times* crossword puzzles. Monday morning was a particularly vivid day as hospital doctors and nurses would bring Sims their unfinished puzzles.

Marks talked and his residents huddled around catching each word as if listening to an elder Indian chieftain dispensing wisdom unknown to others. Marks turned to Dirk Eldridge, tallest of the group.

"Dirk, what are you, about 7 feet?"

"No sir, 6-10."

"Dirk, I told you that basketball was a better bet than medicine. And, Dirk, how do you fit in the cockpit when you fly in those small planes?"

"It's easy, sir. I love flying. There's room if you want a ride. Too bad. I never could get Simsy to go with me."

Marks joked that his residents were hired by height. Dirk Eldridge was the tallest and "Simsy" the shortest.

The other five on Marks' team were Allen Fiengold, Nancy Debbs, Gaetano "Guy" Piccard, Karen Ferris and most recognizable of all, Ernie Green. Rumpled and disorganized from head to toe, Green's feet melted into his aging and dark brown tennis sneakers. Each resident was very different. All had earned the title of medical superstar through their own special exploits. They combined clinical skills with a detective nose for clues.

Toledo was cloudy and calm as their flight landed. The funeral for "Simsy" was not crowded. Most of her hometown friends had scattered and lost touch when she moved to Boston. Marks kept hoping for some magical parade to pass by with "Simsy" waving. After the funeral everyone stopped at the Sims' home and settled in for small talk with her parents and twin sister. Marks had met her parents a few times during family visits to Boston. Scattered on the kitchen table were school yearbooks, letters, and pictures of family vacations including a reunion on Cape Cod in 1993.

Marks saw the many pictures that showed "Simsy" and Dirk together.

For several hours they talked and then Marks gently moved towards the door for the inevitable and uncomfortable good-byes. Marks hugged Simsy's mother. Sally Marks looked on and felt her husband's pain, masked by his years of experience at saying "good-bye" to patients. She knew he died a little with each farewell.

Simsy's mother reached out and clutched Marks' hand tightly. She would not let go.

"Dr. Marks, who do I tell this to? About two weeks ago my little girl called from Boston and said she thought someone was following her home at night."

Marks saw the pain written across her face as she held his hand even tighter.

"She didn't want me to bother anyone and asked me not to call the police."

"Well, I called them and they never called back", Simsy's father interrupted. He had little to say all day, but the tone of his voice echoed rage and uncertainty about what happened to his daughter.

Still clutching Marks' hand, Mrs. Sims pulled Marks closer to her.

"And something else Dr. Marks, Simsy said something wonderful happened with one of her patients. I never heard her sound so excited. She said it was a miracle. But she also said the other doctors wouldn't believe it. What did she mean?"

"I'm so sorry Mrs. Sims. I just don't know."

The flight to Boston was a solemn time for everyone. For Dirk Eldridge it was more time to ponder what happened. Silly thoughts, too, like what if the *Tigers* win the next World Series. He also remembered the words of Simsy's mother. Why hadn't Simsy told him? He would have reacted instantly. Then, of course, that may be why she had not.

The sun was setting on a beautiful late summer day in September as their jet circled and began its final approach into Logan Airport. Dirk had brought his family's private plane into Logan many times using the same approach pattern. Off to the

12 Woody Tanger

West was the Boston skyline, the Charles River, Cambridge to the north and the tall tower stack that dominates the medical center.

Chapter Two:
The Big Sleep

A thletic and healthy 27 year old women don't go to sleep and sleep forever. The medical examiner said Dr. Judith Sims died on Saturday, September 11th. Dirk discovered her body when he returned Monday morning from a family visit in New Hampshire. They shared an apartment in Brookline, an easy bike ride from the Charles. Dirk and Sims were best friends and lovers for more than two years. They were roommates who thrilled at the chance to compete with each other on the 7th Floor. They agreed on virtually nothing except their shared love of baseball, medicine, and each other.

Sims was a walking, talking *Detroit Tigers* baseball encyclopedia, while Dirk loved the *Boston Red Sox* in blissful ignorance. When Sims was 17, the *Tigers* made it to the 1984 World Series with the *San Diego Padres*. For her, that World Series was yesterday. She still had T shirts and caps from the Series. Detroit was about an hour's drive north of her home in Toledo. Sims got tickets for games 3,4, and 5. She reminded anyone who'd listen that she was in the stands when the *Tigers* won the World Series, beating the *Padres* 8-4. No baseball fact was too obscure for her to discard.

"Did you know the Tigers scored the first run in the first game of the World Series when two batters hit safely? How about the Tigers beating the Cubs in the 1935 World Series, 4 games to 2. And I'll bet you didn't know that 10 years later my Tigers beat the Cubs again in the World Series, this time 4 games to 3.

"Hey, is any one listening?"

With Dirk towering at 6 feet 10 and Sims just barely 5 feet, they mastered the art of handling jokes and innuendoes about their height difference. No, they didn't use props. Near her side of the bed, Sims kept a picture of Dirk in an old 1930's flying costume. The master at hassling them was their best friend, Ernie Green. Sims always kidded Dirk that she really loved Ernie most, except she thought his brown sneakers were a health hazard. Not content to lay back and take it, Dirk would dare Ernie and Simsy to date--saying he could not see her anyway without getting down on his knees. The banter back and forth between Dirk, Sims, and Green was their public way of affirming the affection that bound them together.

When Dirk found Simsy sprawled on the bedroom floor, she was wearing her 1984 Tigers World Series T shirt and socks. Suddenly all her baseball trivia about the *Tigers* seemed so very precious and so lost. That's exactly how she was dressed Saturday morning when Dirk went to New Hampshire. The phone was on the floor near her right hand. When he saw her, Dirk knew there was nothing to do except dial 911.

He called the police. Then he rushed to the bathroom and vomited.

Their apartment was filled with cops. There were more than he had ever seen at one time. Dirk slumped on their bed. Simsy's body was covered with a pink sheet. A female cop sat next to him and opened a ringed notebook. Her questions came gently. Dirk never remembered those first questions or how he answered.

"Did you call her folks? They're in Toledo" The cop said, "No."

For two hours, Dirk sat and answered questions. Yes, he thought the Boston police should notify the police in Toledo and they should visit Simsy's home. Then he would call her parents. A detective joined the circle of questioners.

"I'm Detective Rico Santori, Division 3...I know this isn't easy, but we're almost done.

"When did you leave for New Hampshire? Where did you stay and who did you stay with? Why didn't you bring your girlfriend along? How long did it take for you to call the police after finding her? Did she have any illnesses? What sort of doctor was she? Did she handle drugs a lot? What about her friends?

Who were the neighbors? Who else did she work with? Did they talk during the weekend?"

Someone new entered the room and Dirk knew instantly that he was no cop.

This new face was the medical examiner, the *ME*. His face had witnessed so much it could no longer reflect. It was a dead face, empty of everything except huge cut crevices of skin that formed a checkered design. When Dirk looked in his eyes, nothing came back. His eyes were hollow. In all his time at the Charles treating terminal patients, he had never seen a death mask like the one worn by this *ME*.

"Dr. Eldridge, meet Dr. Jim McCann, our medical examiner."

Dirk couldn't reach out to touch a hand that was moving across the body of Simsy. He simply acknowledged him with a look.

Detective Santori turned to Dirk, "Listen, maybe you should call and get a lawyer. I mean, you'd just be doing that for yourself. Don't worry, this is accidental, we figure, but, well...".

Dirk shot up from the bed, "I don't need a lawyer."

Santori pulled off the sheet covering Simsy and looked.

"What the hell are you doing; she's just wearing a T shirt."

Dirk spoke as if the detective was violating her privacy, as if she were a breathing person.

Santori asked, "Is that how you last saw her dressed?"

Dirk sat on the bed and picked up her Tigers baseball cap. "Yeah, she was in bed when I left. She was awake and wearing the T shirt."

Santori leaned close and whispered, "...and did you two, you know."

Dirk knew what the question was and said softly, "Yes, just before I left, we made love."

Dirk needed something to drink and went to the refrigerator to pour some orange juice. When he returned, Santori took a whiff and said, "Smells great! What is it, fresh squeezed? Bet that's expensive."

Dirk shrugged his shoulders, "Guess so, I didn't buy it."

What struck everyone in the apartment was that here was a young woman with no medical history of any kind, lying dead on the floor, with no bruise marks or slightest hint of abuse.

"OK Simsy, very funny, you can get up now!"

Dirk thought she looked healthier than the medical examiner who was standing over her body and telling a photographer what to shoot.

Santori asked Dirk to walk with him to the door.

Nothing in Dirk's life had prepared him for a moment like this. Everything in life, from his clothes to his schooling and family, was so neatly packaged. From head to toe he looked like a Ralph Lauren model with wavy hair and a strong face.

His family owned a chain of factory outlet stores that originated in Manchester and expanded across New England. It was his dad who taught him how to fly. His father had been a bomber pilot in the Air Force during World War II and their home was filled with memorabilia from those flying days. His two sisters were active in the business. Every Christmas the Eldridge family would send out nearly 1,000 custom designed cards with the family settled around the fireplace. Dirk's parents and sisters were very fond of Sims and on several occasions when Dirk worked weekends, she came up alone.

Dirk thought, "Things like this don't happen to good people".

"Tough one, kid. Take my advise, pack a bag and get out of here for a few nights. Have you got some friends you can stay with? Let us know where you'll be. This isn't where you want to be. I'll wait and give you a ride. Questions?"

Dirk called Ernie Green. Green was not home. Dirk paged him and within minutes the phone rang.

"Ernie, where are you? I need you. Simsy's dead."

Dirk hung up without waiting for Ernie to answer.

Dirk packed a bag and prepared to leave for Ernie's apartment. Then he remembered.

"Santori, we each had telephones because Simsy is left handed. She never used that phone they found next to her body. It was mine."

Santori scribbled something in his book.

Then the detective drove Dirk to Ernie Green's apartment.

Chapter Three:
'Till Love Do Us Part

When Dirk arrived at Ernie's apartment, it was already crowded with doctors, nurses and staff from the Charles. Like cramming for a mid term, everyone talked and asked questions--their conversations, like their lives, lost in a time warp between day and night.

"Dr. Tim!" someone announced. As he walked in, everyone looked to see the expression on his face. There was none.

"This is a bad time for us and I don't have any answers. We'll get through this together and that's all I can say."

That was enough, coming from the creator of the 7th Floor and the force around which his staff orbited. Marks looked tired but strong as he moved around grabbing each person's hand for a few moments of private talk. He was in Ernie's apartment no more than 15 minutes. No one could ever remember a visit like this, but no resident from the 7th Floor had ever died.

Ernie and Dirk talked through the night. They reminisced about Simsy. They talked by telephone with her parents. This was their first "all-nighter" together since medical school. Then, suddenly, it was eight AM.

"Hey Dirk, it's that detective on the phone." Ernie huddled near Dirk.

"Dirk, this is Detective Santori. Feeling any better today?"

"Guess I'm OK."

"Can you come down for a blood test?"

"Hold on."

"Hey, Ernie, they want me down there for a blood test."

Ernie shrugged his shoulders.

"Detective, why?"

"Look, the ME thinks he has a handle on your friend's cause of death and it's a bit wild. Just come in and we'll take some blood and wrap it up. Don't worry. You know where we are?"

Division 3, Boston Police, is a red brick building near Copley Square. It could double as a library or art gallery. Outside it is wrapped in Boston charm, with twin columns and turn of the century blue lights. Inside, nothing is quaint. Dirk and Ernie walked up one flight of stairs and into a bullpen of ugly wooden desks and scratched metal filing cabinets.

Santori ushered them into his cubicle office. Slumped in a chair at the rear of the room was the "dead face".

"You know Dr. Jim McCann."

Santori turned to McCann pointing, "Remember, this is Dr. Eldridge. You haven't met his friend, Dr. Ernie Green. They work together."

Dirk fixed his eyes on McCann, amazed that his face looked the same. His eyes were nothing but empty holes. Ernie nudged Dirk in confirmation.

Dirk and Ernie parked themselves against a wall, saying "thanks-but-no-thanks" to the offered chairs.

"Detective, you asked me to tell you about anything that came to mind later. Simsy and I never bought fresh squeezed OJ. It cost too much. There was a quart in the 'frig' and I don't remember either of us buying it. I'm sure it's no big deal. Maybe she splurged. And there's one other thing. This is really going to sound silly. Whenever Simsy and I went to baseball games, I'd buy peanuts. You know, peanuts is baseball. Simsy never ate peanuts. I asked her why and the answer was always that she didn't like them."

Without any indication of having heard him, Dr. McCann suddenly began to speak.

"Anaphylaxis is one of those things that should not happen. I don't have to tell you both what it is. Anaphylaxis is to common allergies what the hydrogen bomb is to a firecracker."

The doctors knew exactly what he meant. Anaphylaxis is a speeding train that only goes in one direction...downhill. Within seconds victims are run over by a vicious stampede of sneezing, pounding of the eyes, itching in the mouth, numbness around the mouth, then a pounding heart, faintness, loss of consciousness, shock and death.

"Dr. Eldridge," McCann continued, "we think your girlfriend died of anaphylactic shock."

Dirk shot up, "No, no, not possible! We lived together for years and I would have known if she had any allergies. We're all tested at the Hospital. They are very strict about allergies on the 7th Floor. Simsy never had any physical problem except for her bicycle accident last year. We went to the ER after she fell. She lost a lot of blood, and they transfused her with one pint. She had stitches on her arm and was out of work for about a week."

"Listen, young man", as McCann lowered his voice, "we found semen in her vagina and we believe that triggered post coital anaphylactic shock."

Detective Santori watched the reaction of the two doctors. There was none. Each was vacant of any visible emotion. Dirk knew what McCann said was impossible since he and Simsy had been lovers and she never had any adverse physical reaction to sex.

McCann was saying that someone had accidentally killed her because she had sex with him after Dirk left. Sims had an allergic reaction to some proteins in that man's seminal fluids. While Dirk was on his way to New Hampshire his girlfriend was being unfaithful to him and then died as she lay helpless on the floor, searching for the strength to make a 911 call. They were loading his head with "what ifs". What if Dirk had insisted and brought her along. These were "what ifs" that could hang like a leaden tire around his neck for the rest of his life.

Gentle was not in McCann's nature. Maybe all the work over the years as an ME killed his soul.

McCann said, "Dr. Eldridge, you're off the hook. The Charles says your blood type is O. The semen that killed her wasn't your blood type. She was allergic to some proteins in his semen. The anaphylactic shock killed her very fast. It was just one of those fluke things."

For Dirk, each word from McCann was a stab. Where was Simsy to tell him it wasn't so? Where was Simsy to jump up, yell

"Strike Three!...you're OUT Mr. Medical Examiner!" He missed her so much, and she couldn't defend herself. He wanted to reach out and hold her hand. Together they could straighten this out. Dirk and Ernie knew that the ME was wrong. It didn't happen this way. Dirk had to find the strength to be faithful to Simsy despite what he had just heard.

Detective Santori then took over with a series of short questions. With each one, Dirk looked at Ernie.

"How soon after sex with your girlfriend did you leave?

"Why did you leave so quickly?

"Was she dating someone else?"

The medical examiner continued. "I called some people out in Los Angeles at the medical examiner's office there. They've had similar cases. We're getting some more input from one of the hospitals here."

Dirk Eldridge and Ernie Green were no ordinary physicians. None of those from the 7th Floor at the Charles were average in any way. But what they heard from the police was off the wall, off the charts, and off any plate of logic they knew.

SELECTIVE   DESENSITIZATION   TO   SEMINAL
PLASMA PROTEIN FRACTIONS AFTER IMMUNO-
THERAPY FOR POST COITAL ANAPHYLAXIS.

Dirk and Ernie read in disbelief. There in the library's computer was the story of a young girl who reported sexual intercourse related pruritus, hives, wheezing and dyspnea within ten minutes of ejaculation. Dirk, the medical detective, was reading in stunned silence. The studies dated back to 1967. Simsy wasn't even born then. The study detailed findings of elevated levels of serum-specific IgE antibodies to human seminal plasma (HuSePl). Dirk sat while Ernie peered over his shoulder as he continued to scan the computer screen. They were mesmerized by the what they read. Anaphylactic, or allergic, shock, is rare and usually caused by IgE-mediated sensitization to HuSePl protein allergens. There can be allergic reactions to bee stings, foods like shellfish or peanuts or drug antigens transferred via the HuSePl of male to female partners.

Dirk's thoughts swirled back and forth. He remembered Simsy said she felt a little "off" as he was leaving, but after a long bike ride she was sure she'd feel better. "Did that have anything to do with it?"

Now Dirk knew how Simsy felt when she told him about her patient who was diagnosed with pancreatic cancer and then survived. Sims was tending to him and messed up his treatment protocol. His condition improved so she adopted the treatment error as her protocol. She thought he was cured. Except there is no cure for advanced pancreatic cancer and so the Hospital labeled it as MIS-DIAGNOSIS. Simsy never believed that. Now Dirk was in the same place. He could not believe.

The trouble was the police did believe. They concluded there existed enough facts to classify Dr. Judith Sim's death ACCI-DENTAL and move onto the next case.

Dirk reached over to Ernie, "We'll figure this out. We have to."

Chapter Four:
Primum Non Nocere

(First Do No Harm)

Dr. Ernie Green's Brooklyn accent was his badge of honor. The fit was perfect. Green's high-top sneakers might have been white in some distant time, but they evolved into the deepest mahogany brown anyone had seen. His sneakers combined dirt and wear and blended into a montage of earthen colors. Green's sneakers were the anthropological link between those who knew him in medical school, the "white sneaker days", and those schoolday friends who know him now in his "deep brown sneaker days" as the most brilliant clinical detective on the 7th Floor at the Charles.

Dirk's and Ernie's lives were interwoven through years together in medical school and now at the Charles. Dirk's good looks and basketball height contrast sharply with Ernie's slumping 5 ft 10 inches. Yet, in matters of medicine, Dirk looked up to Ernie. While Dirk's heritage stems from the Mayflower and New England's social elite, Ernie's family extends from Brooklyn to the Warsaw ghetto. Ernie's accent is a powerful reminder to him that he was only one generation removed from Ellis Island.

That night Dirk and Ernie talked. Ernie shared Dirk's feelings. They did not believe the medical examiner's initial findings. Both thought Simsy's computer might hold some answers. She used it as a combination personal diary, medical log, and keeper of various other items ranging from charge card balances to Detroit Tiger's box scores. They knew the computer sign on, but not her password. At eight o'clock they met at Dirk's apartment to try and pull some answers from inside Simsy's computer.

Ernie settled in front of the computer keyboard with the confidence of a maestro preparing for another command performance. His confidence was reassuring to Dirk. Ernie loved computers. He was the unofficial free-lance computer guru for the 7th Floor.

"Dirk, what's the sign on?"

"RED SOX"

"How come Simsy went with that; she's no Sox fan?"

Dirk smiled, remembering the warm summer nights they spent at Fenway Park watching the *Tigers* and *Red Sox* play.

"OK my friend, now the part that separates the boys from men. What's her password?"

"Hey Ernie, if I knew that you could've stayed home."

"Dirk, the password must have four letters in her computer setup. Maybe it's a baseball thing."

They ran through a list of four letter baseball words. BATS. BALL. HOME. LEFT. BABE. RUTH. BALK. HITS. RUNS. Each entry prompted the same computer response: WRONG PASSWORD: TRY AGAIN.

Dirk offered a frustrated look at Ernie.

"You know what, bet she used a medical..." and before he finished they burst out in laughter.

There are no four letter words in medicine. Except when something goes wrong.

"Oh, shit. Go ahead, try it."

That was Dirk's first laugh since finding Simsy.

Evening stretched into morning as the hunt continued. Around two AM, they ordered in pizza. During "all-nighters" in medical school the only food that tasted OK after midnight was pizza. They could not find the password.

"Dirk, I've got another idea. Ever hear of the movie, *War Games*?"

Dirk shook his head NO, but knew that Ernie's mind was getting sharper as the night got shorter. That's how Ernie was with computers. He seems better able to bond with them in the early morning.

War Games was a movie about a computer that liked to play simple games such as tick tack toe. This imaginary computer with incredible thinking skills was given command over the US nuclear arsenal, ostensibly to avoid a mistaken launch of nuclear weapons. The computer played games to stay sharp when not re-tasking (re-targeting) US missiles. Like a six year old, when it couldn't play games, the computer lost its temper. Then it played nuclear war games. Without the unlock password, the war games computer would destroy the human race. Ernie had seen *War Games* ten times, about once a month in the past year. That's when he wasn't watching *Star Trek* for the 25th time. Science fiction and computers were the perfect combination for Ernie, and he had seen movies about them dozens of times.

"Dirk, this computer in *War Games* had a password that was its creator's name. A person's name. What was Simsy's mother's name?"

Dirk's face brightened.

"Jane."

As Ernie punched in the four letters, they both expected success. But again the computer said NO. Without even asking, Ernie typed J-U-D-Y. Again, nothing happened.

"Damn it Dirk, Judy should have been it. I was so sure on that one."

"Hey, listen Ernie. If we bomb out, I've got some friends in Washington who can take this computer apart and get the information we need. They're world class. I'll tell you about them someday."

"Dirk, and here I thought I knew everything about you. Who are your friends in Washington? You never mentioned them before."

Dirk just shrugged his shoulders and did not answer.

Ernie made a mental note, "Now that's something I'll ask him about later."

Then Ernie typed in D-I-R-K. The computer seemed to get up and dance as it sprung to life. Ernie had found Simsy's password.

With Ernie at the keyboard and Dirk hunched over, they scanned everything that Simsy had catalogued.

"You know, Dirk, you might not want to see all this stuff. Want me to go through it first?" Dirk's look gave his answer.

"Look at this, Dirk, everything about the Tigers, from batting averages to pitching and base stealing. Simsy was amazing!"

Dirk didn't need Ernie or anyone else to remind him how true that was.

Simsy had filed things randomly, not alphabetically or chronologically. It was a helter-skelter of facts and notes. There were even some words about Ernie's sneakers. Ernie looked down, paused, and then smiled. He felt like Simsy was in the room, telling him to get on with it.

Finally, a series of entries starting in March about patient Steven Hays.

"PRIMUM NON NOCERE: FIRST DO NO HARM" REALLY SCREWED THIS UP. ADMINISTERED 17,500mg/m2 OF GW'S XM2 INSTEAD OF 175 mg/m2. SHOULD HAVE KILLED HIM. DID NOT GIVE GCSF. NO EPO. ADVISED MARKS. TOLD PATIENT OF ERROR IN DOSAGE. NO CHANGE APPARENT. 3/23.

CA 19-9 RESULTS BACK. AMAZING. LEVEL DOWN FROM 4,800 TO 2,900. MARKS ADVISED AGAIN. CAN'T BE. MUST BE INACCURATE TEST RESULTS. COUNTS ALL THE SAME. JUST NO WAY...ORDER ANOTHER SET OF TESTS ASAP. RESULTS BACK TWO DAYS LATER. LEVEL NOW EVEN BETTER AND DOWN TO 2,300. TELL MARKS. GET IMMEDIATE LFT'S AND THEY'RE BETTER TOO. THIS IS AMAZING. PATIENT HAS WEIGHT GAIN. 4/10. MARKS TELLS ME TO BREAK CYCLE AND ADMINISTER AGAIN AT LEVEL OF 17,500 mg/m2. INFORM PATIENT. HAYS SAYS GO FOR IT, NOTHING TO LOSE. CA 19-9 DOWN TO 1,200. 4/12. CONTINUE OVERDOSE LEVELS MAY-SEPTEMBER. MARKS GETS RESULTS. MEET WITH MARKS, DORY, GENE WORLD LAWYER, DEPT OF DEFENSE LIAISON BEECHER. WHAT'S HER THING? SHE'S THE ONLY ONE AROUND THAT LIKES THAT JERK DORY. WHAT'S HE DO FOR HER? SIGN DOCUMENTS ABOUT RESULTS, SOMETHING TO DO WITH NATIONAL

SECRECY. THINK IT'S WASTE OF TIME. MAYBE I'LL TELL FOLKS AND DIRK AND ERNIE. THEY'D FLIP. TOLD PATIENT HE WAS IMPROVING. MARKS SAID ADVISE HIM WE MAY HAVE MADE MISDIAGNOSIS. MARKS KNOWS THAT'S NOT TRUE. NO WAY WE MADE MISTAKE. HE HAD ADVANCED PANCREATIC. WHY'S EVERYONE SO UPTIGHT ABOUT? 9/2.

BULLSHIT. MISDIAGNOSIS PAPERS ISSUED. MADE ME SIGN. GARBAGE. I ALWAYS THOUGHT MARKS SPECIAL; THIS IS NOT THE MARKS WHO HIRED ME. HE KNOWS THIS IS WRONG. CA 19-9 NORMAL. PATIENT OK. MUST TELL HIM OF MISDIAGNOSIS. PATIENT DISCHARGE 9/5. THOUGHT I WAS FOL-LOWED HOME LAST NIGHT. GUY IN DARK CAR WAS IN GARAGE WHEN I LEFT AND SAW HIM AS I GOT OUT AT APARTMENT. HE KEPT DRIVING. GUESS THIS THING AT HOSPITAL IS GETTING TO ME. MARKS AND DORY TELL ME ALL PAPERS AND COMPUTER FILES ON PATIENT HAYS TURNED OVER TO LAWYERS TO PROTECT AGAINST SUIT FOR MISDIAGNOSIS. MEET WITH DORY ALONE. WARNS ME THAT ANY WORD OF THIS WOULD AFFECT GENE WORLD STOCK AND PUT FUNDING AT RISK FOR THE 7TH FLOOR. WHAT AN ASSHOLE. 9/6.

Dirk and Ernie read in horror. It is every doctor's nightmare from hell to be the proximate cause of harm to their patient. Doctors are sworn to beneficence-doing their healing according to the Hippocratic Oath. Dirk and Ernie knew the cliff that Simsy looked down that night. She was alone on the 7th Floor with her patient. The proscription against doing harm is pre-eminent and owns a mandate over the uncertainties of beneficial treatments. Simsy was face to face that night with the Greek physician Hippocrates. His words echoed loudly from 460 BC to 1994. Dirk and Ernie could only imagine the torment she must have endured that night after administering a potentially fatal dosage of XM2. The computer had no more to offer. The night was silent. Perhaps Hippocrates had offered her inspiration and guidance during that lonely night on the 7th Floor. She had a little sign in the apartment from the Hippocratic Oath: PRIMUM NON NOCERE.

Chapter Five:
The 7th Floor

T he next day, Dirk took the elevator up to the 7th Floor at the Charles River Medical Center, or as everyone in Boston calls it, "The Charles". In all of America, few places are as special.

Admission to the 7th Floor is through a screening committee. The committee includes: Dr. Marks, one resident (whose term rotates each year), and Atwood Dory from Gene World. Unanimous approval is required.

Applications for consideration for admission are received from doctors around the world. It is not uncommon to see a request accompanied by a letter from a senator. On a few occasions, the President of the United States has written at the request of a member of Congress. All applications are initially graded on a Marks'-created scale that uses the names of Boston subway stops to denote the level of priority. PARK STREET is the highest priority and is also Boston's subway hub. Other names, drawn from the "Green Line" which he has ridden for decades, include: BOYLSTON, COPLEY, ARLINGTON, KENMORE and more. If someone is designated PARK, they will get the next available opening. Every applicant is fighting a terminal illness.

There exists a "subculture" on the 7th Floor which is a five bed sealed section reserved for those afflicted with unknown and presumed fatal viruses. This area, known as the *Zipper*, works off an independent air filtration system and all those who enter wear spacesuits and follow a protocol of decontamination outlined by the Center for Disease Control. Three US Embassy personnel have been "entombed" in the *Zipper* during the past year, two from the consulate in Saõ Paulo, Brazil and one from the embassy in San Josè, Costa Rica. All were secretly flown by the

Air Force to Hanscom Field outside Boston and transported to the 7th Floor. None left alive and all were cremated, as required by rules governing the *Zipper*.

There is also an adjunct to the 7th Floor called the Bunker. Buried deep below the hospital grounds, it is a specially constructed containment facility for the storage and study of "biohazards" such as viruses, bacterium and protozoa. The Bunker requires an elaborate process for entrance. It was built by the military, and its blueprints never saw the light of day. No Boston building permits were requested. According to records at City Hall, the Bunker does not exist. The Bunker was built adjacent to the hospital's basement and under Louis Pasteur Avenue in Boston's medical center.

The 7th Floor requires all patients to sign a unique consent form which permits the Hospital to determine, and pay for, all matters relating to burial except location of internment.

All patients admitted are presumed to be in the late stages of a terminal illness and go through a lengthy interview process and psychological evaluation. Each must sign a consent form that gives the 7th Floor authority beyond that enjoyed by any hospital in the world. Many of the advanced experimental treatments are administered when patients are unable to make choices about their care. Patients grant power of attorney to Dr. Marks, thus excluding family members from decisions in care. In return, those patients accepted for admission receive care that is paid for in its entirety by the 7th Floor. And the level of care is extraordinary. There are seven residents for 50 patients, plus visiting professors, as invited. The nursing staff numbers an astounding 80, with approximately 25 on duty at any given time. Many of the nurses have their masters degrees and some have military backgrounds. The Department of Defense liaison office has provided a continuing list of job applicants from Air Force bases around the world. It is the extraordinary nurse-to-patient ratio that enhances the effectiveness of the residents, visiting professors, and Dr. Marks.

Patients enjoy a recreational area including a billiards table, small library, and sun room. All rooms are private and include cable TV, a shower and telephone. Marked in bold letters on each phone is:

ALL TELEPHONE CALLS ARE MONITORED. CONVER-SATIONS IN ROOMS ARE RECORDED

There is no such thing as visiting hours. Relatives call for appointments that are processed through the medical and security staff. Clergy are not allowed to visit unless accompanied by a relative.

Elevators to the 7th Floor empty at the security desk. It's a semi- circle enclosure with TV monitors and two armed guards on duty at all times. With them is a nurse receptionist.

Classical music is played around the clock through hallway speakers, and volume is adjusted automatically by the time of day. Each patient's room is sound proofed, although there is a speaker system that permits nurses to monitor all sounds coming from the rooms. Many of the patients are electronically monitored either in bed or as they walk around. Those readings are visible both at the nurses' desk and in Dr. Marks' office. The 7th Floor cafeteria is open around the clock and the food is more reminiscent of an executive dining room than a hospital. Doctors designate which patients can use the cafeteria instead of specially prepared meals delivered to their rooms.

The 7th Floor has its own pharmacy, blood bank, and medical library. It is a hospital within a hospital. Those who work outside the 7th Floor know that they are working above or below one of the world's crown jewels in medicine.

The Charles is nestled not far from the banks of the Charles River. Named for an English King, the Charles River divides Boston and Cambridge and runs a long meandering course from its source in Hopkington along the course of the Boston Marathon until its waters complete the long slide into Boston Harbor. The Hospital was founded just after the Civil War and sits on a prized piece of real estate with million dollar brownstones within walking distance.

At the turn of the century, the Charles was led by Dr. James Berrymore, an eccentric collector of everything from medical science to art to antiques and voluminous amounts of alcohol. He was bigger than life and his bronzed statue still stands in the main hospital entrance. Berrymore raised money in quantity, if not from quality sources. No one asked where all the money came from, especially not the doctors and patients who were the recipients of his donors' largesse. He competed for medical talent the way baseball owners hunt down a 20 game winner or next home run king. New medical treatments were his pennants, and cures his World Series rings.

No one is modest about the Charles' reputation for excellence in the field of scientific exploration. What hospital in America has a central admitting office adorned with a 50 foot long *Star Trek* painting?

Each successor to Berrymore has hand picked his Board of Trustees, and in turn, his successor. Dr. Irizome "Iri" Shiri, a Japanese-American whose fund raising exploits in Los Angeles earned her a world-wide reputation, when she was given a choice between United States Surgeon General and President of the Charles her choice was easy. She quickly infiltrated Boston's social elite with her grace and charm. Irizome constantly talked of the hospital's crown jewel, the mysterious 7th Floor.

The central building of the Charles is brick and ivory covered with an old world elegance. There are 15 floors at the Charles.

The 7th Floor is not listed in the Charles directory. Dr. Timothy Marks' office is at the northwest corner of the 7th Floor. His office sports rich mahogany wood that climbs from the floor to the ceiling. The giant bay windows offer a panoramic view of Boston, including a partial view of the Charles River. Marks' view would be even better if it were the 15th floor, but no one is there for the scenery. Special exterior window treatments block all views from the outside and an invisible metallic treatment provided by the Defense Department eliminates any chance of electronic sound gathering. Marks' office is cluttered with photographs of world famous dignitaries from reigning kings to presidents. His prized map of the Boston subway system, with its intersecting lines, looks like a military battle plan. Encased in glass shelves are his Nobel Prizes. Throughout the office are wall and floor speakers, with an ever present offering of classical music. Pictures of his family are on his desk. The desk, with its bank of telephones and computers, looks more like one of a wartime commander-in-chief than a Chief of Medicine.

Doctors rarely ventured into Mark's kingdom without an invitation.

"Talk!"

For Dirk, this was the second time he had been inside Marks' office. The last was a farewell party for a departing doctor.

"Sir, if it's OK, I'd like the stand. Ernie and I worked through the night and I'm really bushed."

Dirk watched as Marks' eyes stayed glued to his. He tells Marks of the all-night computer search of Simsy's files and her patient notes on Steven Hays. Then he recalled the words of Simsy's mother. Dirk told Mark's that Simsy never told him she thought she was followed home or about her patient and his "miracle" recovery.

While he spun his story, mixing fact and assumption and fear, Dirk felt increasingly uncomfortable as Marks' expression never changed. Not even a word or a move or a question. Was he listening? Or did he know it already?

"Dirk, do you really believe there's more to this than the police findings?"

"Yes, I do."

Marks stood and walked around his desk and put his arm around Dirk.

"You know, Dirk, this whole thing might be easier to understand if there were some dark cloud hovering over Simsy's death. It'd make it easier for all of us, especially you. I talked with the police and they faxed me their findings. Anaphylactic shock is a pretty big pill for you to swallow. Now you tell me about her computer notes and patient Hays. You're probably trying to make some sense out of all this. I'm afraid you may not succeed. These things happen. It's not the first misdiagnosis and it won't be the last."

Dirk stood in silence, but Marks' gesture of comfort made him feel a bit easier.

"Sir, I just wish we could do something more to double check, please."

Marks moved away and stared at the gray carpeted floor.

"Tell you what Dirk, keep your thoughts to yourself. And tell Green to do the same. I'll check some other things out. Make some phone calls. Let's leave this open and we'll talk again."

Dirk acknowledged his words and left. As he walked to the elevator and signed out, he felt better. Marks was his hero.

Dirk's next stop was the apartment. It was time to pack up Simsy's things.

Dirk didn't have to open the door to his apartment. It was already opened. The computer, TV, CD's and the answering machine were gone. The apartment was ransacked. Even the refrigerator was gutted. A-sick-deep-in-the-gut feeling hit him. It was deeper than anything he had felt before.

Dirk could feel a throbbing sense of trouble. His stomach cramped as he looked at the mess. Things were slipping and he was not in control.

Someone had followed Simsy home.

Chapter Six:
Falling

Ernie Green came barreling through the door into Dirk's apartment. The police were everywhere. For Dirk it was an instant replay of the hours after he found Simsy's body. He was replaying the first moments after he found her body and then fast forwarding with disbelief to the present. If he could just erase the whole thing and get back to New Hampshire.

"Damn, you OK, Dirk?" Ernie focused on the empty computer table with a sick feeling. Were they trapped in a bad dream?

The apartment was in turmoil as police moved around taking pictures and talking. Then Dirk noticed a man standing by a window looking outside. He didn't move or talk. Others came to him and whispered in his ear. He nodded and pointed.

Dirk walked over to him and stood at his side.

"Excuse me, who are you?"

"Street, Detective Jimmy Street."

Street was in his mid 40's and looked tough with hair cut short and tinged with gray. His skin was baby face smooth. His eyes were famous. One eye was hazel and the other as brown as late fall leaves. Street knew all the jokes. What he could not handle were the questions at crime scenes. Witnesses and victims zoomed in on his different colored eyes. They became a distraction. His solution was contact lenses of which he had three sets: one was hazel, another brown, and the third clear. The clear contacts were necessary to balance the colored contact in use. Some days it was Jimmy Street with hazel eyes and other days with brown eyes. He almost always wore hazel contacts. Street's condition was called heterochromia iridis. The short description was "dog eyes."

Some days, Street let nature take its course, and he went out with one hazel and one brown eye. Those were his angry days.

Street usually wore a dark suit and a striped tie. His shoes were polished and his shirt always a crisp white. He looked like a banker. Inside his wallet, he carried a plastic calendar that counted the days till mid April.

Street ran the Boston Marathon each year in April. That was his spiritual pilgrimage. He celebrated each marathon finish with a thick and smelly cigar. A few years ago, Street got his picture in the paper as he crossed the finish line and a cop handed him his traditional victory cigar. The newspaper caption said:

RUNNING FOR HIS HEALTH? DETECTIVE JIMMY STREET OF THE BOSTON POLICE.

Street finished one hour after the winning runner and it made no difference to him. He ran for love, for the thrill, and for the chance to be part of history.

Street told Dirk he was in the area when the burglary call came in and he took it for one reason. Over the radio they said it was the same address where a doctor died earlier in the week.

"The only thing I dislike more than paperwork are coincidences. I don't get along well with them. I'm curious. Like you. So, what the hell, figured I'd stop by and take a look."

Street explained that break-ins are common just after a death. Criminals read newspapers. A lot of times people clear out of an apartment for a while after something like his girlfriend's death.

Street asked Dirk to run through the whole story about his girlfriend. As he did, Dirk motioned for Ernie to come over.

"This is my friend, Ernie Green. He was with me last night when we went through the computer files. Now, they're all gone."

Dirk explained what happened to his girlfriend. With almost every sentence he'd ask to make sure Street understood. Dirk talked about the ME, the one with the dead face.

"Bet that's McCann. He's a real piece of work--colder than the coldest day in January." Hearing Street say that made Dirk feel comfortable.

"So you think dead face McCann was wrong about what happened to your girlfriend? What happened when you told Detective Santori about someone following her home, what happened with that? Santori's a good guy and very careful."

Dirk explained that the police never called Simsy's father. And Simsy never told him about it.

"Those computer files, what's so important about them?"

Dirk answered, "They had my girlfriend's notes on a patient she treated. It was a guy who should have died but Simsy says was cured. The Hospital says no way. They claim it was a goof on the diagnosis. Simsy didn't believe that. It was all in the computer--and now that's gone."

Street asked, "And you think it's all connected? The cured patient, her being followed home, her death and now this. Is that it? Aren't you guys supposed to cure people? What's the big deal about this patient, Hays, or whatever his name is?"

As Dirk heard Street recount it, it did seem a bit wild.

"Ernie, what are you doing?" Ernie had been shuffling through his pockets for a few minutes and both he and the detective noticed.

"Got it!"

Ernie pulled some computer disks from his pocket.

"This, Dirk, is everything inside Simsy's computer."

"Ernie, when did you do that?" Ernie smiled.

For no reason except instinct cultivated over 20 years, Street turned to Ernie and took the computer disks. "Let's take a ride guys. Ernie, I'll bet you have a computer at your place."

Ernie asked, "You're right. How'd you know?"

Street's silent look said that was a dumb question. It was a five minute drive to Ernie's apartment.

"Amazing, detective, you just park wherever. No big deal, right?" Ernie was like a little kid getting his first ride in a police car.

Street issued a forced smile, "Ernie, sometimes they even give me tickets."

Ernie shot back, "And you pay them?"

Street looked over at Ernie with a blank expression. Street watched the data from the disk scroll across Ernie's computer. Street read it without expression. For almost two hours, he watched the writings of a dead doctor move in green across the screen. It was eerie, like an interrogation of someone whose words were only written, never spoken.

Street said, "Make more copies of these."

In less than 30 minutes, Ernie finished with three sets. He handed them to Street.

Then Street handed them back: "One for me, one for Dirk, and the third one I want you to mail to some sister or aunt, someone who is family and doesn't have your last name. Leave your original set here in the apartment."

Ernie asked why.

"Don't you ever go fishing? Ever hear of bait. If someone was after the computer files, and if that someone knows you and Dirk got into the files, then they're going to want your disks."

Dirk said, "Does that mean you think I'm right about Simsy?"

Street gave Dirk a quick course in PYA (Protect Your Ass). He said he didn't know what, if anything, was going on. Making the extra computer files was like sticking some money under a pillow. It's there so you sleep a little better. It could all be a waste of time or maybe there was something to all this.

As Street got up to leave, he put his arms around both Dirk and Ernie. It was like a football huddle.

"Listen carefully guys cause I'm going to give you the bottom line and skip the rest. There's no proof of anything except an accidental death, some shadows following a girl home, and now a break-in. There are no suspects, no motive; in fact, there is nothing I can take to headquarters. But I'll check it out...maybe because you guys look so helpless."

For the first time since finding Simsy's body, Dirk felt safe. Street walked to the door. That was when Dirk noticed Street's right hand. From the thumb to his shirt cuff was a six inch scar.

"Detective, what happened to your hand?"

"Some druggie autographed my hand with a knife. He was going for my face. It's dirty outside, guys."

Chapter Seven:
Cranial Airiness

Next day at the Charles, Dirk and the remaining five residents of the 7th Floor met. Ernie had moved some schedules around and managed to get all six residents together in the cafeteria at 12:30 PM. With beepers on but instructions left with nurses not to call except for emergencies, the six talked. Ernie thought this might help get Dirk out of his funk. He also had a surprise. Dr. Marks joined the residents. As far back as anyone could remember, Marks didn't **do** lunch with his residents *en masse*.

The residents were not all personally close and it showed when the issues were people and not procedures. Allen Fiengold's claim to fame was immunology and a two year stint with the Peace Corps in Zaire. He had authored a well received paper on native esoteric herbal treatments. Fiengold, "Mr. LA", wore his usual California outfit. His sunglasses were always within reach, even in the dead of winter. Unlike Ernie's brown sneakers, Fiengold enjoyed showcasing a rotating set of designer sneakers with colors, and pumps, and gadgets like compression lights that illuminated when he ran. Patients and nurses would ask him to turn the lights low and jump, providing a few seconds of bright light as he impacted on the floor. They were laughing at, not with, him. Fiengold enjoyed the attention.

This California beach boy was one of the ten most renowned immunologists in the world. If beach volleyball wasn't so important to him, he'd probably be the king of immunology. His family in LA was wealthy and he traveled cross country with the same enthusiasm as Marks on the subway.

Nancy Debbs was a kindred soul for Fiengold. She saw something serious and special about him that others thought was shallow and false. While they were not best friends, Fiengold was smart enough to know she liked him for what he was. Debbs came from Houston and her specialty was hematology. There was not one thing that was spectacular about her intellectually, but she always managed to win the special appointments. Her personality was bubbly like "Simsy", and there was a small similarity in the blue eyes and golden hair. Her thick Texan accent was a charming apostrophe after the sterilized and mechanical voices of the other residents.

Gaetano *Guy* Piccard looked as if he had been air dropped from Parma, Italy. Toscanini was born in Parma and just outside of town is Roncole, where Verdi grew up. The area is known for both its traditions of opera and food. When he wasn't talking about medicine, it was almost a sure bet he was discussing *prosciutto di Parma* and *parmigiano-reggiano* with anyone who'd listen. If there is a gastronomical heaven on earth, then this is how ham and cheese would be offered. The nurses would often crowd around him, some taking notes as he described the origins and preparation of *prosciutto*. In Italian it simply means ham. But then he'd explain the word actually comes from the verb *prosciugare* to dry, and refers to the cured, dried ham. It seemed as if his descriptions were from some textbook by nature of the precision of the words used. Like a presentation before a doctoral committee, Gaetano would explain that great cured ham depended on three qualities: the pigs, the skills of the artisans in processing, and the air that dries it. *Prosciutto di Parma* comes from two breeds of pigs: *Landrace* and *Suino Tipico Italiano*. While these words didn't mean much to those listening, they sounded delicious.

By now, anyone listening was transfixed by his mastery of this ancient and honored delicacy. And with each passing word, he looked more like a great chef and less like a world class doctor. Whether medicine or food, Gaetano looked for a sense of history and place. He could recount the *1963 Consorzio del Prosciutto di Parma* rules established to govern the production of *prosciutto*, according to which pigs must be slaughtered at an age from 10-12

months and a weigh in excess of 300 pounds. The ham comes
from the rear haunches. On and on he would go, stopping only
when reminded he was in a hospital and his patients had priorities
beyond the preparation of *prosciutto.*

Sometimes when leaving work, Gaetano would stick a little
post-it on the bulletin board, announcing that the next day was
leftover day. His definition of leftovers coincided neatly with a
great dinner in a five star restaurant. Leftovers brought into the
hospital by Gaetano never saw the clock strike 12 noon. It was
impossible not to like him; but, despite all this, he was a loner
who never joined in the social life at the Hospital. His family
secrets were tightly locked away in Marks' office and that seemed
to be what *Guy* preferred.

Gaetano and Karen Ferris were both clinicians, as was Sims.
Their interests focused on the administration and management of
patient care and not on research. Both were University of
Pennsylvania graduates and had used their contacts at school for
acceptance by Marks. One of their professors, a friend of Marks
and sometimes visiting professor on the 7th Floor, had picked
both as ideal candidates.

Each had a proclivity to publish and their work regularly
appeared in respected medical journals. It was that skill that
elevated both beyond their peers.

Karen Ferris also came from a family of physicians and always
wanted a medical career. Ferris had taken one year after medical
school to join a computer firm in Cambridge, BTTF (Back To
Tomorrow's Future), Inc. Armed with a multimillion dollar
contract from the CDC (Centers for Disease Control), BTTF was
creating software programs that would model the activities of
viruses. Using existing data, and high speed parallel computers,
BTTF was creating theoretical viruses and cures. The CDC
would map a rare virus in captivity, then BTTF would grow it
using its computer software. There were two doctors on staff,
and Ferris was one. Whatever happened while at BTTF, Ferris
had decided that real patients, not computer models, interested
her.

While Sims was midwestern cute, Ferris was big city pretty.
She dressed *hot*, never succumbing to the drab browns and blacks

so often seen around hospitals. Her wardrobe included bright purple and yellow outfits. The more serious the day, the more outrageous she dressed. And she relished the moments when someone would hint that she should get on board with a more sedate dress code. Marks loved the way she rocked the boat and made it a point to compliment her daily.

Dirk, Ernie, and Simsy had been the core of the resident group at the Charles by pure force of personality and skill. The others seemed to orbit the trio; but, with the death of Sims, they sensed that Dirk and Ernie seemed less confident.

Lunch went on for an hour, the longest anyone could remember staying in the cafeteria. After no more than 15 minutes, the conversation moved from Simsy to medicine, despite the efforts of Marks to bring the topic back to her. It seemed as if Marks was trying to create a cafeteria encounter group, aimed primarily at helping Dirk and Ernie. That was not going to happen.

There was a transparent eagerness to avoid the encounter and everyone felt it. Dirk and Ernie suddenly understood how truly alone they were. Marks seemed to feel a sense of failure as they started to leave. The dynamics weren't there and he couldn't make it happen. Except for Dirk and Ernie, the others seemed anxious to retreat to the ordered chaos of the 7th Floor and their patients and research.

Dirk tugged on Ernie's elbow, "Give me a second, OK?" Dirk's face was in distress.

"Why did you send a messenger over to my place for the computer disk? Thought you already had one."

Ernie stopped and laughed, "Dirk, don't do this. You never were good at jokes."

Dirk unconsciously moved his hands across his mouth.

"Ernie, please tell me you sent a messenger for the disk."

Ernie softly replied, "No."

"Is Detective Street there, please? This is Dr. Dirk Eldridge."

A female voice came back, "He's out now. We'll leave a message."

"Could you reach him. This is an emergency."

"Like I said, he's out. Can someone else help? I'll page him. He'll call back."

"Ask him to call me at home; he has the number. I'll be there in about two hours, around four PM."

Ernie saw a spaced-out look on Dirk's face. "Where are you going Dirk? I'll come with you. I'll borrow someone's bike."

"I'm going to see that teacher, Steven Hays, the one Simsy treated. Call me at home later. If Street calls, let him know where I went. And tell him about the messenger who picked up my disk. The messenger you didn't call. Tell Marks I had to take a few hours off. Hays teaches over at Copley Square High School. I checked his file...or what's left in his file."

"Why don't you let Street handle that?"

Dirk was already heading towards the elevator. Ernie went to Marks' office. Marks was meeting with Atwood Dory, and Ernie was told to return after 4 PM.

"Ernie, this is Street. What's going on? I got Dirk's message." Ernie explained about the messenger. He called him the messenger from hell--the messenger no one sent and no one knew but the messenger who now had a copy of Simsy's computer files.

"Where's Dirk now?" Ernie heard the tension in Street's voice.

"Well, damn it, where's this teacher at? How'd he go there?"

Ernie started to answer, but the phone went dead. Street had hung up. Ernie rushed back to Mark's office.

"Q, you've got to interrupt Dr. Marks and Mr. Dory. I just talked with the police and I think something's wrong, again."

Chapter Eight:
Deadline

Doris Questra, Q to everyone on the 7th Floor, was secretary to Dr. Marks for as long as anyone could remember. She alone had the "keys" to his office and mind. Her access was without bounds. Access is power and Q practiced with the confidence of a first violinist. She used it carefully but always to promote and protect Dr. Marks. Since her husband died in the late 60's, Marks and the 7th Floor has been her whole life. She has always been as formal as the doorman at the Ritz or when Marks was threatened, as crazy as a rabid raccoon doing circles at high noon. One slight scratch below the surface and her blood ran whatever color Marks wished. Q was in many ways an outlaw on the 7th Floor, wanted by everyone who wanted access to Marks, yet an outcast when Marks was out of town.

"Ernie, Dr. Marks and Mr. Dory are going through Gene World budgets. They've got a Defense Department person in there, plus accountants. Can't this wait till four?"

Green stood motionless. Inside he was sick. The alarm in Street's voice pushed him forward. Green could not wait. Green felt pushed into Marks' office. He walked past Q and into Marks' office.

"Ernie, we're meeting and you're interrupting us. Where's Q?"

"Sorry, Dr. Marks, I told him you were meeting and he just barged in. Ernie, leave now."

Marks motioned otherwise to Q.

"Excuse me. I'm going to take a little walk with one of our doctors here. Be right back."

Marks got up and ushered Ernie out of the room. Ernie noticed that only Atwood Dory seemed unmoved with all the commotion. He sat there with his standard mean and smug look.

Atwood Dory and Gene World were one and the same for everyone on the 7th Floor. Dory was the man with the money, handing it out like candy to kids on their birthdays. He was the absolute opposite of Green, and the two barely spoke. Atwood Dory, Wall Street and financial wizard with a law degree, was overseer of Gene World's investment in the 7th Floor. His black Mercedes parked against the orange painted hospital garage was a daily reminder that Halloween was always there somewhere.

For Dory, internal medicine translated to the internal rate of return. And the 7th Floor had served the stockholders of GW well over the years. Several GW patents had yielded hundreds of millions of dollars and were directly attributable to experiments originating from the 7th Floor. Atwood Dory had become a cult figure at GW headquarters. Sometimes he had questions as to why a terminal patient had not died within the targeted time frame. Those were the first words he ever asked Ernie Green, and it was the first time Green had imagined other uses for some of the sharper medical instruments he carried.

There were lots of stories about Dory. Were they only rumors?

A couple of the nurses, the young and very pretty ones, seemed to enjoy unusual access with Dory. Some of the doctors heard them saying thank you, but thank you for what. And others in the hospital had their stories, too. Gene World's winter sales meeting in Martinique coincided with a trip that three hospital nurses took to the same hotel at the same time. The JASPER Hotel was Martinique's most exclusive and expensive, not a nurse's natural destination. Marks and his wife were there along with Dory...and the three nurses.

Then, there was the story of a cleaning lady on the 7th Floor who claimed she discovered pictures in Dory's office of a female patient somewhere in the hospital. The pictures seemed posed and non medical. The pictures disappeared after the cleaning lady was fired. There were rumors about Dory's collection of books about the infamous Nazi doctor Josef Mengele, who experimented on Jews in the concentration camps.

Like everyone else on the 7th Floor, the Defense Department had run a security check on Dory and it came back squeaky clean. No military service, no arrests for drugs, and a wife and two kids settled in a western Boston suburb.

Dory was raised in New York City and grew up in a co-op on 5th Avenue. His family business ties extended to several of the blue chip brokerage houses. He favored three-piece suits, even when they were out of style. Inside the suit was a man wound as tightly as any ball of string. When a visitor in his office spilled coffee, Dory's screams bounced off the corridor walls like a fire drill. But, tell him a patient had died, and all was well, provided the empty bed was quickly filled.

While Marks tolerated Dory, Ernie Green sought the role of Dory's constant antagonist. Green believed Dory was an empty shell held together with paste and dollar bills. Simsy felt the same way and both expressed their feelings about Dory to all who would listen. Dirk often told them to keep their thoughts private. Atwood Dory, for good or evil, was the spigot that controlled the flow of dollars from GW to the 7th Floor. Those dollars were measured in millions. Dirk tolerated Dory and kept his feelings to himself.

"OK Ernie, what's so important you have to come barging in?"

Ernie told Marks about Detective Street's call and Dirk's departure to find Simsy's patient, Steven Hays. As they walked up and down the corridor, Marks listened.

Marks told Ernie he had met with Detective Street and turned over files on all 7th Floor patients going back to 1990. That included medical logs on Simsy's patient.

"I'll tell you more, Ernie, since you're so involved. As far as I know, nothing sinister has happened. Dirk is having trouble accepting Simy's passing. She was an excellent doctor. Her computer notes say it all. She made a mistake and administered the wrong dosage to a patient. He got a misdiagnosis discharge from the hospital. It's time for all of us to move on."

Marks continued, "None of the others doctors know this; but they will soon. It's why we're meeting today. The Defense

Department is transporting a small batch of Variola for storage in the bunker. You haven't logged much time down there recently."

Green had not been down to the subterranean bunker, the repository of a colony of viruses, bacterium, and protozoa, in a long time. In fact, he went out of his way to avoid going to that bunker.

"Ernie, you know what Variloa virus is? And 1600 Clifton Road sounds familiar, doesn't it?"

"I know what it is. How'd you know what was on Simsy's computer?"

"There you go again, Ernie. Don't add one and one and come up with five. Simsy kept me informed about everything with her patient. I knew she kept computer files at home on her patients. She told me, plain and simple. Now back to this Variola, ok?"

Marks knew getting some Variola virus for storage was a major medical coup. Variola, or smallpox, as it's commonly known, traces its tentacles to the beginning of mankind. Variola comes from the Latin word *varius*, which means *changing*. Alone viruses are impotent. With no cellular casing or inner nucleus, they are nomads. Outside a host cell, they are as dangerous as a piece of paper. They exist in limbo, neither living or nonliving. Only when joined with a host cell can they commence their killing mission.

Smallpox was mankind's silent nuclear bomb for much of history. It killed each day with the screams and terror of its victims still reverberating. Black vomit was its most visible calling card, besides the pustules that pitted its victims until their skin vanished. POX originally appeared in domesticated animals, then took an Olympic leap called a cross species transfer. It found a home amongst humans. Its victims were anonymous millions and the famous. The Egyptian pharaoh Ramses was a probable victim as was the Emperor Marcus Aurelius. European royalty was cut down until the end of the 19th century. Smallpox crossed oceans and visited major American cities in the 1800's. As recently as 1947, there was an outbreak in New York City.

1600 Clifton Road in Atlanta is the address of the Centers for Disease Control and Prevention, the CDC.

Ernie knew what Marks was talking about. He was more interested in how Marks knew about Simsy's computer disks. Marks continued to ramble on about viruses. Ernie felt he was getting a medical school lecture.

"You know Ernie, smallpox was a genetic link to our past and perhaps is a key to unlocking future medical treatments." He then meandered onto the subject of DNA. Maybe age was catching up to him.

Marks continued in lecture style recitation: DNA is the genetic coding that links all living things...four nucleotides make up DNA--guanine, cytosine, adenine, and thymine. Many virologists and biologists believe smallpox might offer clues about other killing viruses.

"Yes sir, I understand all that. But, Dr. Marks, didn't the CDC destroy the last samples of smallpox?"

"Ernie, don't believe everything you read. Several batches are left, none in use. And one of them will be here on the 7th Floor. Dory tells us GW scientists may have found a use for it. This could be our next great adventure."

"Dr. Marks, this is dangerous stuff. Remember that Yale doctor who got infected with Sabia arenavirus?"

Sabia, like smallpox, is a lethal rodent-borne disease. It was first discovered in Brazil about four years ago and, if untreated, its symptoms include bleeding, fever pulmonary failure and eventually death. Ernie sensed that Marks was extending the safety envelope in hopes of snatching another Nobel prize. Marks droned on more, as if killing time. Ernie knew everything Marks was saying, and couldn't understand why he was wasting his time. This wasn't a speech before the press association. Marks continued anyway and all Green could do was listen politely.

"Ernie, we both know the exploration process of viruses is complex and expensive. For GW and companies like it, the chase is high risk and high reward. Dory has done a great job keeping the money flowing."

Now Marks' lecture was nearing the point of annoyance. Was Marks showboating his capacity to talk endlessly? Was this senility in action?

"Bits of DNA are lifted from a virus like smallpox. Then enzymes are used to literally **eat** all the surrounding proteins. Detergents get rid of the fats. So called "restriction enzymes" are introduced and they adhere to the DNA in selected areas, leaving so-called bits. These bits are placed in a bacteria within a specific part called a plasmid."

Ernie looked down at his watch in hopes that Marks might get a message. That was not to be the case.

"When this plasmid replicates, it also replicates the DNA that was inserted. More enzymes and detergents are introduced, clearing away bacterial elements. This process is repeated, like sifting through mined dirt searching for a glistening nugget of gold. When it's found, the DNA is placed between two sheets of glass with a jelly inside, and then an electrical charge is applied. A laser detector excites different dyes. And from this process, it's possible to map the sequence of tens of thousands of nucleotides that provide a book size code to a virus, and perhaps a cure."

"Hallelujah, it's over." Ernie was wrong.

"And Ernie, there's even more exciting news. Did you ever hear of The Decapitator?"

Ernie looked puzzled, not knowing what wild ideas were now percolating in Mark's mind. Mark's eyes were brimming with excitement.

He explained that The Decapitator was a golden ornamental deity for an ancient Peruvian tribe called the Moches. It was found in a Moche tomb near Sipan in northern Peru. These tombs were discovered by grave diggers. Well, they were caught, arrested and then they started getting sick and dying in prison. It seems the poor devils got themselves infected by some virus inside the burial vaults. The vaults were very deep and almost ice cold.

The Peruvian government called the US for help and the Center for Disease Control got involved. Using their military connections, GW heard about what was happening down there and volunteered to send a scientific mission to do a preliminary on-site analysis. It was all hush hush. Marks said some of the viral samples are on site at the Charles. The Decapitator was found in one of the royal coffins. It's a golden figure with a knife in its left hand and a human head in the right. Small copper balls were inserted in the art.

"Ernie, they found something else in these tombs. What they found were turquoise beads."

"Dr. Marks, so who cares if they found little beads or whatever." Ernie realized that asking any question was a mistake.

"Suppose I told you these beads were nearly microscopic in size and you could fit hundreds on a fingertip. Remember, this is the first millennium, roughly AD 100. That's 1,800 years ago, young man!"

Marks continued, "It seems that these royal families may have been decapitating their enemies not with swords, but with a virus. These Moche people were farmers. One of their most important crops was peanuts. GW and CDC scientists think this virus may have some value in our work."

Then Marks' eyes opened and his face glistened with excitement. Ernie had never seen Marks so animated. Waving his hands up like saying, Touchdown!, Marks' voice was louder.

"Ernie, listen. We know viruses exist to duplicate themselves. They're guerrillas that sneak in and infect cells and take over their genetic works. These viruses are like FED X delivering new genes. XM2 is our experimental cancer drug and imagine it invades cells' enzymes to make more copies of itself. Suppose we created a defective virus? We'd take out part of the adenovirus that controls the virus' capacity to replicate itself. If we took out enough of the adenoviral genome, well then, the virus would not reproduce. But, if we left enough in, it'd no longer be infectious. It'd deliver itself like FED X with all the genetic information."

Marks was on a roll.

"But the package delivered would be the cure, not the killer. With XM2, maybe we can use the virus to cure."

Now Marks had Ernie's attention. Marks and Gene World were trying to create defective viruses. Or maybe they had succeeded.

"Ernie, the 7th Floor was my dream. Many people in the medical research community thought it was a waste of money. They laughed. Now the world is coming to me. It's my time; it's our time!"

Q ran from Marks' office, "Excuse me, Dr. Marks, there's an urgent call for you."

In a setting like the 7th Floor, the word *urgent* is rarely used. Ernie had a sinking feeling in his stomach.

"Ernie, stay here. I'll be right back and we'll finish."

Ernie watched as Marks hurried to a house telephone. He watched as Marks listened and never spoke. Then he let the phone slide from his hands and dangle.

Marks walked towards Ernie.

"Ernie, that was Detective Street."

"Did he find Dirk yet?"

"Ernie, they found Dirk--he was struck by a car on Commonwealth Avenue. He's dead."

Chapter Nine:
The Hunter

Jimmy Street rushed his unmarked blue Ford through Boston's Back Bay from Copley Square to the corner of Commonwealth and Fairfield Streets. He heard the police call a 10-55: Coroner's case. The radio report said a bicyclist was hit and killed by a late model sedan. Street knew instinctively whom he'd find at the accident scene.

Street saw Dirk Eldridge's body, about 50 feet from his bicycle. He had apparently been hit from behind and launched like someone tossed a basketball in the air. His body lay crumpled against a willow tree on the sidewalk. Street never got used to the faces and scenes of death; he was the first officer on the scene and he was going to treat this like a homicide. He knew the routine.

Note time of arrival. Prevent anyone from disturbing the scene pending arrival of medical examiner and crime lab. Prevent unauthorized persons from entering crime scene and anyone present from leaving. Take names, addresses and phone numbers. Verify those with drivers licenses. Note position of body and clothing. Preserve evidence. Take statements. Check personal effects of victim.

Street knew hit and runs usually attracted rookie cops, the ones more likely to get in his way. He moved quickly to get things in order.

"Where are the damn skid marks." There were none.

"How about witnesses?"

Someone pointed out some kids on the curb. They were full of things to say.

"Yeah, man, we saw it all come down. Lady in that new white Monte C (Chevrolet Monte Carlo) with the orange dent; she hit him straight on...then some guy in another car picks her up and they split towards the expressway. Gone! That guy on the bike never had a chance."

Street pointed to the white Monte Carlo. "I want this thing dusted. Where's the VIN?

All cars sold in the US have a VIN (Vehicle Identification Number) inscribed on a metal plaque on the dashboard. Another set of VIN's is carved inside the car's engine. VINs are metal fingerprints. Every cop at the scene knew Street and they knew he didn't **do** hit and runs.

"Boston dispatch, this is Detective Street. Get me a secure channel. I want a Code Zebra."

Code Zebra was Boston's alert squad. For most hours of most days it's a well dressed coffee klatch. But, when needed, it's a special unit of the city's top cops on ready standby. The Zebra team handles terrorism, pursuits, hostages, and cases with "special circumstances." Street was one of the few detectives authorized to call a Zebra. They were never used in hit and runs. Street was sending a message across the entire Boston Police radio network that something a lot bigger than a hit and run was in progress. Within 30 minutes, a fingerprint and fiber team joined Street.

There was not a single fingerprint inside the car. There were none on the steering wheel, seats, or push button radio.

"So what we've got here is a ghost rider, right?"

Street's voice mixed anger with frustration. Street added and subtracted on the spot. No fingerprints, no skid marks, no suspect. And, yes, the woman who hits this kid opens her door, casually walks out and into another car and gets a ride off into a blazing sunset. She's a very cool customer. The Zebra team called back on Street's radio.

"Street, get ready for this one. The plates are registered to a Jane Smith, and her address turns out to be a parking lot. That car is registered to no one and comes from nowhere."

Street checked the odometer and it read 117 miles.

"We checked local dealers and new car purchases during the last two weeks. No one reports selling a car exactly like that white Chevy. That means someone either trucked it in or garaged it."

Street got in his car and looked at the scene. Everything was so clean, except for an orange dent on the driver's door. What marks great detectives are their sense of orbit. It's the capacity to visualize people and objects in orbit. They know when some element is out of place. It's like a satellite decaying in orbit. Detectives like Street aren't astronomers; but they can look into a blackened night sky and see things others cannot.

The orange dent was the wrong color at the wrong time on a new car. Street got out of his car and took a sample of the orange paint. He knew this was murder. Why use a new white car with an identifying orange dent? Whoever drove the car hit something orange and did so just before hitting Dirk Eldridge. For some reason, they had to kill him on quick order. They didn't have time to clean up the car and get rid of the orange paint. That was a mistake. That orange dent was Street's guiding light in the night sky of a sunny Boston afternoon.

Street looked at Dirk sprawled on the ground. He died young and he died dirty. He could not accept that his girlfriend had been with another man. Street barely knew Dirk, but he admired his loyalty--a rare commodity. It was worth fighting for. In Dirk's case, he died for it. Every time Street experienced death, it seemed to bring back memories.

Jimmy Street was born in New York City, 46 years ago. His father was a New York City detective and his mother was a teacher. They lived in Queens, within eyesight of the Manhattan skyscrapers.

Street remembered Saturdays when his dad took him to the police station. Sometimes he would bring along a friend from school. Street remembered going around collecting dollars and doing coffee and sandwich runs. One of the cops would take him in a cruiser and turn on the flashing lights and sirens as they zipped through Queens to a local deli. It was better than any amusement park ride. When he returned loaded with food, the cops gave him tips. It was usually quarters or little things like bullet casings.

Street remembered exactly what his dad ate: always a cheeseburger with a coffee, two sugars and no cream. Despite the noise and jokes inside the station house, it felt so empty. His dad always looked so beat up from the work. No matter how tired he was, Street's dad always had a smile for Jimmy when they looked at each other. Street's dad was one of the hero cops in Queens. The cops told him how special his dad was.

When they told him that, he was 17 and a high school senior and he was standing in front of his dad's coffin on a rainy Saturday in June, five days after his dad was gunned down in a convenience store. Detective Charles James Street was on a stake out when three men came in with sawed-off shotguns. They killed his dad and another cop.

Young Jimmy Street answered the doorbell. It was 9:30 PM. There were three detectives and a bunch of police cars outside. They asked to talk with his mother. Street never asked where his dad was. He knew he wasn't coming home. Street stayed at the door and stared outside at the police cars.

Then he heard his mother and sister start screaming.

At that instant, he also knew that he would be a detective some day. From that moment on, death became a permanent part of his life.

He looked down at Dirk. Street knew there would be more screaming. This time it would be a family in New Hampshire. Street screamed inside, but no one heard. No one ever heard. Silent screams are always the loudest.

Chapter Ten:
The Colordome

T he color orange oozed across Street's windshield as he raced to the Charles Hospital. Halloween, with its orange and black candies and pumpkins, was a great time of year for Street. He thought of all the times he went trick or treating with his brother's kids. Street remembered when a man saw his police gun and lectured him about trick or treating at his age.

Like all police, Street had been in and out of the Charles, interviewing and visiting. All his life he stared at:

WELCOME TO THE CHARLES RIVER MEDICAL CENTER

And all his life he had hated the ugly orange color that was the Charles trademark.

Street did not fear much in his life, but hospitals scared him to death. Perhaps it was that rainy Saturday night when the police took him to Queens Hospital to identify his father's body. He remembers that ride to the hospital.

Street sat in the back seat of an unmarked police car with a police chaplain and a detective on each side. The car zipped through back streets and through red lights. There was no siren but he imagined it was another coffee run on a Saturday. When they reached the hospital, it was ringed with reporters. The police steadied him as they moved downstairs along a dimly lit green corridor. And then they reached the last stop. The sign said: MORGUE.

Street looked but never saw. He nodded *yes* and was back in the police car in less than three minutes.

Street had lots of questions to ask at the Charles, but first he needed a sample of paint from the orange colored garage. Inside Street felt himself changing by the minute, as if transformed like some late night B Hollywood movie. Detective Street was melting away, and in its place *the hunter* of the jungle, locked in combat with an elusive prey whose moves were lightning fast. He had more than his game face on, he was in his possessed mode, the one that knows no clock and no limits. He had radioed for a Zebra team to meet him at the garage with a portable paint test kit. Street ordered a list of all current employees of the hospital and a separate list of those on the 7th Floor, plus all former employees dating back to 1990. A Zebra team member was standing in the hospital's personnel office, watching as the list was computer generated. Each name included an address, telephone and social security number. Social security numbers would produce credit card records, bank transfers in excess of $10,000, all court records and UCCs (Universal Commercial Code). The buying and selling of property and securities would be ripped from computer banks across the country. That list would be instantly cross checked with the NCIC (National Crime Information Center). Everything except parking tickets would be available.

Perhaps Dr. Judith Sims and Dr. Dirk Eldridge had been murdered. If so, were they killed by the same person or persons and for the same reason? But, what was the motive and was anyone else at risk? Street already had doubled checked the bank records of Sims, Eldridge, and Green and they were **Dr.-Resident-Poor**.

"Damn, forgot something. Zebra, this is Street. I want 24 hour coverage on Dr. Ernie Green. You'll find his address and stuff in my computer files."

The Zebra team already had paint samples and was doing a quick on site evaluation. Street had given them orange paint chips from the white Chevy. Getting off on the 7th Floor, Street moved past one of the guards and into Marks' office. As he had requested by radio, it was filled with all the 7th Floor doctors, nurses, the Department of Defense liaison, Marks, and his secretary. Street motioned to Green, who was slumped in a chair. Green's eyes were reddened and offered a blank, dazed look. Green had taken a sedative.

"Ernie, what do I say, 'take a short walk with me'?"

Street moved Ernie away from everyone else.

"You gotta be clear for me. I can't unwind what's happened, but maybe I can find out why and who. Maybe I can keep you alive, too. You understand, I think your life is in danger. I need your help right across the boards. Right now I need to know why you think this happened."

"There's only one reason. The patient that Simsy took care of, the one Dirk was going to visit--something to do with that teacher, Hays. That's all I can figure. Somehow their deaths were connected."

Street told him he just wanted a confirmation--that's what he thought, too. He just couldn't figure why.

"Ernie, I want you out of here now. I've ordered a cop to watch you, for your protection. The cop's in plain clothes, you probably won't even notice him or her. Don't change your habits. We've got you covered and you're safe. Just get out of the hospital today. We'll talk later."

"Detective Street, this is Zebra Six; come to your orange location, please."

Street went back into Marks' office and told everyone to sit tight for a few minutes.

In the garage, one of the Zebra team members was holding two small vials of a black liquid. He motioned for Street to look under a microscope sitting inside the trunk of an unmarked car. The trunk is a mini crime laboratory.

Street tossed his fist in the air, "Knew it, damn straight, I knew it. Perfect match."

Street went upstairs. As the elevator doors opened, the guard handed him the extra copy of an employee list. He slipped it inside his blue blazer. Street moved into Marks' office. It was stilled as those inside huddled and talked.

"I've got a photographer on the way up, and we're going to take everyone's picture."

Marks stood and asked the questions on everyone's lips.

"Why the pictures? Was Dirk's death an accident like Simsy? Why all the requests for employee names? What happened to Ernie, why wasn't he in the room?"

The unknown can be a hunter's tool. Street was not going to share anything. He was asking and not answering questions. Street was observing and looking for giveaway glances. He looked silently, and, after a few more questions, Street left the room. Street knew during the next few hours the computers would do their work. Then there'd be a lot more questions.

There are over 500 full time employees of the hospital, and another 300 part timers. The payroll records turned over were fed into a national social security check, including a comparison of employees salaries vs. expenditures. Sometimes it yields credit card expenditures that don't seem logical with earned income. Until the death of Dirk, everything with the Charles had been a solo act for Street. He didn't think it deserved more personnel. Dirk's death changed that. Street pulled his partner, Mike Mickey McCoy, off another case and re-assigned him to the Charles. By the time he arrived back at police headquarters, Mike already had some news from the computer files. There were about ten employees who had charge card expenses that exceeded 20% of their earned income in the last 12 months. Three were nurses, two doctors, and several administrators. None worked on the 7th Floor. Except for the nurses, the charge expenses were for large home purchases like carpeting and furniture. The nurses had accumulated large charge expenses for a stay at the JASPER hotel in Martinique. They charged for items like clothing, first class air travel, and a sailboat rental. Each earned nearly $50,000 and paid just under $10,000 for the two weeks at the world famous JASPER, romping ground for the very rich and famous. There were some other items the computer search unearthed.

Captain Kate Beecher, of the United States Air Force, 35 years old, enjoyed the rare privilege and high honor of having two social security numbers. One framed the outline of a rising star in the Air Force with a record as distinguished and as clean as any operating room at the Charles. The second Kate Beecher had no beginning, middle, or end.

There was more. The social security check had found a match between Dr. Timothy Marks and the late Dr. Judith Sims. Both their social security numbers coincided at the Beacon Bank and Trust where they had a joint account. Why was the Chief of Medicine on the 7th Floor sharing a bank account with Sims?

Chapter Eleven:
Fiat Lux

S treet could not wait to meet both Kate Beechers.

He and Mickey read her file with amazement. It read like one of those biographies they print about astronauts every time a shuttle goes into orbit.

Captain Kate Beecher graduated from the University of California, San Diego in 1986 with a bachelor's degree in the science of nursing. Three months after graduation, she was commissioned as a 2nd Lieutenant in the United States Air Force and sent to Sheppard Air Force Base in Wichita Fall, Texas for two weeks of MIMSO (Military Indoctrination for Medical Service Officers) in Air Force jargon. She had two weeks to learn how to salute, march, wear a uniform, and recite backwards and forwards the Air Force code of conduct. She was born in LA and from her high school activities seemed targeted for beach volleyball, not Air Force blues. The two week crash course at Sheppard included the infamous Air Force Regulations 35-10, *Weight and Appearance*. Kate Beecher needed little coaching from the AFR 35-10's and its myriad of do's, don'ts, and maybes. The regulations were very specific:

HAIR ABOVE THE BOTTOM COLLAR OF THE BLOUSE, FRONT HAIR CANNOT TOUCH EYEBROWS, ONLY 3 RINGS ALLOWED, ONE BRACELET NO WIDER THAN 1 INCH, NECKLACES ONLY IF HIDDEN, BLOUSE BUTTONED WITH A "W" SHAPED BOW TIE WITH A VELCRO BACKING, AND EARRINGS MUST BE

SILVER OR GOLD AND SPHERICAL, WITH PEARLS AND DIAMONDS ALLOWED

From this two-week *miracle* school, Beecher went to an Air Force hospital, Wilford Hall at Lackland Air Force Base in San Antonio. Within four years, she had advanced to 03 pay grade: O for Officer and 3 for Captain--now, Captain Beecher. For two years, she shuttled through Europe as an Infection Control Officer. Her home base continued to be Lackland and according to her records she saw little of it.

Finally in 1990, she was assigned to Hanscom Field, northwest of Boston. She moved onto the 7th Floor as the Department of Defense liaison officer.

Her career was punctuated with special commendations and letters from her superiors. Street and McCoy were impressed-- Street more than McCoy.

"Mickey, you know what really impresses me about this Beecher? She's marching up this ladder in the Air Force, going here and there, flying all over the place. Then, for about two years, there's this big hole. No letters from her supervisors, no travel to Europe, no vacations, nothing. She was just swallowed by the Air Force. In 1990, presto, she's back and shows up on the 7th Floor. OK, you figure that one."

It was past six PM when Street finished reading about Captain Kate Beecher. Or at least the Kate Beecher assigned to one of the social security numbers. The other Kate Beecher was missing. The *Celtics* were playing a game that night; and, as Street watched it on TV, he couldn't get Beecher too far away from his thoughts. Tomorrow, he would get his chance to toss a jump ball in the air and see which Kate Beecher went for it.

It was exactly nine AM when Street and McCoy pulled into the Charles garage. The Captain Kate Beecher he had met through computer files matched nicely with the real person. She was much prettier than he had imagined and looked so *military*, so put together and official in her formal dress blue uniform. Her jacket was off, and her long sleeved blouse was decorated with two silver bars, called *railroad tracks*, on the blue epaulets. Beecher had short dirty blonde hair and was trim and very healthy looking.

Street, the runner, noticed things like that whenever he met people. Her office was small, decorated only with a few pictures of airplanes on the walls. Street thought what was not on the walls was much more interesting.

Street was a student of the art of interrogation. He noted every gesture, nonverbal sign and voice tone. He always tried to mentally disarm the other person while his eyes looked for voice changes, checking a wristwatch, clenched teeth, crossing and uncrossing feet, difficulty in eye contact, playing with hands, reddening of the face and tapping of fingers. No move, no matter how slight, went undetected.

"Captain Beecher, thanks for seeing us on short notice."

If Street were expecting a warm hello, those thoughts were blown right out of the air with Beecher's silent nod. Not a single word.

"You know, Captain, I've read your file and it's impressive. But I'm probably not very smart on things like this, so I'm sure you can straighten me out. You're in the Air Force, you travel all over the world, you meet lots of interesting people, you have family back in California, and yet I don't see one single picture in your office of anyone. Not one person. Not even pets. What am I missing?"

Street saw her legs moving under the desk.

"Detective, that's just how I am. I'm a private person. My pictures are at home."

"Lie." Beecher never heard him whisper the word.

Street did not need to hear a lie. After all his years on the force, he could feel one rattle through his bones like an earthquake. Street thought to himself, "Why would she lie about that?"

"Something else, Captain: we looked at your service record and it's a real hum dinger. But there's this big hole in it for a couple of years. You sort of disappear--you know what I mean? All those nice commendation letters stopped. Did you hit a bad streak?"

"Detective, I don't know what you mean. My military record is what it says it is. Any other questions?"

Street lived for these moments. The times when he came to the plate with the bases loaded, a chance to kick a winning Super Bowl point, or nail the giant lion he tracked all night in his imagination.

"Captain Beecher, you have two social security numbers. Explain that to me."

"I didn't know that; so I can't help you."

"You know Captain. With all due respect, you've really not been much help. Just a couple of other things and we're out of here. I couldn't help but notice the initials ED all over your calendar. Who's ED?"

"You're funny, detective. Are you jealous? That stands for eye doctor. I have some appointments for new glasses."

Street reached into his pocket and pulled out a fat blue and white pen with the Boston Police logo on it. He always carried a couple with him. Then he rolled it across the desk to Beecher.

"Could you write down your home address and telephone number, please."

Beecher took the pen and wrote the information.

"Detective, can I keep this as a souvenir?" Street didn't know whether she had figured out what he was doing, or simply wanted a Boston Police pen.

"I'll look around for an extra one." Beecher returned the pen.

Street and McCoy got up and left. Street high-fived McCoy as they approached their car.

Street said, "Captain Beecher's a smooth customer, a very classy liar." Street called the Zebra team from his car. "They still haven't heard. So we wait and see what our FBI contact says about this Beecher."

"Mickey, bet she's OSI (Office of Special Investigations)."

The OSI is exactly what it says it is. It's Air Force officers who specialize in counterintelligence operations and conduct criminal investigations. OSI Special Agents train at their academy at Bolling Air Force Base, Washington, DC. The OSI has its own forensic laboratories and criminal records center. Most persons do not volunteer for the OSI. Officers are picked, then groomed and inducted into one of the most elite branches of the military. Agents of the OSI dress in civilian clothes. It's rare to find an

OSI agent in a military uniform, unless the uniform is, itself, a disguise. If Captain Kate Beecher is also Agent Kate Beecher, then the 7th Floor at the Charles is a lot more special than Street imagined. He wondered if Dr. Marks suspected Beecher's double role.

If she were an Agent, it might explain why there were no pictures of people in her office. ED probably did not stand for eye doctor. Street was no doctor, but he bet she had 20/20 vision.

"Mickey, I'll talk with Beecher again. We've got questions for Dr. Marks and most everyone else on the 7th. The more I learn, the less I understand. That'll change."

Chapter Twelve:
Nocturnal Nightmares

In a chilling preview of Halloween, Detective Jimmy Street met a killer on an early October night.

The killer left no fingerprints and pummeled its victims without remorse or fear of being caught. Like every serial killer, the screams of those who are about to die can never be silenced until the killer is no more. There is no surrender and no chance of respite. Those chosen to die do so in measured time. Death visits not with the speed of a bullet or slash of a knife; it lingers for agonizing months. This killer does evil on his time.

The profile of pancreatic cancer is four victims an hour, 168 hours a week, but not one minute on *America's Most Wanted* or *Crime Stoppers*.

Street was transfixed by its orgy of death. Victims were tortured with nocturnal pain described as a drill boring through the gut. Doctors call it epigastric ache. Simple human pleasures like eating or reclining make the pain worse. Bloating, flatulence, malaise and vomiting join jaundice and weight loss in a sickening circular dance around the victim. Each minute awake is an hour of torment, deadened only by pain killers so strong that they make numb any senses left mercifully at peace. Medical management is emasculated. Doctors are humbled in its shadow and can offer only pain reduction, nutritional help and so called, *general support*. Those are funny words, "general support" for, in this battle, the disease is the general and the doctors only silent witnesses at a slow execution.

Pancreatic cancer kills as it chooses---with renal failure, cardiovascular collapse, respiratory insufficiency and gastrointestinal bleeding.

Alone at home, Street could imagine Sims fighting this night stalker as it welcomed each new victim into its bowels. If she had stumbled upon a cure for advanced pancreatic cancer, she was perhaps the most important person in our lifetime. That mistaken dosage was perhaps a cure delivered through divine intervention or even a fluke.

Reading about this killer who saved his painful moments for the dead of night, he saw the ghost of a dead doctor running next to him in the Marathon. At his side was Dr. Judith Sims urging him to cross the finish line. Street saw her rolling over cold marble floors trying to break the grip of this killer. Somehow, all five feet of her managed to trip it and break the strangle hold on Hays. She fought not for glory or a Nobel Prize; she fought to save the life of a 40-year old English teacher. Police reports have her neatly tucked away as the victim of a freak assault of anaphylactic shock. Dirk might soon follow her into the kingdom of nowhere files as another hit and run victim. At home, Street saw the emerging face of this pancreatic cancer along with the faces of Sims and Dirk. He promised that when he next crossed the finish line of the Boston Marathon in April, he would do so with Sims and Dirk running at his side.

As he spoke to himself, the words were like an aphrodisiac, bringing him closer to this evil. This cancer had human partners that, for unknown reasons, wanted Sims and Dirk dead and the killer disease to live.

Street could not put the medical journal down despite so many words that made no sense to him. In many ways, it read like a homicide report, methodical and without emotion. Words like *unfortunate outcome* or *ineffective* or *increased incidence* were now obscene. Damn, these were people being described. Fathers and mothers of real children with homes and jobs. They were little league coaches and cops and the people who collect toys for children each year. Street was 46 and he had nephews and a sister and parents. Street knew that he and his Zebra Team and all the cops of Boston combined were nothing but ornaments for this killer. Were there humans protecting this monster that Sims may have stripped naked? If he could hunt down the humans, perhaps he could find what Sims had found. If she had found anything at all.

He put the journal down and picked up a book. It read like a telephone book with mostly numbers and charts. There was an increased incidence of pancreatic carcinoma in males and blacks and people in developed countries. More of the same crap, the same unemotional gobble-de-gook. It says chemical carcinogens are strongly suspected. Street wouldn't recognize a chemical carcinogen even if it were between the lettuce and tomato of his next tuna sandwich. The book says anthracene derivatives induce cancer of the pancreas in experimental animals. Sims wasn't experimenting with animals! Finally, Street saw words he recognized. It was like finding a desert oasis after a long night search. It says, "Cystic Fibrosis is the most common cause of childhood exocrine pancreatic insufficiency in the US." So now, they're talking about little kids.

It was three AM when Street awoke, fully dressed on his living room sofa. Was all this an ugly dream? The medical books and journals scattered across the floor said no.

Street was trapped. His mind flipped through names and phone numbers. Could he call his partner Mickey? What about his sister Anne? No, the middle of the night call would scare her. Boston Police had a 24 hour hotline for cops who need to talk. That was no good because every caller was logged in and got a call from a staff psychologist the next day. Street remembered six months of required therapy after his partner was shot and killed. The sessions always went back to the shooting of his father.

Perhaps somewhere in the Charles walked a human killing machine. Street put a face on his villain. It was in partnership with a disease whose face was pocketed with craters filled with sewage. This killer was so cold when it looked inside, it froze at the sight of its own hellish reflection.

Street pictured combat in the Charles between those dedicated to helping people in need and those whose need to help was dead. Street knew that evil needed both power and greed to sustain itself.

Chapter Thirteen:
The Fury

A furious storm rocked Street during the night as he labored through medical journals and books. He was imploding. Street began to make phone calls. The time was four AM.

"Dr. Marks, this is Detective Street."

"What the hell's going on?"

Beecher and Dory also received middle of the night phone calls from Street.

At nine AM, all three assembled in Marks' office, with Marks and Beecher drowsy in their chairs. Dory was not seated. He was walking circles around one of Marks' oriental rugs. His face was red with anger and he wasted no time.

"Detective, you've got a lot of nerve calling my house in the middle of the night. You think you've got some license to do that. There are laws. And what right do you have to call Beecher and Marks? You're off the wall, a real loony. I've got a meeting in New York; so, if you've got any questions, make them quick."

Street put his hand on Dory's shoulder, then gently pinched.

"That's a charming little speech we just heard. Fly away Dory. When you come back we'll meet you at the airport and take you downtown in a blue and white with flashing lights. You can answer my questions overnight. Then we'll take you back to your ritzy home in another squad car. This time we'll add sirens to the flashing lights. Before you know it, Dory, why they'll be a big crowd in front of your house. Tell you what, we'll take all the

kids in the neighborhood for rides. You can tell them about your
night at headquarters. So go catch that flight."

Atwood Dory plunked himself down in a chair. Marks and
Beecher glanced at each other with wide eyes. They had never
seen Dory back down to anyone. He was the town bully. He
used every centimeter of his power every day and in every way.
This morning they watched as he was on the receiving end.

Street looked at Dory with satisfaction.

"That son-of-a-bitch probably had himself a nice breakfast. I
had shit. No breakfast, no shave, no clean shirt."

What Street did have on was his game face and his mind
riveted to images of Dr. Judith Sims. He was tired, irritable, and
angry.

"You three are going to answer my questions. The first time
I hear *no*, we'll all parade down to the garage where my partner
Mickey is waiting. He'll drive you downtown while I wait for a
search warrant. Then we go through every last pencil holder on
this whole damn floor."

Everyone was paying attention.

"I want some medical things translated into English, preferably
with no more than a couple of syllables. I'm sure you can help
me with that."

First, Street tried a little experiment.

"Dr. Marks, would you please pick up your phone."

Marks looked around the room with a big question mark on
his face. He reached for the phone with his right hand.

"That's fine. Now, Captain Beecher, would you please do the
same."

She also extended her right hand.

"Now, my friend Dory, it's your turn. Let's pretend it's 10 PM
and you're going to call your wife to tell her you'll be at police
headquarters all night."

Dory did not like the sarcasm. He reached for the phone with
his left hand.

"OK, folks, here's what I see. I see two right-handers and one
southpaw. Is that correct?"

All three signaled, Yes.

Street reached into his pocket and pulled out some notes on yellow lined paper.

"I'm reading from notes taken by Detective Rico Santori last September while he was in Dr. Judith Sims' apartment. Quote: *Deceased is left handed and right hand extended to telephone.* Now why would she reach for a telephone with the wrong hand?"

Street didn't expect any answers. He wanted to send a message.

"Now here's another one for you. Maybe you can help with this. Dr. Dirk Eldridge, roommate of Dr. Sims got himself hit by a car the other day. A nice new white car with a woman driver who never used her brakes, left no fingerprints, and walked over to another car and vanished. The only thing she left for us was some nasty orange paint on the side of this new car. Guess she must have hit something before she hit your doctor. Would anyone like to guess where that orange paint came from?"

Marks stood up, "Detective, obviously you're saying it came from here, right?"

"Thank you, Dr. Marks. It did come from here. Weren't you the one that Dr. Sims' mother talked to about someone following her home?"

"I was, indeed."

"Let's get into some of these medical words." The door to Marks' office sprung open and his secretary motioned to Street.

"Detective, there's a call for you and they say it's important."

Street had a hunch who was calling.

"I'll be right back, folks; so, just get comfortable." No one in the room was comfortable.

"Street, this is Bill. I've got some answers." The *Bill* was Bill Winters, Special Agent in the Boston office of the FBI.

"We've got some answers on that pen you sent over."

Street interrupted Winters, "Wait a minute, Bill. Can I reach you at your number. I'll go down to my car and give you a call. This is kind of public, you know what I mean?"

Street went back to Marks' office, "Folks, I'm going to be busy for a few minutes. When I get back, we'll continue. Be back in about 15 minutes."

It took two minutes to make it down the elevator to his car.

"Bill, this is Street. We can talk now. I'm on a scrambled cellular line. So what did you find?"

"We ran the fingerprints on the pen and lifted a few really good ones. Do you want to hear about Beecher or yourself?" Street laughed at Winter's joke. Over the years, Street had been an occasional 1st baseman for one of the Boston Police softball teams that played against Winter's FBI team. The Boston Police team always won.

The FBI has more than 200 million fingerprint files indexed alphabetically at their Washington, DC headquarters. More than half contain criminal history data, while the rest cover federal employees, alien registration, military personnel and individuals requesting their prints on file for the purpose of identification. In addition, the FBI also maintains technical files on such things as anonymous letters, hair and fiber references, national automotive paint and altered numbers, and national stolen property. These files are used regularly by city, state and federal agencies.

"Captain Kate Susan Beecher is Special Agent Beecher of the OSI, just like you figured."

Street sat in the car and thought about what to do next. Was Beecher an OSI agent who was managing the 7th Floor liaison office, or was she there for some specific reason? Who knew she was more than a Captain in the Air Force? There were so many possibilities. Street needed to talk with her without putting her in the spotlight.

"Well, everyone, thanks for waiting."

Street eyed Marks, Beecher and Dory.

"Captain Beecher, may I call you Kate? Would you mind running across the street and pick us up some bagels?"

Street reached into his wallet and pulled out a crisp new $20 bill. Beecher's reaction was easy to predict.

"Detective, you're a prehistoric creature. The sun's going to rise in the west before I ever get you anything. I'm an Officer in the United States Air Force and you speak to me like some kind of kitchen help. Why don't you go to hell."

Street walked over to Beecher and grabbed her by the elbow. He whispered in her ear, "Let's take a walk, now, Agent Kate Beecher or do you want me to start speaking louder?"

Beecher was on her way out of the room.

"Excuse me, gentlemen. Dr. Marks and Mr. Dory: I'll talk with you in a little while. Anyone going anywhere?"

Beecher and Street rode the elevator down to the lobby, exchanging not one word. Now every time he saw the hospital lobby and its orange colors, his mind reversed to the scene of the white *Monte Carlo* and Dirk's body not far away. Orange was never his favorite color anyway. When they got outside the building, Beecher broke the silence.

"Are you for real, Street? You've got a hell of a lot of nerve to embarrass me like that. Do you have some serious male ego problem. Maybe your hormones are out of whack."

Beecher would have continued, but Street ended her speech.

"What I said upstairs was intentional. I wanted you out of there without creating a hassle, Agent Beecher. I didn't want to put you under suspicion."

Beecher asked, "Suspicion for what? I don't know what you're rambling on about. You're strange, Detective. Do you handle all people this way?"

"Enough, Beecher. Let's get across the street, sit down, and have a cup of coffee. We can help each other."

After they sat down, Street absorbed how physically appealing Beecher was. The uniform was one thing, but her thin hands and fingers were so feminine. Her eyes, when not ablaze in anger, were a stunning shade of hazel in perfect color harmony with her dirt blonde hair. He noticed that she was in great physical shape. Beecher was very different from his ex-wife in so many ways.

Street's mind reversed to Susan Street. He met her while a beat cop. He walked a beat that included the big newsstand at the corner of Boylston and Dartmouth Streets in Boston's ritzy Back Bay. They smiled and, after a few encounters, Street walked with her to the travel agency where she worked. She traveled to Europe every three months. Within a year Street had a collection of postcards from London and Paris. Two years after meeting, they went to Paris together on their honeymoon. It was the last good time he could remember with her. After the marriage, she changed. She put on weight and cut back to part time at the travel agency. Soon, she seemed totally absorbed in daytime TV soaps and complaints about Street and his long work days.

"Detective, testing one-two-three. Are you in space?"

"Sorry, just thinking."

This detective had burst into her life, disrupting it with questions and obnoxious asides. She was about six inches shorter than Street and thought he was physically appealing--when his mouth was closed. Beecher sensed they were both consumed. When she looked at his worn white shirt and scruffy face, she instinctively wanted to reach over the table and clean him. There was no chance that was going to happen. Not now, anyway.

"Can I start calling you Kate, or do you want it to be Agent Beecher?"

There was an ever so slight smile. "It's not Agent anything, but if it'll make your life easier, go for it, call me Kate."

"Kate, was that just a speck of a smile I saw, like a coming attraction? I want you to call me Jimmy, not Street and not Detective, OK?"

At last, they had agreed on one thing besides two black coffees, no sugar.

"Let me share some stuff with you, Kate. I've got a confession to make. When we talked before, remember when I handed over that big fat blue and white pen and asked you to write your address. You wanted to keep it. Well, I carry a bunch of those around and they're real handy for getting fingerprints. That's exactly what I did. By the way, you asked to keep a pen, and that's OK now."

Street pushed one across the table. Beecher took the pen and grudgingly mustered a half smile.

"Jimmy, you're funny. If I was an agent, like you imagine, then don't you think I would have figured out that silly pen trick? I hope you got a good set of fingerprints."

"Yeah, sure, but what could you do, wipe it off in front of me? I had you. You knew it."

"So, tell me why you think I'm some sort of agent?"

Street reached over the table and touched her hand.

"I know for a fact that you're in the OSI. I've got friends at the FBI and they ran your fingerprints. That extra social security number was a clerical error and you ought to get it fixed. It's like a big red flag, even to an amateur like myself."

"You're not an amateur, and this probably sounds silly to you Jimmy, but all I can give you is my name, rank and serial number, if you get the gist of what I'm saying. Speaking of names, I like Street better."

"Can I inspect your dog tags?"

"Cute."

Street knew they had connected. The words came easier.

"Kate, I've been alone for a long time in my life, so this detective stuff is about all I've got. Most people say I'm real good at it. So here's a little wager. Sometime today you're going to call that so called eye doctor, the ED on your calendar and tell him about our little chat. Then he's going to call so and so, who'll call so and so, and before you know it, my boss will be on the phone with yours. Then, you're going to get the OK to tell me what I already know, Agent Beecher. If I'm right, we have dinner together."

"And what do I win if you're wrong?"

"Tell you what, if I'm wrong, you're looking at your very own delivery service for lunch. You'll order it, and I'll pick it up and serve it right at your desk."

"Detective, you've got a deal."

Beecher looked at Street without expression. She looked into his eyes. She kept looking in silence. Street noticed and knew something was wrong.

"Kate, why are you looking? What's wrong?"

"Street, it's your eyes. You wear contacts, right?"

"Yeah, so what?"

"Well, under that hazel colored contact is a brown eye. I can see brown on the edges. And I'll bet the other contact is a dummy. It's there to balance the other contact. Your eyes are different colors. Street, why didn't you tell me you're a walking medical marvel?"

"Very funny."

Street was not laughing inside. Never in his career had anyone noticed his colored contacts.

"Guess the only thing you haven't done is read my mind."

Beecher smiled, "You'll never know, Street."

Street sent Beecher back to the 7th Floor while he made a phone call to the Zebra Team.

"What about that account at Beacon Bank and Trust? When was it opened and how much went in?"

One of the team members reported the bank account was opened in late April and deposits totaled about $25,000. The deposits came in monthly amounts of $5,000.

Street had gone 24 hours without sleep. The dynamics with Beecher were changing quickly. As for Dr. Marks, *King and Creator* of the 7th Floor, Street was puzzled. Everything about this man's life and habits were impeccable. He was honored, revered, and had dedicated his life to savings lives through the development of new medical treatments. There had to be an explanation for the $25,000 joint bank account with Sims. More importantly, there had to be a reason he had not told the police. Surely he knew it would be discovered.

Then there was Atwood Edward Dory, a man Street could never like. He was smug and nasty. Dory was a spoiled brat whose toy, the 7th Floor, was being touched by other *kids*. Dory did not share and it seemed to Street that he did not care, except for himself. Street was prepared to donate to Dr. Marks the benefit of every doubt and to farm from Dory every explanation, no matter how reasonable.

It was almost 12 noon and Street found Marks in his office.

"Street, I've been on the phone with Dirk's parents in New Hampshire and we're all going up tomorrow for the funeral. That's two of my people gone in just a few days. Ernie's taking all this really hard. His parents came up to spend time with him. I'm really proud of my doctors and how they've rallied around the team. You know they've still got patients to care for while they try and help themselves. Social services in the hospital has arranged some counseling for the residents, especially Gaetano and Ernie."

Street saw the pain in Marks' eyes and for a moment he thought of calling off the questioning till after the funeral. But he could not do it.

"Dr. Marks, this is a rotten time to ask questions, but, I just don't have any choice. You understand?"

As a master at medicine and research, Marks understood more than most that time was a perishable commodity. It could never be put aside. The only timeless things in his life were the great classical music works he enjoyed at Symphony Hall. Often he would ponder how men like Beethoven and Mozart could reach across time and touch people with their music.

"I need your help to translate all the medical things I read last night, this morning, whenever it was. First, I've got to know why you and Dr. Sims shared a bank account at Beacon Bank and Trust. What's that all bout?"

"Detective, I was going to tell you about that. The answer is quite harmless and logical. Did you find out about it from her computer files? As you know, Judith thought she had stumbled on some sort of cure for this patient Hays and his advanced pancreatic cancer. She told me all about it. We've got a discretionary fund here on the 7th Floor provided as a block grant for use as I see fit. It totals about $100,000. I told her to proceed with experimental care for her patient, but that without more data, we were going to release him as a misdiagnosis. There was no other choice. I respected Judith. She believed this patient was going into remission from advanced pancreatic cancer. Now that just does not happen. And she thought it had to do with her mistaken dosage of the experimental drug, XM2. I didn't want her to stop looking, reading, and experimenting. It had to be done outside regular 7th Floor channels. So, I made a note in my diary, set up a joint account with her, and disbursed the money each month. That's it. You can verify all that through the canceled checks. Hindsight is 20/20 vision, and in light of what's happened, it was probably a mistake."

Street took notes as Marks talked. "Doctor, how did you know she had computer files. How did you know she had a computer?"

Marks again answered quickly and directly. "She sent me notes on her E-mail."

"OK, Dr. Marks, you can probably see the lines under my eyes. Last night I tried to digest a bunch of medical books and journals.

I got some information, and a hell of a case of indigestion. I need your help, kind of like a translator."

Marks pressed a buzzer for his secretary, Q. She brought in coffee and sandwiches. Marks moved over to a large chalkboard in the corner of the office. The chalkboard was black and the chalk, Charles River orange.

"Dr. Marks, do you have another color chalk. This *orange* thing is getting to me. I hate the damn color!"

"OK, Detective Street, fire away with questions." Marks picked up a few long yellow pieces of chalk.

"Our medical examiner says Dr. Sims died of anaphylactic shock. Well, I've never gotten on that horse, if you know what I mean. See, I just don't understand how it all works. Can you explain?"

Street could see Marks, the teacher, light up like a lighthouse to guide someone lost. This was his element.

"Detective, I'll do my best to keep it simple and short. In most people, the immune system protects the body. That immune system is like radar. Sometimes it malfunctions and misreads signals. If it did nothing else, then there'd be no problem. The trouble is that our immune system can do more than react; it can also respond to these benign--call them harmless--substances. And that's because the immune system thinks they are harmful antigens. I'll explain *antigens* as we go along. This reaction involves an interaction between the foreign substances known as allergens and specific antibodies. The allergens are antigens that stimulate antibody production. I know this a bit complex; so, keep your eyes on the chalkboard."

Street was walking a high wire across two tall peaks. He was shaking and twisting, trying to hold his balance. Every time he thought of falling, the images of Sims and Dirk ran across his face. He had to hold on and stay focused.

"Street, when these foreign substances, allergens, enter the body, they react with antibodies called, and I'll write it out, *IgE*, on the surface of a circulating white blood cell, something we call basophils. They do the same with cells in the respiratory and gastrointestinal tracks and skin--we call those mast cells. Hang in there detective. These basophils and mast cells release Histamine. Now you've heard that word before on the radio or TV. There's another circulating white blood cell called Eosinophil. The number of IgE antibodies that are present in the body controls the severity of the symptoms, sort of like a lever. Anaphylactic shock is simply a severe allergic reaction when the blood vessels dilate and air passages narrow. These reactions can come from things like food, preservatives, bee stings, and blood. I saw the report of the medical examiner. He claims that Dr. Sims died of anaphylactic shock due to human seminal fluids. In other words, she had sex with someone and had an allergic reaction to the fluids in his sperm."

Marks continued, "Truth is, as difficult as it is to accept, she was with someone else after Dirk left for New Hampshire. No one seems willing to accept that fact. That man's semen caused the reaction that sent her spinning to disaster. Why he didn't call police as she was dying is beyond me."

"How long would it take for Sims to have this allergic reaction after sex?"

Marks' answer hit Street like a pinprick. "Street, she would have been in big trouble within ten minutes."

"You mean, this guy has sex with her, then she had this terrible allergic reaction and is fighting for her life, and he gets up, gets dressed, and walks out without calling police?"

"Its hard to believe someone could do that."

"Well, Dr. Marks, that's not good enough for me. I don't buy it. Even if this guy's a jerk, he's going to call the police for help and then leave. He just wouldn't bolt without doing something."

Street knew the other answer. If this was murder, then the rules change.

"Dr. Marks, thanks for your help. I don't have more questions. I will later." Street pulled out one of his big Boston Police pens and gave it to Marks. "Could you make a note of your home address and telephone?"

Unlike Kate Beecher, Marks was not interested in a souvenir pen from the Boston Police and he returned it with no questions. Street believed Marks, but he also believed checking his finger-prints was wise.

"Dr. Marks, one last thing. Tell Dory I'll see him tomorrow while you and your staff are at Dirk's funeral. I'm sure he's not going."

"How'd you know that?"

"Twenty years on the police force and ten of them as a detective. I know about people. The only funeral he's going to attend is his own."

Atwood Edward Dory was waiting for Street when he returned the next day at 10 AM. He struggled to find the most effective approach for his interrogation. It could be confrontational, using Dory's overplayed anger from the other day. Or, Street could try to slide gently into Dory's mind with an easy approach. The bottom line for Street was he was going into Dory's head whether Dory liked it or not.

"Mr. Dory, we got off to a real lousy start the other day. I was dog tired and you're probably right, I shouldn't have called in the middle of the night. That's just me. So, I'm sorry about the other day, and we can make this day number one."

Street never scripted the dialogue; instead, the words flowed from his mouth. He was going for a soft and cuddly approach.

"Detective Street, that's very humble of you to admit you messed up and if you're apologizing, I certainly accept. These haven't been the best of days up here on the 7th recently. Everyone's on edge. I'm here to help; so, I'm ready when you are. Please, call me Atwood."

Street thought to himself, "Nice, now I can call this pompous ass by his first name, Atwood. Let's do it man, and try to stay cool."

"Atwood, before we start, take just a second to write your home address, telephone, close family members. It's just routine, for the files only. Here's a pen."

Street rolled one of his *big blues* across the table.

"That's OK detective, I've got my own *Mont Blanc* right here."

Street was always ready for comebacks like that. "Humor me, Atwood. I know this sounds silly, but I'm one of those superstitious types, you know: Friday the 13th, black cats, the whole routine. That pen is good luck for everyone who uses it."

Dory took it and complied with Street's request. He handed the pen over, and Street carefully, but nonchalantly, placed it inside his suit coat. Dory had joined Beecher and Marks in Street's great fingerprint parade. Now Street was ready to notch up his intensity level.

"Atwood, this has nothing to do directly with Sims and Dirk's deaths, but how come you don't go to funerals for co-workers?"

"Street, let's not pretend I'm *one of the guys* up here. They tolerate me at best, and only then because I've got the money that let's them do all their creative research. They resent the power I have and that's tough luck. Without me and Gene World, they'd all be dicking around in some hospital somewhere, just nameless faces doing what thousands of other doctors do. Instead, they're up here, princes of the medical world. And it's all because of my Company and the risk capital we invest here. Don't get me wrong, I knew both Sims and Eldridge, and it's not personal. They had this one friend, Ernie Green, who really grates me. He's the one with the smelly brown sneakers, the know-it-all. He's a trouble maker with a mouth that's way too big. He'll be at the funeral and that alone is good enough reason for me not to be there."

"Fair enough, Atwood. I understand where you're coming from on this."

There are crossroads during every interrogation. Those are the moments when the outcome is in doubt. Street was in Dory's office to take a measure of him. He was doing this interview alone to put him at ease, increasing the chance that he would reveal something useful. But Street disliked Dory in a visceral way. None of the dislike was objective. He knew his next question would break the façade.

"I understand you're a big Nazi fan. Is that right Atwood?"

Right before Street's eyes, he watched Dory's face change color to red. The words zoomed in as if a smart bomb and they ignited dead center on target.

"Street, you were doing so well. What's this crap? I'm a student of World War II, particularly the European conflict. It's a hobby of mine. Any problems?"

Welcome back, the Atwood Dory that Street had just met. For a detective like Street, who doesn't like someone, Dory's words were like an invitation for lunch. Street was hungry.

"Atwood, I did some reading last night. Who's this Nazi, Dr. Josef Mengele? Wasn't he called the *Angel of Death* and he did medical experiments in concentration camps. That Mengele, wasn't he doing medical experiments at Auschwitz? Sort of like here on your 7th Floor. I'll bet he's in some of your books. Did you read about these two doctors who were trying to figure out how fast infections spread in war wounds. So what these doctors did is remove part of, let's see, I wrote it down...yeah, they removed part of the tibia and infected it with bacteria. They called that *kroliky* in Polish. It means guinea pig. So, is that what you're doing up here Dory?"

"Get out of here, you scum bag! You're crazy. You think I'm some Nazi lover? I'm all done talking. Interview over."

Dory's face was redder than a stop light. He leaped from his chair and started towards him. Street was not surprised. That's why he pulled his *big blue pen* trick at the start of the interview. Dory was on fire and Street would pour more gasoline.

"Sit down, Dory; we've just started."

"No detective, you can take your carnival show and get lost."

"OK, I'll do just that." Street took Dory's phone and dialed.

"Mickey, come on upstairs. Our friend here, Mr. Atwood Edward Dory, has decided he doesn't wish to answer any more questions here. We're taking him to headquarters."

Street turned to Dory, "You can call your lawyer from here."

Atwood Dory's face turned white as Street's words sunk in.

"I'm sorry, Detective; really, I apologize. Ask me anything you want. I've never even been in a police station."

"Well then, today's your lucky day, Dory. We'll give you the tour at no cost. I never bluff, not in this business. We're going for a ride. We'll wait for my partner and then leave. I suggest you sit down and chill. Say Dory, are any of your Nazi books autographed?"

Chapter Fourteen:
The Sysop

Street sat in the back seat of his cruiser with Dory as they drove to headquarters. He felt like a *Sysop*, a computer operator who manages a computer bulletin board with all its varying interests, conflicts and needs. This was like returning to his days as a rookie cop directing traffic. Look what was in motion around him. He was riding to police headquarters with a hot shot Wall Street investment banker. In New Hampshire, they were burying Dr. Dirk Eldridge, someone Street knew briefly but liked. In Toledo, Ohio the parents of Dr. Judith Sims were trying to understand what happened to their daughter while stunned by the news of her boyfriend's death. Add to that a Captain in the Air Force charged with overseeing the Department of Defense and its involvement in the 7th Floor at the Charles River Medical Center. A captain who, it appears, was a Special Agent of the OSI, the Air Force's counterintelligence agency. Then he thought of the clouds that blocked a clear view of the death of Dr. Sims and Eldridge. There was the white Monte Carlo with an orange dent and a hit and run driver who left no fingerprints and vanished. And a promising young physician dying of an allergic reaction while the man who may have caused it is unknown. Implanted within Street's brain were the chilling thoughts about pancreatic cancer and what, if anything, did Dr. Judith Sims discover while treating her patient, Steven Hays. Street wished he had never met this pancreatic cancer, for, it was a killer that made him ponder his own mortality.

Street always connected death and criminals. That night in Queens, After his father was gunned down, the memory visited him every day. Now, Street had met a killer without fingerprints. He met a killer that did not care about Miranda rights and lawyers.

Few things in life scared him and this was one. At least his instincts were intact. He remembered the *Code 10-67: Person Calling For Help* when Dirk reported the break-in at his apartment. Something inside said, "Take the call," and he did. Now he was arriving at police headquarters with Atwood Dory.

Dory's bad attitude was hijacked somewhere between the hospital and police headquarters. The most defining word to describe him was contrite. Not an idiot, Dory figured that he had overplayed his hand with Street. Kick-ass was OK in the hospital where he controlled the money. Now it was two PM and Dory knew and the next few hours were going to be difficult.

"Dory, before we start, you need to get a lawyer. Whatever you say in here will be video taped."

"Are you charging me with anything?"

Street thought the suggestion of a lawyer would help expand Dory's anxiety, and it succeeded.

"Like I said, Dory; if you want a lawyer, this is the time to make some calls and get one. We'll wait as long as it takes for your lawyer to get here. It's your choice."

"I don't want a lawyer, just get on with it."

Street and Mickey McCoy ushered Dory into a plain looking room with a beat up wooden desk and some chairs. There were a clock and fan inside and a couple of windows with the drapes pulled. In one corner was a video tape recorder mounted on a tripod and a young man in a Boston Police trainee uniform standing with it.

"OK, Mr. Atwood Dory, the camera is on. So, for the record, we recommend you say nothing and get a lawyer. You have indicated you wish to proceed and answer our questions, right?"

Dory nodded, Yes, in silence.

Street said, "Mr. Dory, would you please respond to my question with a verbal answer."

"Just get on with this. I don't need or want a lawyer. I want to answer your questions and get out of here." His discomfort, particularly matched against a privileged lifestyle, was a weapon

Street could use. Street knew he would get only one chance with Dory like this unless he uncovered something material to the deaths of Sims or Eldridge.

"For the record, I was questioning you in your office at the Charles today. I inquired about some books you have on Hitler. For example, I understand you have books containing materials on Dr. Josef Mengele, who did medical experiments at the death camp of Auschwitz. Why do you have those books?"

This time Dory answered in a measured voice. The red came back to his face, but he was not going to make the same mistake again and lose his temper. He explained that he was student of World War II and that the subject of medical experiments conducted by the Nazis interested him. While saying these experiments on concentration victims was despicable, he pointed out that they were considered important enough to be in the possession of the US Government.

"Dory, this is Detective Santori. He was the detective called to Dr. Sims' apartment when Dirk found her dead. He's going to ask you a couple of background questions while I step outside with my partner. We'll be back in a few minutes."

"Mickey, we'll let his mind wonder a bit. How long will it take to get back the info on his fingerprints?" Twenty-four hours was about average in cases like this.

"Mickey, I figure we're going to ring his bell about that corporate sales trip to the JASPER in Martinique. Remember, we've got proof three nurses in that hospital were there at the same time. That's a very ritzy place and a nice little coincidence. Is there anything else I can use?"

"Afraid not; you're going to have to wing it, Street."

Street and McCoy went back in the room as Santori was finishing.

"Rico, I'll take over; we've got the info." Street had no information but made sure Dory heard those words.

"Mickey, what are the names of those three nurses from Dory's hospital, the ones who went down to his company's sales meeting in Martinique?"

Dory interrupted, "They didn't go to our sales meeting. They weren't invited and they didn't attend any function." Street thought how accommodating it was for Dory to interrupt and help things along.

"Mr. Dory, we have a variety of sources to verify facts and it's important you give your memory a real good test here. Mickey, what are those names?"

"Well, we have Patricia Luis, another Patricia with the last name of Goldberg, and a Cindy MetCalfe. All are nurses in their mid 20's, and none work on the 7th Floor."

Street motioned to his partner and then turned to the cadet operating the video recorder.

"Hey kid, turn that off for a few minutes and grab some coffee. Mickey, leave me alone with Mr. Dory for a few minutes."

Both retreated, with McCoy going next door and peering back into the room through a one-way mirror.

"Atwood, you and I should talk off the record. This is about your last chance on this one. How about I tell you a little story and you tell me if it's fact or fiction. You're married. But, you get a little bored. One of these nurses happens to be, you know, a diversion. So it's real cold over the winter and you're heading down to Martinique for a medical conference. You're a nice guy; so, you give this nurse the money for a trip to Martinique while you're there. She can't go because if anyone sees her there alone, well, people always ask questions. Bingo, some rich aunt dies and leaves her some money and she decides to take two friends along. She gives them the bucks for the trip and off they all go. So, Atwood, just between us guys, is that fact or fiction?"

Dory's *eyes-down* look gave Street the answer. "Atwood, which one?"

"Cindy."

Street pressed a buzzer and his partner and the cadet operating the video recorder returned.

"Mr. Dory, exactly what does Gene World do?"

Dory felt relieved at a question that seemed not to have spikes on the outside. He thought this one was harmless.

"We test, develop, and market drugs for use worldwide in the treatment of diseases. That's a simple answer but it covers almost everything. We use the 7th Floor at the Charles as a place to initiate experiments on human beings. It's all legal and we do so with a special exemption. These drugs have very long chemical names like Benzodiazepines, Acetophenazine, Methotrexate..." Street was already overdosing on medical names with more than three syllables. "Stop, we get the picture."

"Mr. Dory, how well do you know the other people who work up on the 7th Floor?"

"I don't know anyone that well. I'm there solely to administer the funds allocated by Gene World and to protect our investment. All medical decisions regarding testing is in the hands of Dr. Marks. So, I don't really have much contact with the doctors or the medical staff. I told you, they don't like me very much because I control the money. That's the way it goes and I can handle it."

"Mr. Dory, do you know of any reason, no matter how far fetched, why anyone would kill Dr. Sims and Dr. Eldridge?"

"Absolutely not. No reason at all."

Street looked at Dory as he answered. He leaned over to his partner and whispered, "Lie." Street knew a lie when he met one and he knew he just met one. What he didn't know was why Dory would lie.

Street was ready to show Dory out the door and offer him a ride back to the hospital. He could have kept the questions coming for hours. This was not the time. For the hunter, there is a time to hunt and a time to wait.

Hard as it was for him, this was the time to wait and let things settle down. For Street, waiting was a bad back, toothache, and 24 hours without sleep combined. Only with his prized collection of French wines did he enjoy letting time work its magic.

Chapter Fifteen:
Hello

Street was in the middle of a 60 minute Stairmaster at level 15 when his beeper sounded. It was 6:30 PM. He had finished with Dory Atwood by four PM and then cleared paperwork off his desk. The sweat pouring down his face felt like a warm salty shower with all his stress dripping to the floor. His beeper read the phone number of headquarters.

"The hell with it, I've got 27 minutes to go; it'll keep."

Like so many detectives, Street found it difficult to keep his work in balance with the rest of his life. His ex-wife blamed the Boston Police for the end of their marriage. Street would not deny that might be true. He was one of many cops *who heard the clock*. The *clock* was that unknown time in the future when they would might face death. Time was a mystery for Street. When it came to exercise and great wines, time was different. Then it was a comforter. Whoever was calling would wait.

Exactly 27 minutes later, Street went to the front desk at the gym to get a telephone.

"This is Street, you paged me."

The police operator asked him to wait a moment. "Yes, Detective. At 6:25 PM, a Miss Beecher called and left a phone number." Street already had the phone number in his notes. The notes were in his gym locker with clothes.

"Captain Beecher, I thought you went to Dirk's funeral in New Hampshire."

"Well, I did and I'm back, and how would you like to take me to dinner tonight?"

Street won his bet or Kate Beecher was hungry and lonely.

"Detective, why don't you meet me in front of the Ritz at eight PM." She gave Street no chance to think of any alternatives. Eight PM it would be.

Beecher was waiting outside in a light blue dress, definitely too short and tight to be military issue. "Hop in."

"No, park the car and let's go inside."

Street did not want dinner at the Ritz. He got out and received the customary hello from Charlie at the front door. Every door attendant in the City of Boston knew Street and most of the other detectives. Doorkeepers, with their instant replay eyes and high fidelity ears, are prized contacts for detectives on the hunt. In return, detectives always plowed an *All Clear* zone around parking meters designated for hotel valets.

"Jimmy, let's go the bar and have a chat." Street was aware that Beecher, starting with her phone call, was orchestrating everything.

"Do you have any *Chateau Talbot* vintage '86? That's my first choice. Otherwise a *Lynch Bages* '89."

Beecher had already ordered her gin and tonic, and Street's inquiry surprised her. "What, you're not having a beer? I didn't know you're into wines."

"Kate, there's a lot you don't know about me. What I don't know is why you called me. Did I win that little bet, Agent Beecher?"

Street did not have to wait long. As he was talking, a young man in a conservative blue suit and pin striped tie approached. He appeared no more than 27, but looked like someone had sucked all the youth out and replaced it with a seriousness way beyond his years.

"Detective Street, my name is Tom Adler, may I sit down?" Street looked at Beecher and instantly got the message. Whoever he is, he knew Kate Beecher.

"Kate told me about your investigation at the Charles. You're asking lots of questions, Street. Maybe I can answer them."

Street got his second choice, the *Lynch Bages* '89.

"Adler, I presume you're in the Air Force?"

"Wrong, Detective, have you heard of the DCIS?"

"Nope."

Street had worked on cases with all the big name federal investigative agencies, including the Air Force's OSI. But, he never heard of the DCIS.

"DCIS stands for the Defense Criminal Investigative Service. We work with the Department of Defense to combat and prosecute fraud. Things like product substitution, overcharging, false charges, misuse of government funds and resources. We have a special arrangement with Dr. Marks and the Charles Hospital. We provide them with lots of benefits, things like military transport of people, the transfer of viruses and chemicals in a protected environment, and access to classified research ongoing at some of our facilities. Dr. Marks set all this up years ago, and your two US senators have made the 7th Floor sacred ground. The Senate Intelligence Committee is up to speed on it. Captain Beecher is on site to protect our interests. She gets audits of drugs, viruses and chemicals. She's also responsible for the security of the bunker. We built it like a missile silo. In 1992 we were made aware of the misuse of some materials that we transported to the 7th. Beecher has been looking into it. That, Detective, is it."

"No Mr. Adler, that is not it. You're joining a list of people who are giving me all these polite answers that add up to zero. There's a lot more to it. I'm investigating two deaths listed as accidental that may be murders. That's what I care about. So if that's your little speech, thanks and have a nice trip back to Washington. When you get there, tell them there's this *buckaroo* loose in Boston who's about to call some friends at a newspaper. Adler, I'll make sure they spell your name correctly in the story. Same for you, Kate."

Street got up and moved for the door.

"See, Tom, I told you. I knew he wouldn't buy it."

Adler turned to Street, "Detective, meet Special Agent Kate Beecher of the OSI. We've got big problems in that hospital. Give us 24 hours and we'll make arrangements for a meeting in Washington. We'll notify your Chief of Detectives."

Adler shook hands and left.

"Well, Kate, guess we can have dinner now."

Chapter Sixteen:
Dinner For Two

For the first time, Street looked at Kate as a woman, not a captain or special agent or someone who worked on the 7th Floor. He thought she was looking at him as a man, not a detective. They lingered over drinks at the Ritz, feeling each other out. It seemed so easy, sliding into this other world. Street saw a woman about ten years younger whose profiled face and dirt blonde hair tempted him. Her legs were long and tight and her dress was far enough above her knees that he had to concentrate on not looking. She wore a white silk blouse which he could easily see through.

"Wow, a *Victoria Secrets* catalogue right in front of my eyes'""

Street didn't know what Kate was thinking, and they talked about a common interest, wine. If Street had gotten inside her head at that moment, he would have felt a burst of confidence. Kate liked Street's hard body from the first time they met. She liked his height and the way he carried himself. His stomach was flat as a sidewalk and she knew under his clothes he was very well put together. She liked his little boy eyes and innocence, real or imagined. Street's eyes intrigued her. They were hazel now.

"Street, how come you always go with hazel eyes. Why not go brown?"

"Kate, my eyes are not a toy. They're not a fashion statement. I've taken a lot of shit on them for years. Let's leave it."

"Sure Street, but don't get sensitive on me."

"Kate, let's stop at my place and I'll pick up a bottle of wine. I know an Italian restaurant on Newbury Street that'll open it for us with dinner."

"Street, why do I like your last name better than Jimmy? Let's go."

Street's condo was in the fashionable part of Beacon Hill. It was a duplex, with first and basement levels. Street parked outside and left his police ID on the dashboard. There were twin doors, the outer was solid green and the inner a white French door. Walking inside, Kate saw what she had not expected. The condo had hardwood floors, antique furniture throughout, and two beautifully appointed fireplaces. Street took her by the hand downstairs to a small wine cellar. Kate quickly guessed there must have been about 500 bottles in the wooden bins.

"Street, I'm surprised. They must be paying very well in the Boston Police these days."

"You're not the first to say that. You've seen too many movies. We don't all live in beat up, bad part of town apartments with newspapers and trash tossed around. Truth is when I was divorced, I needed a change. I asked for some personal time off. It turned out to be almost two years. I worked as an investigator for a couple of law firms in town. One of the cases was huge and involved some contingency fees and bonuses. I got some big money, and you're standing in it now. I put it all in this place, a little house in Nantucket and the wines."

"Street, let's open that bottle of wine here. Do you have pasta around? I'll cook something up. You'll owe me dinner some other time." They walked upstairs to the first floor.

"You'll find some pasta in the drawer near the telephone. I'm going to take a quick shower and change into some casual clothes. My sister usually leaves some stuff around here, and you're welcome to change into them. You'll be a lot more comfortable. Things like a sweatshirt, pants, sneakers."

"Street, maybe I'll take you up on that after you shower. Just pour me a little wine before you go."

His bathroom was colored in hunter green with maroon colored drapes and towels. It was very masculine. Street's answering machine was in the bathroom, next to a radio. He could undress, shave, and hit the playback button all at the same time. Street thought of them as survival tactics for bachelors. There were three messages.

"Jimmy boy, it's Ellen. Your nephews are missing their favorite uncle. Give us a call. Where have you been?" "Mr. Street, it's 5 PM and this is Lee Tams Laundry and we've got a problem with one of your shirts. We've can't get the spot out. It's grease of some kind. Stop by and tell us what you want us to do. Thanks." "Detective Street, this is Dr. Ernie Green. Just got back from Dirk's funeral and need to see you. Please call as soon as..."

The message stopped in mid sentence. The last time the machine stopped in mid sentence was when he played back messages and one of his nephews picked up another phone. That caused some kind of electrical stop that re-cycled the tape.

Street wrapped a towel around and went into the kitchen. Kate was there boiling water and looking at one of his wine books. "Kate, did you pick up the phone by any chance. I'm having trouble with my answering machine."

Kate was right about his hard body as she looked at him wrapped in a towel.

"Street, is that your idea of casual? No, I didn't make a call."

He went back to the bathroom. She eyed him all the way.

"I'll be right back."

Street thought Ernie's voice sounded stressed. You can take the man out of the detective, but never the detective out of the man. He was not going to enjoy the rest of the night without answering Green. Night time in America is a cacophony of answering machines talking to answering machines. Street called Mickey at his home.

"Mickey, it's about eight PM. Green just called and he sounded off. Any chance you could stop by. I'll try to call him. When you get this message, call me, I'm home."

"Street, what is this, an encore performance?"

He returned to the kitchen, this time with the shower warming up and his maroon towel still his only clothing. "Sorry Kate, if this bothers you... I need to get a phone number out of my briefcase. How's the wine taste? That's a 1976 *Lafite*, first growth."

"Damn, another lousy answering machine." Street waited for the tone. "Ernie, this is Detective Street, I got your message. I asked my partner to stop by for a few moments. If there's a problem, call me at home. Ask Mickey for the number when he gets there. Otherwise, I'll call you tomorrow at the hospital."

Street jumped in the shower and was shaving when there was a knock on the bathroom door. "Street, since you're taking so much time, here's some wine." He changed into some slacks and a polo shirt and sneakers.

"Better late than never, right Kate? Do you want to change?" She said no. Maybe it was the wine or the time of night, but Kate was looking better by the second. Dinner was pasta in a white clam sauce.

"Pretty good for last minute and considering how little you had to work with."

Street went to his stereo and turned on the radio. It was perfect timing as the announcer said, "Now, Leonard Bernstein conducts the New York Philharmonic as they perform Ravel's *Bolero*."

"Kate, do you know anything about classical music?"

"Street, between the antiques, the wine collection, the classical music, well, I'm impressed."

Kate's eyes fastened on Street as she spoke. Her voice was silky smooth, a perfect match for the *feminine* taste of the *Lafite* wine.

"Kate, see the legs from the *Lafite*". Street whirled his glass and little leg shaped lines oozed down from the rim of the glass. Kate looked and fantasized they were Street's fingers moving down her thighs. "The bouquet is so silky and smooth. You can smell the juices of fruit in perfect harmony with the tannin." Kate imagined juices, but they were not coming from the wine.

Out of uniform she seemed so relaxed. Was she coming on to him, or him to her. Dinner did not take much time. It had been a long time since Street was invited to undress a woman. Kate showed him how to do it slowly, button by button, inch by inch, layer by layer. Maneuvering through the lingerie, Street was out of control. Kate stretched her hands behind her head. Her hazel eyes were opening and closing as he moved his hands across her blouse. She felt her nipples rising with each pass of Street's fingers across her breasts. They were not going to make it to the bedroom. Kate lay back on the couch in the living room, dropping her shoes to the floor. She was very smooth and confident. Street slid her blouse partly off. "Don't take the rest off, yet. Leave it on for a while."

She touched his hand and guided it down to her knees. "Rub the back of my knees, kiss them; it drives me crazy." Street turned her over and put his lips behind her knees and soaked them with his tongue. Kate started to moan quietly. "Now, go higher." Street moved his hands inside her dress and pulled it up to her waist. He had nothing on but his polo shirt and some socks. Kate was not far behind. "Take me, Street, now! Do it, be slow but don't be gentle. You can do it as hard as you want. Don't hold back." They rolled onto the floor and she opened her legs. She was still wearing some clothes. Street looked in her eyes, which never closed.

"Street, stop, take your contact out. I've never done this looking into two different eyes. Do it."

"Damn Kate, you want it out now?"

"Now."

Street moved his hand to his eye and lifted the contact off his brown eye. Kate dug her nails into his back and never took her eyes off him. They fell to the floor in a bundle of heat and sweat.

Street picked her up and carried her into the bedroom.

Street awoke at two am. He was tucked in bed under the covers. There was a note next to him.

Street, you were delicious. The food and wine were good, too.
I wanted this to happen and hope you did too. Didn't want
to wake you up. Sleep well. See you. Agent Beecher.

"Agent Beecher, guess that's supposed to be funny now."

It was two AM and Street realized neither his partner nor Ernie had called back.

Chapter Seventeen:
Moxie

Mickey, you never called back last night, what happened?"

Street's partner spun his story. He retrieved Street's message and went to Ernie Green's apartment. It was 11 PM when he arrived. Before going in, McCoy talked for a couple of minutes with the police woman assigned to watch him. She said Green was in his apartment, but he had visitors. As McCoy was about to go inside, Green emerged with two other persons. McCoy recognized them as doctors on the 7th Floor, Gaetano Piccard and Karen Ferris. All three got in a car driven by Ferris. McCoy ordered the police woman to stay outside Green's apartment while he followed the doctors. After just a couple of minutes, McCoy knew they were heading for the Charles Hospital. McCoy followed them inside and watched as the elevator they boarded stopped on the 7th Floor. He decided not to go upstairs.

It was after two AM when they headed back to Green's apartment. McCoy radioed to the police woman. He arrived back at Green's apartment and joined the police woman on watch. The doctors remained inside all night. What happened outside was much more interesting. Around 2:30 AM a late model car with a woman drove by Green's apartment, slowed, then continued past. A couple of minutes later she returned. This went on for about half an hour. McCoy got the license number.

"Street, ready for this one. I ran the plate and guess who's car it is? It's our friend, Special Agent Beecher."

Street recoiled as he fast forwarded what this meant. She must have picked up the phone while he was in the bathroom getting messages off his answering machine. She heard the message from Green. Why would she circle around Ernie Green's? What was their connection?

"Mickey, where's Green now?"

"He's at the hospital, I think."

"Then that's where I'll be." Call the medical examiner. I need to talk with him. I've got an idea."

Street approached the security desk.

"Page Dr. Green and tell him it's Detective Street."

Green came to the desk and told Street he needed to talk with him soon. It would be better if they talked outside the hospital.

"What about lunchtime, Ernie?" There was not enough time and too much risk. "Ernie, here's the address of my gym. Be there tonight at six. Can you do it?" Green said, "yes."

Street's drive back to headquarters gave him some time to play 'what ifs.' What if the guy he met last night with Kate, Adler, did not call back as promised within the next 24 hours? What if Ernie's involved in all this and that's why Kate was driving by his place?

McCoy was waiting for Street when he arrived at headquarters. "I set up a meeting with the ME. Anytime you want it."

"Now is not too soon." Street and McCoy walked into McCann's office.

Street always figured McCann was an ME because he did not have what it takes to make it in the world of private medicine. The detective suspected his work. He thought McCann was a *meat packer*. Like handing out parking tickets, he had his quota and he filled it. Street did not feel comfortable being around him. Every time he met the ME, it meant another case and more questions to answer. McCann had trouble with criticism. He was right, period. But, now Street needed McCann's help to understand the lingering questions that kept visiting him.

"McCann, let's play a little game here. Remember, I'm no doctor. I'll spell it out, and you take it apart."

McCoy and McCann listened carefully. This was vintage Street, the hunter who goes with his senses and has more solved cases on file than any active detective in the police force. This was not some rookie day dreaming.

"Let's go back to the very beginning, way back to the death of Dr. Sims on September 11th. Now, suppose I need her dead. Forget the reason why. So here's what I do. First, I can't have her death look like murder. Now I'm very smart and I know my way around medicine. I figure there must be some way to kill her and make it look like an accident."

"So here's what happens. Somehow I find out that she's going to be alone for few days because her boyfriend is going home. She knows me from the hospital; so, I ring the door bell and she let's me in. Being sociable, I bring along a quart of fresh squeezed orange juice. Who doesn't love fresh squeezed at breakfast? We talk for a little while. Then I go to the kitchen and offer her a glass of this fresh OJ. What better way to start a weekend? While I'm pouring her glass of OJ, I mix up a neat little cocktail. You won't find this on the breakfast menu at McDonalds."

"I mix Methaqualone with some Valium. Did I pronounce that first word OK? See Doc, I've been studying. Anyway that Metha-something is called a Super Quaalude. She gets about 50 mg of the Metha and 50 mg of the Valium in her OJ. Soon Dr. Sims gets very relaxed and drowsy. Basically, her eyes are open and she's sleeping."

Street reminded McCoy and McCann that Detective Santori's notes include a mention by Dirk Eldridge about finding fresh squeezed OJ in the apartment. Dirk said they never bought fresh squeezed OJ.

McCoy and the medical examiner looked at each other. Where did this story come from? Where's Street going with this? If it were anyone else, they'd be giving thumbs down by now. But, like Dr. Marks at the Charles, Street also dominates a room when he enters and speaks. Street's hardcore, and he doesn't play mind games. Street's eyes demand attention. He had bottled a lot inside and was finally pulling the cork. Street was too excited to sit down and he walked a circle around both men as he continued.

"Put yourself in her room, guys. Sims is lying on the bed, with her eyes drilled to the ceiling above. She knows bad stuff is happening. She can hear and see. But, the killer owns her body. So what the killer does is this. With a little homework, and access to Sims medical files, our killer knows her blood type. Maybe it's more than one person. So, they have a vial of semen and load it into a syringe with no needle. They take her panties off and spread her legs. Sims can't do a thing. She's like silly putty. She wants to scream like it's a bad dream. She can't get it out. Sims is looking in the eyes of her killer. This semen has peanut extract purified in it. The killer knows she's allergic to peanuts because it's in her medical records at the hospital. The 7th Floor has detailed medical records on all the doctors there. And Sims probably had a history of reactions to peanuts. That would be on her record. That's why she never eats peanuts at baseball games. It's right here in my notes.

"So, in goes the semen with a peanut extract. Now the clock is ticking. In the first minute, she feels nothing. But, each second the mucous membrane in her vagina is absorbing the deadly semen. In two minutes she's coughing and her breathing is faster. Her heart rate picks up and it's shallow. Her breathing tube starts to close up. Now she's gasping for air. She can't move. Her killer watches as she dies. Cause of death is anaphylactic shock. The doctor who may have stumbled on the cure for pancreatic cancer is dead."

Street's a tough cop. Inside, he hopes it didn't happen this way. What he described was a slow, tortured death. Street's dad was always very gentle and kind with everyone. Street inherited that tenderness and gentle inside. Death was death, but Street knew the difference between a bullet to the head and slow death.

"Detective, I've already ruled that Dr. Sims died from anaphylactic shock. We found no signs of any struggle and no bruise marks. She got it on with someone after her boyfriend left and it happens she was allergic to something in his semen. These things are rare, but they happen. So what's the big deal?"

Street was getting impatient with *dead face* McCann.

"We know she died of anaphylactic shock. If there was a killer and he was in this room, he'd say, 'Thanks Dr. McCann, that's just what we hoped you'd say.' Maybe the allergic bomb that killed her was no accident. I think Sims received an injection of semen that was mixed like a cocktail.

"If there's a killer, he made one gamble and two mistakes. First, he gambled that you wouldn't find any bruise marks. That gamble he won. Then the mistakes. The smarter a killer, and whoever may have killed her was brilliant, the more ridiculous the mistakes. With all the research they did on Sims, they assumed she was right handed. They were wrong. That's why Santori's notes say the telephone was near her right hand. She was probably already dead, and the killer moved the phone near her right hand. And the OJ. Leaving that quart of fresh squeezed OJ at the scene was stupid. So, Doc, tell me, what do you think? Did you check for any bruise marks? Did you check to see if she had been drugged?"

Street knew his words were changing as he described what happened. Words like *accidental* and *maybe* were vanishing. But the word *killer* was everywhere.

McCann was getting impatient with Street's assumptions. McCann was the ME, not Street.

"Street, this is pretty far outside the ballpark. We didn't see any bruise marks and, no, we didn't check to see if she was drugged. The anaphylactic shock was right in front of our face. It was obvious. Those were our findings."

"Well, that's great, McCann. You missed your calling. You should have handed out parking tickets. Then you wouldn't have to think. Like right now."

McCann was not amused.

"Street, we could exhume and then do a GCMS--that's a gas chromatography-mass spectroscopy test. It can positively identify a narcotic or poison. We could also do a HPLC--that's high pressure liquid chromatography and it separates drugs and other organic compounds for toxicology or narcotics. And who's going to pay for all that?"

"Damn it, why didn't you do all this before? Don't you have any moxie?"

"Street, we've got budgets and timetables. This was anaphylactic shock."

"Sure it was, McCann, but maybe it was also murder. That's what those tests might have shown. McCann, we're going to see the Chief on this. I want to get her body exhumed and I want these tests done."

Street was at his gym when Ernie arrived.

"Ernie, get some towels and we're going to talk in private. Ever use a steam room, Ernie?"

"Hey Joey, do me a big favor. I'm using the steam room for a little while. I need to talk to someone alone. Can you help me and keep it off limits for about 30 minutes?"

"It's done Street. And next time maybe you'll handle a ticket for me, right?"

"Ernie, these are great for you outside and inside. They sweat out all the tension. You'll like this. No one's coming in. Start talking, I'm listening."

Street had been inside the steam room so many times he settled onto a section of the wooden deck that was *his corner*. Six months ago, Ernie, Sims and Dirk were very special for each other. Their medical careers were on a fast track and they still made the time to enjoy each other's company. Now, only one was alive. Street thought for a moment about how lonely it must be for Ernie talking to a virtual stranger about his two dead friends. Street had suffered the same sense of loss.

He remembered coming home one night to a note scotch taped to the refrigerator. It was more than a good-bye note from his wife Susan. She said it was not all his fault and that she had met someone else. Street called his sister that night and then cried himself to sleep.

He also remembered losing a partner just after his wife left. They had found an abandoned car in Boston's South End. While they were looking it over, several men came over to talk. With no warning they pulled out a Beretta Cougar .32 automatic. Street and his partner had stumbled upon a drug buy. They were disarmed and watched the deal get done. Both were down on their knees. They heard a police siren and one of the men unloaded the gun in his partner's face. Everyone scattered while Street was left cradling a dead partner in his arms. The blood was all over his shirt. He thought of Jackie Kennedy cradling the head of her dead President. Street burned all his clothes from that night but the memory was burned into his brain forever.

The thoughts of that night were in the steam room as he listened to Ernie Green.

Ernie started by telling Street about the trip up to New Hampshire for Dirk's funeral. He rode with Gaetano Piccard and Karen Ferris. Dr. Marks was there along with Beecher, the other doctors, and many of the nurses. Sims' parents had flown in from Ohio to console Dirk's family. Sims' parents seemed to gather strength from the trip.

During the trip, Ernie told Piccard and Ferris about everything that had happened to Sims and Dirk. That's when Ernie got back more than he gave. Ferris listened to the story about Sims' patient, Steven Hays. And she said Sims had confided in her about what happened. Not only did she confide in her, she asked Ferris to administer the same treatment to one of her patients, also dying from advanced pancreatic cancer. Ferris was uneasy about it, but Sims arranged for her to meet with Dr. Marks and get an official go ahead. Like Sims' patient, there was a similar reaction. Sims, Ferris and Marks met several times to discuss the treatments. A couple of times, Marks brought Dory and Beecher into the meetings. Ferris' patient was discharged one month earlier than Sims' patient. Like Steven Hays, her patient left the 7th Floor with the label of misdiagnosis. Ferris knew that was wrong. Ferris signed a confidentiality statement like Sims and got a lecture similar to the one Dory had given Sims. It was the Marks' lecture about keeping things quiet.

Street's mind processed the information he was hearing. Now there were two possible cures, not one as he originally thought. And if Sims was murdered because she had stumbled on a cure, why was Ferris still walking around alive. Maybe Sims had challenged someone about the data. Perhaps whoever killed Sims assumed that she had already confided in Dirk.

When Ernie heard Ferris' story, he decided it was time to do something. All three doctors agreed to make a middle of the night visit to the 7th Floor to try and locate anything that might explain what happened. What they did not find was more intriguing than what they found. Other than name, address and *misdiagnosis*, the computer files of both Sims' and Ferris' patients were gone. There were no records. Nothing was in writing. That's why Ernie called Street.

"Ernie, you know we've been watching your place. We knew you and your friends went to the hospital overnight. What you don't know is that a woman in a car drove around your apartment several times last night. Do you have any idea who that might be?"

Ernie shrugged.

"We think we know who it is, but we don't know why. Maybe you can help. We think the woman driving around your place last night was Captain Kate Beecher."

"No shit!"

"Does that surprise you Ernie?"

"It sure does. Obviously I know her. And that's it. She's with the Air Force and that's all I know about her. Someone said she was a nurse going back a few years. She keeps to herself. That's all."

"Tell me about Ferris and the other doctor: what's his name?"

"It's Gaetano *Guy* Piccard. They're both friendly. Not close like Simsy and Dirk and I are...were. Ferris is a clinician, which means she deals with patients instead of research. Simsy never told me about another patient. In fact, she never told Dirk or me about her patient Steven Hays. We only learned that from her computer."

There's a time and place in every case when a detective makes a decision. Their instincts are first to trust no one. Then, during the investigation, it can become risky not to trust. People can get killed that way. Early in this case, Street believed Ernie, and ordered him to receive round the clock protection. Now, he had to extend matters further.

"Ernie, if I'm going to hunt down the persons who killed your friends, I'll need your help. It's not risk free, but I know Sims or Dirk would have done it for you. I want you to think about what I'm going to ask you. Talk to your family about it first. Ernie, I want you to call Sims' parents in Toledo and get their permission to exhume the body of their daughter. That won't be easy. Tell them as little as possible, except that it will be done in a very dignified way with a religious service. Tell them the truth, that their daughter may still be able to help us find her killers. Ernie, the other thing I want you to do is quit your job. There's a good chance we can bring the killers to us instead of trying to find them. If you quit the 7th Floor in a manner that causes our killers to get worried, they may try to--well, who knows what they'll do. So, think it over carefully. There's risk; but I think it'll turn out fine. Confide in no one except your family."

"Street, I don't need to talk with any one about this. My two best friends are dead. I'll do what you want."

"Don't do anything until I tell you. But, it will be soon."

Street sat alone in the steam room. "Ernie, now he's a ballsy guy. A real stand up person." So many times in his life, Street had gone to hell and back for others. His thoughts rambled across so many different landscapes.

He wondered if his ex-wife found life better with him gone. At this point, he didn't give a damn. The holidays aren't that far away. How he wished he had a son like Ernie Green. His nephews were so young and innocent. Guess he was trying to make things a little safer for them. Could one cop make a difference? Why do people do horrible things to others? There are more than enough diseases around for those in search of evil. The human component of evil isn't necessary. Nature's going to kill us all anyway. How about Charlie the doorman at the Ritz? He gets the biggest kick in the world when one of the detectives slips him some *Red Sox* tickets. Or these doctors. They didn't have anything in the medical books on the 7th Floor. Look at Dr. Marks and his Nobel Prizes. The guy's coming apart under that brave exterior. Two of his hand picked doctors are dead. Then there's Beecher. Where's she going in her life? She gets up in the middle of the night and leaves me a little note. Maybe she was embarrassed. Did she hear the message on my machine from Ernie? Of course the whole thing started with that English teacher. Bet he's surprised. He's alive and that's one big surprise.

Who would have thought a 40 year old guy dying of pancreatic cancer would outlive his 20 something doctor. And outlive her boyfriend, too. This is one really messed up deal. There's a second person out there who may have been cured of pancreatic cancer. What am I doing talking with all these doctors about medical words that have ten syllables? Is there really a cure for a disease that's not curable? I sure hope McCoy's taking careful notes of all this. Who do I trust? One minute it's black, then white, then that lousy, rotten orange color. What do normal people do? They get up and go to work. I guess in the movies all this looks pretty snappy.

Who knows what it felt like when I was on my knees with my partner that night in the south end and we both figured we'd get out heads blown off. He's dead and I'm not. No wonder so many of us drink to forget. Who's going to hold you tight and say *I understand* and really mean it. After my partner was killed all the papers put his picture on the front, lined in black. One is still stuck to my refrigerator. By now, hell, no one remembers his name unless they're a cop. The ones that shot him--some of them will get out in the next few years. My partner is never getting out of his box in the ground. Sometimes this job sucks. Other times it's just rotten. When things are going great the job gets better and it only stinks.

Street was on a roll. "Great, I just sent a kid doctor out of a steam room and into who knows what. Is he the next target? Why didn't they go after Ferris? She had a patient like Sims? What's Beecher doing? She goes from my bed to her car and then drives around Ernie's neighborhood. However this comes down, I'm in it to the finish line."

Someone knocked on the steam room door.

"Hey, Joey, what'd I do, stay in the steam too long?"

"Do what you want Street. You've got a call at the front desk. I don't how they tracked you here."

Street knew how they found him. His big blue and white Boston Police pens had a mini transmitter installed by a police consultant from MIT. They were experimental tracking devices. The same devices are used to track stolen cars. If the pen breaks, the signal stops. When that happens the cop is beeped and must call within ten minutes. Most of the cops have dumped their pens. Street liked them.

"It's headquarters, they own me buddy."

"Street, it's not the police. There's some guy on the phone named Adler and he's calling from Washington. He said you'd take his call."

"Great, I'll send you a postcard from Washington."

"Street, this is Tom Adler, remember me?"

"I don't have dementia, not yet anyway. Of course I remember."

"Listen, Street, we just had a talk with your Chief of Detectives and he okayed your trip tomorrow afternoon to Washington. Your flight has been booked and it leaves Logan at two PM, arriving here at 3:30 PM. We'll meet you at National. Any questions."

"Oh, about nine thousand. Is Beecher coming?"

"She's sitting right here, next to me."

"Good, tell you what, Adler, why don't you ask her what the hell she was doing driving around Dr. Ernie Green's apartment in the middle of the night. One of our surveillance teams spotted her. Go ahead, ask, I'll wait."

"Street, she said she'll explain tomorrow."

"Adler, or whoever you are, DCIS or OSI, you and Beecher and everyone else involved with this hospital is taking my blood. There's delay, excuses, and half truths. I'm getting the drip dry treatment. And I'm just about dry. When I come down, I expect answers. If I don't get them, all hell is gonna break loose here in Boston. You and Beecher are going to be media stars after I've talked with my contacts at the papers. Your bosses will be shaking plenty. Adler, are we all on the same page?"

"Detective, don't worry. We'll see you tomorrow."

It was 7:30 PM when Street left the gym. He felt exercised in a bad sense. Never could he remember leaving the gym more stressed than entering. He could go home to an empty house and grind his teeth. He could try to purge his frustrations by working more. This was the syndrome that got him in trouble during his marriage. Street felt as if going home now was retreating in combat.

"This is Detective Jimmy Street, Boston Police. Is Dr. Karen Ferris on duty now?"

It took the hospital operator about three minutes to come back on the line. "Dr. Ferris is not in the hospital, but she is on beeper."

"Please beep her now and give her this call back number. Make sure you tell her it's the police.

Street's car was parked outside the gym and the number he left was his cellular phone. It took Dr. Karen Ferris less than five minutes to call back.

"Detective Street, this is Dr. Ferris."

"Dr. Ferris, I need to talk with you. It's important and I'd like to do it tonight."

"That's not possible. I've got plans to see a movie with friends."

"OK, then meet me at police headquarters after the movie and we'll talk then."

"Are you crazy? That'll be around midnight."

"Two of the doctors you worked with on the 7th Floor are dead. You just went to Dr. Eldridge's funeral. This is a lot more important than any movie you're gonna see. Where are you now?"

"I'm home."

"Make your choice, Dr. Ferris: now or later."

"This better be important. I'll cancel my plans. Where do you want to talk?"

"I'll meet you at your home at eight PM. I have the address from the hospital. I'll be driving a gray unmarked police car. Dr. Ferris, for your own safety, you better get in the habit of verifying who you are talking with. Practice with me. Call police headquarters and ask for the Sergeant on duty and tell him about this call and ask him to verify it and call you back. They'll radio me to confirm that you didn't get a call from an impostor. When I show up, ask me for picture identification. That's your lesson number one in staying alive, and it's a freebie."

"I don't understand. This sounds kind of silly. This isn't a James Bond movie."

"Dr. Ferris, I'll repeat myself. Two of the doctors you worked with on the 7th Floor are dead. Now, if I were a doctor up there, I'd be worried."

"Those were accidents, detective."

"See you at eight PM, Dr. Ferris."

Street drove to her apartment in Cambridge. It was on Massachusetts Avenue with all the noise and honking that comes with a busy street that dissects Harvard University. The apartment building looked like all the others with its brick and small windows. There was no doorman. Steel mailboxes lined the entrance, and somehow the gray linoleum floor was uglier than the mailboxes. There were twin elevators inside. Street waited at the front door. Precisely at 8 PM, one of the elevator doors opened and out walked Ferris.

"Dr. Ferris I presume."

"Detective Street, I assume."

"In all the commotion, I realize now there are a bunch of people on the 7th Floor I don't know. You're one of them."

"OK, Dr. Ferris, let's take a ride across the Charles and we'll get some coffee at a place on Newbury Street and talk."

They headed for the car and Street opened the door. Ferris was wearing tight blue jeans with a big brass belt that punctuated her tiny waist. She wore a white patterned shirt and had on boots. Whatever he imagined, she looked a lot better. As he slammed her door closed, a bomb went off in Street's head. The sound of metal to metal and the sight of Ferris sliding onto his front seat behind the tinted glass set off alarm bells in his head. "Damn, she never asked for my ID like I told her. She's gonna get herself killed just like her friends."

"Dr. Ferris put your seat belt on." Then Street locked the car doors.

SLAM! In a hair trigger instant, Street grabbed her hands and pushed them behind her back. In a split second she was hand cuffed. Then he jammed her face down into the seat.

"Make one noise, one move and I'll take my gun and slide it in your pretty mouth and look you in the eyes while I pull the trigger. Ready to die?"

Street did not pull his gun, but he saw Ferris' eyes riveted to it. Tears were coming from her eyes and her feet and arms were moving back and forth in tiny uncontrolled lurches. Street sped up as they crossed the Mass. Avenue bridge into Boston.

Then Street reached over, "Kick your shoes off. You won't run barefoot."

Like a passing thunderstorm, suddenly it stopped. Street slammed his car to a stop leaving a long row of skid marks. He lifted Ferris out of the seat. She was sobbing and out of control. He moved towards her and unlocked the handcuffs. He handed back her shoes.

"Ferris, you didn't ask for my ID. You are going to get yourself killed. If I'm not a cop and you're in this car with the wrong person, you are dead like Sims and Eldridge. Did you get the message. This was lesson number two and it wasn't free."

"I learned plenty. You're a fuckin' asshole lunatic. I'm getting out of here now and I'm reporting you. You're an animal. You'll pay for this stunt. Now let me out."

Street opened the door and she ran towards police headquarters. Street knew this was a bad scene. Something inside snapped when he slammed the door closed. He knew he'd find Ferris at headquarters.

When he arrived, Ferris was still crying while talking with three detectives. One of them moved her into a room and tried to calm her.

"Street, what the hell did you do? She's going to file a kidnapping complaint against you. Man, you are in big trouble. Are you losing your marbles? You've been on too many of those big game hunts in your head. We can't help you on this. Internal affairs is coming in on this one. And you're not too popular with those folks."

"Hey guys, help me out here. She's one of the doctors on the 7th Floor at the Charles Hospital. That's the case I've been working. Two other doctors up there have been murdered. What I did was set up a meeting with her and told her to demand some ID from me when I got there. I wanted her to get in the habit of being careful. Well she didn't ask for any ID and I went ballistic. I thought I was doing her a favor by scaring her. Guys go in and talk with her before internal affairs gets here."

Street looked at his watch. It was nine PM. Three hours earlier he was at his gym in a steam room talking with another doctor from the 7th Floor, Dr. Ernie Green. He was Detective

Jimmy Street, one of the best in Boston. Only he and a few others had earned the authority to call in the famed Zebra Team. His connections went straight to the Chief of Police and to the Mayor. A few year's ago, they chose him to appear in some public service announcements broadcast by local TV stations. Many cops thought he was first in line for Chief of Detectives when the position opened. His star was shining bright, or at least it was before he picked up Dr. Karen Ferris. More than two decades of work could go up in flames in a couple of hours. All the awards and citations would mean nothing.

Street paced back and forth as he watched shadows move through the glazed windows in the room where Karen Ferris was telling her story. Street knew his buddies were trying to put a sugar coating on what he did. They were trying to dig him out of the hole he dug. Street said, "The hell with it, I'm going in there." In a split second, he was in the room with Ferris and the three detectives. He knew instantly they had not persuaded her to drop the charges. Street thought, "So this how they'll look at my funeral." This was his funeral.

"Dr. Ferris, I'd like to say..."

"Don't say anything; you know what you did. I don't want to listen. And your friends here are not going to change my mind about filing charges."

Street was the pitcher who wanted the ball with the bases loaded and no one out. He lived for the moments when everyone thought he was wrong and he knew he was right. For Street, 4th down and long yardage in the Super Bowl was an opportunity for glory and not a risk of failing. With seconds left in the 7th game of a *Celtics* championship game, give him the ball and he's not afraid to take the final shot. A coward dies a thousand deaths and Street has not died once.

If a young doctor was going to come marching into his territory and blow his career, he was not going to be a silent witness.

"Dr. Ferris, I'm going to say my peace and then you can do what you want."

The three detectives sighed and were certain Street would somehow manage to make matters worse. A diplomat he could never be.

"First, Dr. Ferris, I apologize. What I did was wrong." There was no change in her expression as she sat still in her chair. She was angry and showed it. Then Street reached into his wallet and pulled out a crumpled piece of paper. "I want to read something. It's a poem and I wrote it."

IF ONLY I COULD MIRROR TO THE PAST
WOULD I SEE WRONGS SO LONG AND BADS SO VAST?
PERHAPS THAT BRIEF LOOK BEHIND
WAS INSTEAD PAYMENT OF LOVE IN KIND.
BECAUSE WHEN SPUN FRONT AND BACK
I SAW GOOD AND GAVE MYSELF SOME SLACK.
THE GUILT OF YESTERDAY IS A WILLING GUILLOTINE
WHOSE SHARPENED BLADE GLADLY CUTS DEEP AND
[MEAN.
IN BENDED KNEE I REPLAYED EACH PAST OFFENSE
UNTIL THEY CUT AND CAPTURED MY GOOD SENSE.
ACCEPTANCE OF WRONGS REQUIRES WELCOME OF
THE GOOD AND BURNING OF THAT GUILLOTINE'S
[DIRTY WOOD.
ONLY THEN CAN I ARISE UNITED
[AND UNCONDITIONALLY
PROCLAIM THAT I AM WHOLE AND DECENT
[AND FREE.
AS I TURN BACK FROM THE PAST IT'S HARD
[NOT TO PEER
BACK AT THAT PYRE OF GUILT WHOSE ODOR IS FEAR.
YET IT'S OK TO SAY I'M GOOD AND WALK
[HEAD UP HIGH
NEVER TO MIRROR THE PAST KNOWING THAT
[I DID TRY.

Street finished reading the poem and it was easy to spot a couple of tears falling from his eyes.

"Dr. Ferris, I wrote that poem a few years ago. It was after my partner and I were on our knees in a deserted part of the South End. We could feel the cold hard steel of guns as they pressed against our foreheads. My partner and I had stumbled on a drug deal. The guys with the guns were high on coke. They kept saying 'who gets to kill the pig?' We were just dogs to them. My partner was married with kids and he begged them not to shoot us. They all wore ski masks. One of them called, pushed my head to the side, and I looked in the eyes of my partner. Just like I looked in your eyes tonight. Then he pulled the trigger and blew my partners brains all over me. I vomited. There were sirens all around. For some reason, hell I don't know why even today, they didn't kill me. Sometimes I wish they had."

"Two of your friends at the Charles Hospital are dead. When you pull the covers up over your head at night, don't pretend for one second that those were accidents. Your friends were killed for reasons I don't understand. But Sims and Eldridge are still dead. Whoever killed them is going to try again. I called you because Ernie Green told me about what you said on the way to New Hampshire. You treated a patient like Sims, and he was also cured. I think there are killers out there. Whoever killed Sims thought she had confided everything to Eldridge. And because of that simple assumption, a woman got in a car and hunted down your friend riding his bike in the Back Bay. She accelerated and aimed her car at him. It's like she took a gun out and killed him. The same as when my partner died. I saw Dirk's body just a few minutes after he was murdered. He was lying on the sidewalk like a crumpled piece of paper. The woman got in a waiting card and left your friend to die on Commonwealth Avenue."

"Now, what do you think they're going to do about you? I don't know why they haven't killed you already. So, when you got in my car tonight without so much as asking for a driver's license, well, I thought of your parents and another funeral. I thought of another dead doctor from the 7th Floor. That's what I was thinking when I made that damn fool mistake to try and scare some sense into you. And there's one more thing I want to say..."

At that instant the door to the room swung open and in walked Sam *the Spider* Field. Sam Field was from internal affairs. He was not a cop's cop. His horn-rimmed glasses was the bullseye for any cop willing to trade their career for one good punch. Field was never a beat cop and out in the field. He graduated from the police academy and had a Ph.D. in psychology. Members of internal affairs do not get invited to police barbecues or softball games. Field never hid his feelings about Street. Over the years, they had run-ins many times before. The *Spider* thought Street was a cult hero with cops for all the wrong reasons. From what he heard on the way downtown, this might be his chance to finally nail Street. And it could be a chance to do it in front of Street's fellow detectives.

No matter what happened in the next few minutes, Street felt content that he had his say. With *Spider* in the room, Street did not look over at Ferris. It hurt too much to look at her. She was still crying.

"Sit down, Street. Dr. Ferris I'm Sam Field from the internal affairs section of the Boston Police." Field turned to Street with a curly smile, "So, Detective, we've expanded into kidnapping these days. You never said that in all those cute TV appearances you did for the Department. Now we'll put you on TV, on the 11 o'clock news. Not one word from you Street. I'll question you alone in a moment. I want some witnesses while I ask Dr. Ferris a few questions."

"Dr. Ferris, are you comfortable in answering a couple of questions. Would you like me to get rid of Street while we talk?" She nodded "No."

"First, I understand that Detective Street called you tonight and said he wanted to ask you some questions. He picked you up at your residence in Cambridge around eight PM. Correct so far?" As Ferris nodded, yes, Field looked over at Street knowing that he was going to cut off his head in just seconds. For Field, this was a moment he had dreamt of for years.

"Then Detective Street hand cuffed you, slammed your head into the seat of his car and told you to take off your shoes. He scared the hell out of you. He kidnapped you in a Boston Police car. Is that about right?"

Ferris looked into Street's eyes, then turned to answer.

"I apologize." Field interrupted. "Dr. Ferris, you don't have anything to apologize about." She continued, "Yes, I do. I'm sorry for all the trouble I caused tonight. What happened to Simsy and Dirk has turned me upside down. I've been so upset.

Detective Street picked me up in his car like you said. He was very polite. He never touched me. Nothing happened in the police car. I had an anxiety attack, probably due to some medication I've been taking. Then I came here. I don't know what made me say those awful things. I'm really sorry."

Street was stunned and could not believe what he was hearing. Like before, Street knew a lie when he heard it. The tears that came as he was reading his poem were back.

Field interrupted again. "Dr. Ferris, you cannot take back what you said. Maybe you're afraid because Street's in the room. Street, get out of here, get lost."

"Mr. Field, you heard what I said. That's it. I'll swear to it."

"Well, Dr. Ferris, if you feel that way, maybe I should tell you that filing false charges against a police officer is a crime. We'll check that one out."

The detectives in the room could not believe what had happened. Street sat slumped in his chair. Field had his gun at Street's head and it misfired over and over with each word from Dr. Ferris. The detectives knew this was going to be the talk of the town.

"Field, you can't charge her with anything. She filed no charges. She signed nothing. And frankly, we don't remember talking with her. Why don't you crawl back into your hole for the night."

Field and the three detectives left the room. Street sat and looked silently at Ferris. Not a single word between the two was spoken. Then they both got up and walked out of headquarters. Street had dodged another bullet, just like the night his partner was killed. And like that night, he could not understand why.

"Dr. Ferris, instead of a cup of coffee, how about a couple of drinks?"

"Detective, let's go."

What do you say to someone who had your career in their hand and could have squeezed the life out of it? Street felt an overwhelming sense of relief. The words *thank you* could not make it to his lips. Ferris thought he looked as if a paralyzed deer that had run into a street and stood transfixed by the lights of oncoming cars. He looked back at headquarters and then down Boylston Street towards the theater district and the bright lights. Ferris knew how uncomfortable he was. Street did not know it at the time, but Ferris also wrote poetry and his words had touched her deeply. When he went to his wallet and pulled out that crumpled piece of paper and read those beautiful words, it meant a lot to her. He did scare the life out of her. He explained that's better than someone taking the life out of her. They both made mistakes that night and it did not matter who was on *first base*. Each had reasons for reacting the way they did. Both were right and wrong. Ferris could sense Street's anguish. She spoke first.

"Detective, if you told me how wild tonight was going to be, I would have canceled my movie plans with joy."

Street managed a slight smile. Now Ferris was confused. Here she was trying to cheer up Street and bring back the gusto and brazen detective that she first met.

"Come on, Detective, you promised me that drink. And you've got questions to ask. Let's go somewhere, anywhere but out here on the sidewalk. No one's taking our drink order out here."

"Dr. Ferris, how about a rain check on the drinks. I'm just not up for it after tonight. I don't know what hit me in the car. I'll call you a taxi; it's on me."

"Street, if you're sending me home, then the least you can do is take me back yourself. I heard what you said upstairs. All of us on the 7th have been pretending that everything's OK. We know that's not true. Detective, my name is Karen. You're not my patient. My patients call me Doctor."

Street and Ferris headed back across the Charles River to her apartment.

How do you talk to someone who held your life in their hands and easily could have sucked the life out of it? Street was unable to bring the words *thank you* to his lips.

Ferris also wrote poetry. She wrote poetry late at night during study breaks. The poetry and a cup of coffee was all she had in her tiny studio apartment. At night she would return from classes with little money and less energy and friends. By force of will alone she would open her books and study into the early morning hours. Like Street, her poetry ended up in her wallet or desk at home. So, when Street pulled out that poem, he lifted Ferris our of her chair and back to days of isolation and loneliness at school. She saw the loneliness carved into Street's face as he read his poem.

All her life, Ferris struggled for acceptance by family. No matter how well she did in school, she never got the crushing kind of hugs that yell *I love you no matter what happens.* There was love in her family but it always came with a price. With each successive achievement in medicine, she became less happy. Amidst her field of plenty, there was always a drought or flood not far distant. Ferris focused more of her energies on work. While she worked she was OK, or sometimes not OK, but too busy to know she was not OK. A vicious little paradox that she understood. Aerobic workouts was the one release she could use. As pretty as she was, and her tight blue jeans reaffirmed her figure was athletic tight, she had a personal life that always seemed incomplete. She would say, "why does the rain always skip my friends roof and find mine?" With the clank of cars and buses and sirens, a good night's sleep in her Cambridge apartment was a rare treat. Still, there was 7th Floor. And now the 7th Floor, her castle of safety, had been overrun with the deaths of two doctors who were also friends. Into this turmoil came Detective Jimmy Street and his wild west ride to remember.

"Detective Street..."

"Call me Street, please."

"Street, you know this whole night started because you wanted to ask me some questions. Do you still want to? It's another five minutes 'till we get to my place."

"Karen, right? That's OK to call you Karen? The questions can keep, I guess. Most of them had to do with your pancreatic cancer patient, the one like Sims. I understand yours was cured, too."

"Street, I don't really understand it all. Simsy, Dr. Sims, had some kind of a deal going with Dr. Marks. She told me there was some extra money available for the purchase of the drugs she was using on her patient. This was really off the wall. I'd never been involved in anything like it before. She would give me money to buy the drugs so that I wouldn't have to log them out of the 7th

Floor. Simsy said the pharmacist was aware, so I gave him the money and he gave me the drugs. I was thinking of reporting it to the hospital oversight committee, but Dr. Marks told me everything was legal. He said what I was doing was special and that for now we had to keep the treatment protocol secret. I copied Simsy's treatment protocol and my patient got better. Hell, he didn't get better; he was cured. Anyway, the hospital discharged him saying it was misdiagnosis. He was a real nice guy, about 55 years old. I think he was a famous stock broker. Some of the doctors said he was on TV shows with his opinions on the stock market. They always asked me to get stock tips from him. I never did."

"Karen, any chance you could get his name and address?"

"Sure, Street, but it won't do any good."

"Why not? All I want to do is talk with him."

"I'm afraid you can't do that. It's strange how life has its twists and turns. This fellow comes in with pancreatic cancer. Then, because Simsy makes a mistake while treating her patient, I'm asked to duplicate it with mine. Both of our patients are cured, except the hospital sends them away saying it was misdiagnosis. There's no way Dr. Marks believes that. A few days after Simsy died, someone tells me that they saw my patient in the paper. They said there was a big picture of my patient in the newspaper. It was in the obituaries. He was killed by a hit and run driver. The same thing happened to Dirk."

"Karen, do you know anything more?"

"Nope. Just his name."

Street grabbed for his police radio. Then he put it back and picked up his cellular phone. "This is Detective Street. Get me up to McCoy or someone up there."

"Who's this?"

"Hey, Jack it's Street, twice in one night." Jack Demarco was one of the three detectives in the room earlier as Ferris was being questioned.

"Jack, I need a name tracked down ASAP." Street looked at Ferris, "Say hello to Dr. Ferris. You met earlier tonight. She's going to give you a name, a hit and run victim and whatever she knows. Call me back. Use the cellular, not the police radio."

"The person's name is Louis Berger. He was a patient of mine. Someone said he was killed by a hit and run driver. It'd be about two weeks ago. I don't know anything more. Not even where it happened... Street, the Detective wants to talk to you again."

"Street, now what's going on? Did you sign her up for the force. How about taking the rest of the night off. Aren't you going to Washington tomorrow? This can wait, right?"

"Wrong. I'm in my car and I'll wait."

Street arrived at Ferris' apartment building just as he hung up.

"Karen, I'm going to wait for a call back."

"Street, do you mind if I wait in the car for a few minutes? I'd like to know what they say about my patient."

It was almost 11 PM. This day stretched on with no beginning or end. After the call back from Demarco, Street was going home. He could steal at least a few hours of sleep and look forward to the next day in Washington. He expected it to be a day very different from today. In Washington, Street expected more answers than questions.

The cellular phone rang at 11:10 PM. Street put the call on the speaker phone so Ferris could listen.

"Street, this' Demarco. Here's what the computer says. The hit and run victim was Louis Berger, age 56. He lived in Brookline and was killed while crossing Beacon Street. The accident occurred around 6:30 PM."

"Demarco, let me guess. It was a white Monte Carlo with a woman driver and she left the scene of the accident. Right?"

"Street, it's refreshing to know you're not always on target. Guess you might just be human. He was hit by a late model blue car. A couple of people saw the accident. The car was abandoned at the scene. You are right about one thing. The driver was a woman."

"Demarco, see what else you can find. Get the whole report and leave it on my desk. Thanks."

Street and Ferris sat in the front seat. Street did not wait for Ferris to ask questions.

"The answer is, I don't know if this has anything to do with the person who hit Dirk. The driver was also a woman. And she left the accident scene. Until I get a better picture, I'll assume it was the same person."

"Street, suddenly I don't feel very safe around here. What should I do?"

It was midnight and the quiet of the Cambridge night was winning the battle against the noise of buses and cars. Street was exhausted and silent. Ferris could see he was thinking. She understood why he had done what he did earlier. She could feel the danger that Street had known. They sat and looked at each other.

"Karen, can you stay with someone else? Can you call that other doctor? What about Ernie or Gaetano or even Marks. It's a good idea for you not to stay here until things get cleared up."

A big yellow transit bus rolled in front of their car with a billboard on the side, *Come to Jamaica.*

"Karen, now there's a great idea. Jamaica!" They laughed.

They were both laughing as the first bullet exploded through the rear right window smashing glass and ripping apart a piece of the front dashboard. Street's instincts were solid while Ferris' were frozen. He threw her to the floor, ducked, and pulled out his service revolver. Street had heard this sound before. It was not a rock. The second blast came within two seconds, this time directly through the rear window, tossing glass everywhere.

"Shit! I'm hit!" Street's right arm pulled back in reflex.

"This is Street, CODE 30, I'm hit. Officer down. Location 421 Sanders off Mass Ave Cambridge."

The police radio burst into red. Street knew help would come in seconds, not minutes. Nothing electrifies police airways like the call that a cop is under fire. It's a chilling sound that breaks through all other calls. Stolen cars, speeding, break-ins, accidents, and all other police calls fade into the background. When a fellow cop is under active fire, it's war.

THIS IS CODE 33, VEHICLE IS IN CAMBRIDGE. GRAY UNMARKED BOSTON POLICE. ALL AVAIL-ABLE RESPOND. OFFICER DOWN.

Street looked at Ferris, who was lying on the floor. She was OK. He was not. His right arm was burning and blood was oozing near his shoulder and running down his right arm. The bullet had knocked the revolver out of his hand.

"Karen, stay in the car. Don't move. Stay put."

"What's happening, what's happening, Oh God!"

Street thought it sounded like a rifle. Rifles use spiral grooves cut in its bore to give the bullet a spinning motion and greater accuracy. It's like a quarterback who spins the football to keep the wobble out. Street thought that whoever was shooting was firing from a roof or window. He couldn't be sure. In fact, he didn't know how many were shooting. He knew the shooter would be gone in an instant. Off in the distance, within 60 seconds of his call for help, Street could hear a rising chorus of sirens.

Most of what Street did came from instinct. Call the report in. Stay in the vehicle for protection. Try and protect others around the scene. Wait for back up. He saw Ferris on the floor. Street was sure she was OK.

"Street you're hit. You're bleeding."

"That's OK; they'll get an ambulance fast"

"Street, remember me. Dr. Karen Ferris. Get your shirt off."

First on the scene was a Cambridge police cruiser which skidded to a stop perpendicular to Street's car. Both cops jumped out and squatted behind their doors. There were no more shots. Total elapsed time was under 60 seconds from Street's call for help.

"You all right in there? Where's the shooter?"

"I'm hit. Look up behind my car."

One of the cops rushed over to Street's car and opened the door.

"More coming. Ambulance here in a minute. Hang in there guy. Let's see what I can do."

Both of the cops were female and one reached over to look at Street's bloody shirt.

"I'm a doctor; I'll take care of him. No internal bleeding I can find. No blood from ears, nose, no vomit blood. I checked for abdominal tenderness and spasms. He's OK there, too. Let's put him down on sidewalk and elevate those legs. Looks like a flesh wound. That bullet skipped through his deltoid. No bones hit. This looks worse than it is."

"Easy for you to say. It hurts like hell."

"Street, you'll be fine. You better have a good laundry to get all the blood out."

"Karen, funny. Got anything for pain?"

"Street, an ambulance is coming. Just relax."

Seconds later, three other cruisers had arrived, including one from Boston. Within five minutes, the 100 yards surrounding Street's car looked like an outdoor disco with blue, white, yellow, red, green, white lights flashing in all directions. It was a ground level 4th of July fireworks display.

Street had never been touched by a bullet in his life. Now, in one six-hour stretch, he went from a steam bath to the brink of professional extinction as a detective to lying on the sidewalk bleeding. Lying there on the sidewalk with Ferris kneeling over him, Street kept thinking of the bus with the billboard *Welcome to Jamaica*.

"Karen, I'm getting some chills and I'm thirsty. Is there something to drink?"

Ferris got up and went to one of the cops. "He may be going into mild shock. I don't think so. Get the ambulance here."

The ambulance already was there. With so many police cars, it couldn't get close. Street was lifted into the ambulance and Ferris went with him.

"Take him to the Charles Hospital. I'm a doctor there."

"Hey, Karen, not the 7th Floor."

They started to laugh and kept doing so most of the way to the Charles. The ambulance pulled up to the Emergency door and Street was wheeled inside.

"Street, I promise, no 7th Floor." He was moved into a partitioned room with two residents and three nurses.

"Hey Dr. Ferris, what are you doing here. Coming down from the Ritz upstairs and joining us ordinary folks down here in the ER?"

"This is a police detective. I think it's just a flesh wound. His pulse and BP are fine."

One AM is a time of night. It is that hour when you are staying out late or starting extra early. One AM is always pitch black. It's the hour when the second hand starts to move downhill towards the six. Clocks are so much in our lives that no one notices them. All cops learn the lessons of *time*. Cops and clocks dance together each day and night. Street knew that lesson as he fixed his eyes on the clock in front of him. The great divide between one day and the next are those few hours when we close our eyes. Was it sleep or no sleep? Street was counting the precious few hours left to do that.

Ferris waited for Street outside the treatment room. Inside, one of the residents was giving Street a short list of do's and don'ts. He lost very little blood. He did have a deep skin wound, however. For the next ten days he would be on antibiotics. He should not have alcohol, and should change the bandages each day. Other than that, he was fine. According to regulations, Street would be required to log in three visits with the Department's psychologist. If the bullet hit three inches lower, chances are that flags at Boston Police headquarters would be at half staff. His shirt was a total loss, or, depending on Street's view, a red badge of honor. It sent a bright message to Ferris.

"Street, this is our endless night." Ferris was the one gentle face in the crowded emergency room. As required by procedure, the Chief of Police had been notified that a cop was shot and he appeared just as Street was leaving. There were about ten other detectives milling about including his partner, Mickey McCoy.

The Chief spoke quickly.

"Street, you get me out of bed 'cause they said you were shot. I come down here and you look great. Have your partner get you home. Rumor around here is that you've crammed about a week into the last few hours. And you're supposed to be in Washington tomorrow for that meeting. Are you still going?"

"Yes sir, I leave late in the afternoon so I can still get some sleep. Mickey, we need to take Dr. Ferris with us."

The three got in Mickey's car with Street in the back seat.

"Karen, next time I call to ask you questions, tell me it's a wrong number."

"Street, where do I go now?"

"We're two steps ahead of you. Mickey has talked with Ernie and you're his house guest for the next few days. Give Mickey a key to your apartment and he'll go in with a female cop and take out what you need. Write out a list. You don't know this, but Ernie has been under police protection. So, now you'll have the same. He promised us that he's taking a mattress on the floor and you get the bed. It'd be smart if you don't talk about tonight beyond what hits the papers. Especially don't talk about your patient Berger. Now you know why I was worried."

The police car arrived at Ernie Green's apartment. "Mickey, take Dr. Ferris upstairs. I'll wait in the car."

"Street, I'm your doctor now. Call me tomorrow and let me know how you are. Here's my beeper number. Street, instead of drinks, I want dinner when this is over. And that's doctor's orders."

She reached over to Street, touched his hand and gave him a very soft and tender kiss on the cheek.

At three AM, Street arrived home. McCoy was leaving for Ferris' apartment to get her things.

"Street, they're working through all night to get the bullets. We've got three crews over there interviewing. Cambridge police has two more. Zebra is over in Cambridge, too. A lot of people aren't going to get much sleep tonight. Are you OK?" Street smiled.

"When you go back to Ernie's tonight, or this morning, or whatever the hell it is, give this to Dr. Ferris. She'll understand." Street reached in his wallet and pulled out a crumpled piece of paper.

Street's answering machine was blinking. It said there was one message.

"Hi Street, this is Kate. Hope you had a nice day. I'm looking forward to seeing you in Washington."

Street was looking forward to a few hours of sleep. There was one question that needed a quick answer. Who was being shot at tonight? Street. Ferris. Or both. And why tonight?

Chapter Eighteen:
Accessories

Mickey McCoy was the designated alarm clock for the morning. It was 10 AM and there was nothing soft about McCoy's hammering on Street's buzzer.

"Mickey, they didn't shoot my ears off. Is that how you wake up a guy who's been shot? Hold it."

When he opened the door, McCoy was standing there with a big grin on his face. "Yeah, and what's so nice about today Mickey?"

McCoy flashed a copy of the 2nd edition of the *Boston Gazette*.

BOSTON COP HERO IN CAMBRIDGE SHOOTING

"Where'd that line come from? All I did was get shot at. Nothing more."

"Well, Street, it seems the angle is you took a bullet intended for the doctor. Those are the words from the Chief."

"That's not true. We don't know who the shooter was going for. Maybe it was a random nothing. Who wrote this crap?"

Street knew how things worked in the Department. The Chief called in a favor from the paper and spun the story the way the Department wanted. The reporter writes it that way and earns an I-O-U the next time something big is brewing.

"Street, your desk has messages all over it. That guy in Washington heard and called to see if you're coming. There's a message from Beecher to call her in Washington. Atwood Dory from Gene World called. Green called and so did your, well, let's say your private doctor called. Karen wants you to call back.

Your sister left a message asking why you didn't call her last night."

"McCoy, enough already. Let me get dressed and pack a bag for Washington."

Across town, the President of the Charles Hospital was in her office with Dr. Marks and Atwood Dory. Dr. Irizome Shiri spoke in a way that never left her feelings in doubt.

"I didn't ask for a gussy-up and I won't take any razzle-dazzle. Did you see this morning's papers? It starts with a shoot-out in Cambridge that includes one of your doctors. And we've lost two other doctors from the same floor due to accidental deaths. We've had police in and out of here constantly. Every employee in this hospital has undergone police checks. Gentlemen, I can continue. And why couldn't Beecher make it?"

Dory answered, "She's in Washington."

Both watched Shiri carefully as she spoke. Her silhouetted figure was elegantly framed by the floor to ceiling tinted glass. Looking outside, her view offered the optical illusion of mid-air suspension at tree top level. Outside was a collage of green trees and grass. Shiri wore a navy blue suit with white silk blouse and a fresh cut carnation. Shiri's instinctive cordiality had been pre-empted by events in the last 24 hours. If Marks thought he was king of his 7th floor castle, then Shiri knew she was Queen of the realm. What she felt was barely controlled rage.

"Dr. Marks, this 7th Floor was your idea. The Board of Trustees entrusted you with the good name of the Charles Hospital. And you, Mr. Dory, you've enjoyed access to some of the greatest medical minds in the world. Don't give me your standard dollars and cents story. We could replace Gene World in New York in a minute. Marks, I asked for a report on the deaths of Dr. Sims and Dr. Eldridge. All I got was a memo that the deaths were accidental. So why do we have homicide detectives all over the hospital? Now, this shooting. I want answers. I could turn your 7th Floor into one big cafeteria. Start at the beginning and get to the point."

Marks stood and answered.

"President Shiri, I have always had the best interests of the hospital and its staff and patients as my top priority. This matter has caused me great pain, both personally and as a physician."

Shiri interrupted, "I told you, I want answers, not editorials. Start with Dr. Judith Sims. I asked for her complete files and all I got was a summary. Why are the police so interested in her death? You told me it was anaphylactic shock. Now, is that true? Get to it."

"The medical examiner ruled that she died of anaphylactic shock as the result of semen from a sexual encounter. Incidentally, the blood type of that semen didn't match her boyfriend, Dr. Eldridge. And that was it."

Shiri, barely five feet, stood and looked up at Marks. "Tell me exactly what she was doing on the 7th Floor. I've heard through the grapevine that she was treating a patient with advanced pancreatic cancer who walked out of here healthy. Explain that one."

"Dr. Shiri, what you heard is not really accurate. Her patient's name was Steven Hays and you're correct that he was discharged in fine shape. But we think it was a gross case of misdiagnosis. I notified the legal department about the error. I personally authorized Dr. Sims to conduct additional tests to verify that misdiagnosis. She unfortunately died before all the tests could be completed. Another physician was doing parallel work. That's all there is to it."

"Tell me about her boyfriend, the one who was hit by a car."

"There's nothing to tell. The police report said he was hit by a female driver in a white car. She left the scene and the police are still looking for her."

"What's the name of the doctor doing parallel work?"

"That would be Dr. Karen Ferris."

"Ferris is the one who's name is in the papers this morning. She was in the car when that detective was shot last night. Marks, this circle of coincidences is rather large. Aren't you suspicious?"

Atwood Dory was silent as he watched Shiri interrogate Marks. Shiri was a fearful force. Dory was present several times when Shiri conducted Board of Trustees meetings. The meetings were severe. She always released a timetable which announced how much time was allocated for every subject. Her gold stop watch was not an ornament but a tool she used. Time was the commodity she prized and idle conversation in board meetings did not occur.

A Boston magazine disclosed that she was the highest paid hospital administrator in New England and the fifth highest paid in the US. Unlike many hospitals, the Charles was profitable. She had masterminded a brilliant strategy of reducing the number of hospital beds and substituting them for medical office space. Since taking control of the Charles, Shiri had cut the Charles Hospital's number of beds from 875 to 650. She added almost 50,000 square feet of new medical office space at rates near $30 per square foot. Much of that $1.5 million in extra annual revenues was converted into profits. Parking prices in the garage, sometimes called the *Orange*, were boosted. Shiri mastered the art of fund raising with donor plaques adorning everything from patient rooms, elevators, chapels, cafeterias, rest rooms, lobbies and halls. There were now three statues scattered across the Charles ten-acre site along with several small gardens. Millions of dollars collected from these donors sat in Boston banks and investment houses. It was this income stream that made the Charles the most profitable of the so called non-profit hospitals. The Board of Trustees never faced the crisis meetings that plagued other hospitals. At the Charles there were never layoffs. Salaries were substantially above the national average. In the medical community, a bright orange *Charles Hospital* ID badge meant someone had hit the top. Dory knew these successes insulated Shiri from criticism. She asked the questions and demanded answers. She gave the orders and they were followed. Shiri countenanced no mistakes.

"Marks, I want a written summary, no longer than two pages. You also need to bring to committee the names of candidates to replace Sims and Eldridge. I want to see the computer disks and paper files on doctors Sims, Eldridge, and Ferris and on those two patients with pancreatic cancer. What are their names?"

"Dr. Shiri, one is Steven Hays; he's a teacher. The other is Louis Berger, formerly a stock broker."

"What does *formerly* mean?"

"Well, very tragically, after Ferris treated him, and he was discharged..."

"He was on the 7th Floor. Why was he discharged?"

"It was another misdiagnosis. We're checking into the whole matter relating to acceptance of patients for the 7th Floor and initial diagnosis."

"What's this Berger doing now if he's not a stock broker?"

"As I was saying, tragically, after Ferris treated him, Berger was killed in a hit and run accident."

Shiri rose, turned her back on Marks, and looked outside as she spoke.

"Marks, why was I ignorant of this? You have been at the Charles a long time and the hospital is your home. Didn't all these events make you concerned. Where's your inside compass. No wonder we've got detectives all over the hospital. Get that written summary to me. Mr. Dory and I are going to speak in private."

Until that moment, Atwood Dory thought the firestorm would hit Marks, leaving him intact. That hope was very short lived.

"Mr. Dory, it's been a long time since we've had a talk alone, and this moment is way overdue. Do you agree with that assessment?"

"Well, Dr. Shiri, I always look forward to talking with you. It's just that you're so busy. You're accomplishing so much here at the Charles. My people at Gene World think this association with the 7th Floor has been immensely successful for everyone."

"Dory, you are a walking, talking piece of cellophane. Don't suck up to me. I can see right through you. Let's talk business."

Dory rolled his eyes up towards the ceiling.

"I've looked at our agreement with Gene World. We've got another couple of years to go. I asked Marks to leave the room because he gets emotionally involved in the 7th Floor. But, Dory, you're a businessman. Health care and treatments and cures means less to you than the closing quote on your Company. Right?"

"Dr. Shiri, that's not really accurate. I've been up on the 7th Floor a while and I feel a real sense of family with those people. So does my Company."

"Dory, it'd be so much easier if you could cut the crap. Isn't there any finesse within you? Those people on the 7th Floor are no more family to you than the homeless guy you probably step over each night to get to your car. I have ears and eyes. You command no respect on the 7th Floor. And that's your fault. You came in as Mr. Moneybags and never let anyone forget."

Nothing Shiri said was from impulse or anger. She was ready to drop a bomb in Dory's lap. It had a time fuse he could not defuse.

"Dory, the short and long of all this is simple."

Shiri, as only she could do, offered an epic tale. No person on earth could frame the purpose of the 7th Floor is such overwhelming words. The 7th Floor was nothing less than the battlefield between good and evil. New drug-resistant bacteria and exotic viruses had wrestled human research to the floor in a strangle hold. For all the bravado that once crowned the human assault on these killers, the 1990's was pay back time.

Deadly infections had fought a guerrilla war against mankind and was emerging from the jungles to claim victory. Only a few private and government research laboratories and the 7th Floor stood as guardians of humanity.

Not a sunset passed without another story of human retreat. Stories of cruise ships racing to home port with victims, not vacationers. It was dinner and dancing under moonlit skies at eight PM and by two AM how many who ate would live to see the sun rise. There was the Yale University researcher who contracted Sabia virus while working in his research laboratory. Sneaking out of the Brazilian jungles and into the town of Sabia, a virus stalked the dirt roads and picked its victims at random. In southern Russia, there was a Cholera outbreak. In England, flesh-eating bacteria provided fodder with grotesque pictures of children watching as their skin was devoured. Antibiotics were being assassinated by emboldened bacteria. Some of these bacterium attacked by producing toxins that cued the human immune system into a giant response so toxic that it killed.

The battle was not limited to bacteria like Vibrio cholerae or organisms like Mycobacterium tuberculosis. There are viruses such as smallpox, HIV, Hepatitis B, or the extravagant killer, Ebola. From the Peruvian jungle there could be thrilling experiments with viruses uncovered in ancient tombs. Then there are protozoa, like Plasmodium known more commonly as Malaria.

The 7th Floor would be ground zero for some specialized testing of smallpox in the *Zipper* section of the Floor. Exciting days were ahead and the 7th Floor would be a national center-piece in the continuing battle. The counterattack was moving into the realm of science fiction. Plans were in progress to use both crystallography and biochemistry to *fingerprint* bacterial genes and enzymes that cause drug resistance. Then antibiotics will be created to fire against a targeted microbe. They had to move fast since some of these microbes could reproduce before a single 30 minute episode of *Married With Children* had played out its laugh lines. Viral diseases were under assault in the same manner. Pharmaceutical companies, including Gene World, were focusing on cancer and viral diseases, especially AIDS.

Dr. Shiri had a special way of framing events in a dramatic fashion. She talked about combinational chemistry. It was another weapon in the battle. The theory is to build blocks of chemicals that join in millions of combinations and then, like a smart radar-guided weapon, zero in on a specific bacterium. The 7th Floor was coming of age. Shiri planned to increase staffing and budgets. This was the moment in time that Marks had dreamed of so many years ago.

"When our contract expires, we're going to end your Gene World's exclusive deal on the 7th Floor. It's time to open the 7th Floor to the marketplace through fair and competitive bidding. Of course, Gene World can participate. I want to see what the marketplace says about the value of our product. I expect the Charles can get substantially more income through competitive bidding."

Dory knew everything she said was true. Over the years, Gene World's arrangement with the 7th Floor had been a bonanza in the development of cancer treatments. It provided

Gene World with access to advanced military medical programs.
Gene World used the relationship with the Charles extensively in
presentations on Wall Street. The Charles 7th Floor was always
a centerpiece of each year's annual stockholder's report. Now
Shiri was throwing a bucket of black paint across the smiling
executive faces that adorned Gene World's annual report to
stockholders. From 200 miles distant, he could feel the tremors
shaking in New York. The lawyers would probably demand that
the contents of this meeting be incorporated within the next
Securities and Exchange filing. That would be public and the
market gurus who followed Gene World would punish the
Company's stock by selling. Dory seethed at the disloyalty of this
little queen of the Charles. Gene World had provided money
when no one else would. Their profits from treatments that were
developed was fair. Now that the 7th Floor had gained world-
wide fame, in large part through Gene World, Shiri was tossing
them in a pile with all the other pharmaceutical companies in the
world.

"Madame President, your words are disingenuous. You're
telling me that my Company's investments were welcomed and
appreciated and in two years we can compete with every other
Tom, Dick, and Harry for a chance to renew our relationship. Is
that your definition of loyalty?"

"Dory, you don't get the picture. So let me elaborate. You
and Gene World have abused your privileges at the Charles. I
know about the three nurses you sent down to Martinique. They
all signed statements and have been terminated. What you did
was unethical and probably illegal. There are other abuses. Our
attorneys advised me that we cannot break the remaining portion
of the contract. If I could, I would. In fact, when the contract
expires, I will bring my influence to bear on the Board of
Directors not to select Gene World. Don't lecture me on loyalty.
Privileges granted Gene World were abused and the good name
of my hospital was endangered. I feel no remorse whatsoever.
Treatments you've developed over the years at the Charles will
provide an income stream for Gene World well into the 21st
Century. These treatments for pancreatic cancer are probably

worth billions of dollars. And you have Dr. Marks to thank for much of it."

"Dr. Shiri, or, President, or, whatever you want to be called, you'll hear from our attorneys. We have a contract that conveys upon my Company the rights of first refusal upon renewal. You can take your dreams for the 7th Floor and toss them out the window. If you want to kick us out we'll create a firestorm that will burn your dreams for the Charles to a crisp. I will make it my mission in life to destroy you."

As Dory spoke, he sensed others in the room. Shiri had pressed a buzzer under her desk and two uniformed security guards appeared.

"Escort Mr. Dory to the 7th Floor. Effective immediately, every document and every computer file that is created on the 7th Floor is to be copied and deposited here. Mr. Dory shall at all times be accompanied by a security guard when he is on the premises of our property. Is that understood?"

"Shiri, like I said, you'll be hearing from our attorneys."

Dory's face looked like he had been slapped around. Shiri's words stung and Dory's ears were ringing. The escort out of Shiri's office did not look like an honor guard.

"Timothy, did you hear all that?"

"Iri, yes I did."

"It's all on tape. Now get those documents for me. And I imagine you might want to get a sedative for Dory. He didn't look very good when he left." Shiri and Marks laughed.

"Only you could do that Iri."

"Timothy, only you could have created the 7th Floor. Talk to you later, my friend."

Street arrived to a hero's welcome. There was no way to tell he had been nicked by a rifle bullet only hours earlier. The bandage inside his shirt was not large and he could move his arm with some pain. His partner, Mickey, had been up most of the night and he looked a lot worse than Street. Several detectives huddled around his desk.

"Well, Street, so you're still going to Washington today? In all those messages, we didn't see one from the President. I guess they forgot to tell him you're a hero."

"Come on guys, give me a break."

McCoy had briefed him on the way over to headquarters. Two bullets were retrieved from his car and ballistics think they came from Remington Model 742. The weapon was not recovered although empty shell casings were found on the roof of an apartment building across from Ferris' place. No witnesses had come forward.

"Street, my hunch is they were after Ferris. She's the logical target. What do they get from killing a cop?"

"Mickey, if they wanted her, they would have waited till she got out of the car and was a clear shot. I don't buy that line. I think they wanted me. And maybe she was going to be a bonus."

Someone yelled that Street had a call on line three. It was Kate Beecher calling from Washington.

"Street, are you OK? I called you and left a message at home and at your office. You had us worried. I was trying to get your beeper number last night and they told me you had been shot. I hear you saved some doctor's life. What a hero."

"Kate, that's garbage. She was in the car and I didn't do a damn thing except duck. You know, I'm still coming down on that two PM flight. Are you going to meet me at the Airport?"

"Street, we'll take good care of you. We've got you booked at the Willard for the night. And I took the liberty of making dinner plans. See you in a few hours. And keep your head down."

Street looked at his desk and it was littered with messages. He scanned them quickly. He'd call his sister. Ernie Green called. Karen Ferris. There were other calls. One from Dr. Nancy Debbs. And Dr. Shiri. That last name registered instantly.

"Charles Hospital, may I direct your call please."

"Dr. Shiri's office."

"This is Dr. Shiri's office. May I help you?"

"I'm Detective Jimmy Street and Dr. Shiri called me."

Street was put on hold. The hospital had classical music on hold. He was listening to Vivaldi's *Four Seasons*. That was one of his favorites. Street would be happy to stay on hold for the next 20 minutes.

"Detective Street, this is President Shiri. You know who I am?"

"Yes, I do. What can I do for you?"

"First, I hope you're OK after what I read in the papers. You know
Dr. Ferris is one of ours. Thank goodness you're both OK. I'd like to meet you and discuss your investigation. Is that possible?"

"I knew we'd meet soon. I'll be in Washington this afternoon and back tomorrow. How does late afternoon sound?"

"It sounds fine. Just call when you return to Boston and I'll be available. Can we meet here at the hospital?"

"No problem. I'll see you then."

"Could you please switch me back to your telephone operator."

"Who are you trying to reach?"

"Dr. Nancy Debbs from the 7th Floor called."

"Hold on. I'll have my secretary round her up."

Street was back on hold which was fine with him. He could hear more of the *Four Seasons*. McCoy was motioning for Street, pointing to the Chief of Detectives, Roy Clark. "Mickey, tell Roy I'll be right with him."

"Detective, this is Dr. Debbs. I know what happened last night. I've talked with Ernie. I'm scared. Am I in danger, too?"

"Hold on Dr. Debbs. First thing is calm down. I think you're OK unless you know something I don't. It seems every day someone tosses me a curve ball up on your floor."

"Well, Detective, I was talking with Simsy on the morning she died. In fact, I was on the phone with her when someone knocked on her door. And I know who it was."

"Stop right there. Not another word. Meet me at that coffee shop across the street at 12 noon. Can you do that? You don't know what I look like so ask for my ID when we meet. I'm bringing my partner along. See you at noon. Relax."

Street jumped out of his chair and followed Mickey into Chief of Detective Clark's office.

"Hey Mickey, we're stopping at the hospital on the way to the airport. We may have a break."

Roy Clark and Jimmy Street started at the police academy together. They worked traffic together. In the early years with no seniority, they worked Christmas and most of the other holidays together. Clark was Street's best friend on the force. After so many years together, they took care of business fast. Their conversations were direct and no nonsense. The silliness came after hours. Street never forgot that Clark was in charge and always addressed him as *Chief* when in the presence of outsiders. Every detective understood the bond between these two men was unbreakable. Clark knew Street's history from Queens. More than anyone, he knew how Street suffered when his dad was gunned down. Clark knew Street was rock outside and sponge inside.

"Street, man you really know how to keep your good buddy here nervous. Operations called me at home last night and told me what happened. Whoever did the shooting, I'd sure like a piece of him."

"Yeah, well Roy, not as much as I would."

"Street, are you all set for your Washington trip? Seems this Beecher is a real hot shot in the Air Force. I don't know what you'll find. She's connected all the way to the top. Keep your chin down. We don't want that pretty face of yours all mucked up."

The total length of time in Clark's office was under five minutes. That was typical of their conversations. Boom, boom, the facts and it was bye-bye. The two men talked in short hand.

"Mickey, let's get going. First that coffee shop across from the Charles and then the airport. And when are they going to get me a new car?"

Street and McCoy arrived 15 minutes early at the coffee shop. It was easy to spot Dr. Nancy Debbs sitting at a table, fingering a coffee spoon. She was a very unsettled woman.

"Dr. Debbs, you're early. I'm Detective Street and this is my partner, Mickey McCoy."

"Do you mind if I see some ID first?"

Street thought back to last night when he picked up Ferris. Dr. Debbs was very different. Street and McCoy pulled out black wallets with gold badges and pictures next to the blue and white official Seal of the City of Boston.

"Detectives, everyone at the hospital is talking about what happened to Karen last night. Say, aren't you the detective who was with her?"

"There are rumors all over the place. This morning Dory went to his office and had two security guards outside his door. The story is that Dr. Shiri had a knock down fight with him. Some people are saying that Simsy and Dirk were killed. Ernie's not talking and has been keeping to himself. Karen called in sick this morning. Dr. Marks has his secretary running all over the place getting papers and documents. Supposedly some nurses were fired by Dr. Shiri for taking money from Dory. It's mad up there."

McCoy interrupted Dr. Debbs. "Doctor, you reeled off a list of people on the 7th Floor. But you skipped two names, Dr. Gaetano Piccard and Dr. Allen Fiengold. Why?"

One constant with Detective McCoy was his computer mind. What he lacked in charisma he made up for in attention to detail. Street gave him an approving glance.

"Well, that's why I called you, Detective Street. I forgot about Fiengold. He's that type of person, very forgettable. Let me continue. On the Saturday morning when they say Simsy died, I was talking with her on the phone."

McCoy asked, "About what time was that?"

"I'd guess it was about nine AM. So, I was talking to her. She told me Dirk had left to go up north. She was planning on taking a run in the morning and then going to the hospital to get some paperwork done. She also said that some former patient, I don't know his name, had invited her out for lunch and she was going. Something was strange because on the 7th Floor we don't have *former* patients. You know what we do up there. So that struck me as unusual. And, we don't socialize with patients. We were talking for about five minutes when the buzzer rang. I could hear it over the phone. Simsy said *Guy* was downstairs and was coming up to leave off some *prosciutto*. He did that a lot for people. He's a real nut on *prosciutto*. Simsy said she had to go and said good-bye."

Debbs noticed the look between Street and McCoy.

"Did I say anything wrong? That's all I know. I would have mentioned it sooner but it skipped my mind. And *Guy* is one of the nicest and kindest people there is. He's friends with everyone. So now, tell me, am I safe?"

McCoy answered as Street remained silent. "I'm sure you are. If you feel uncomfortable, stay with friends. If you do that, make sure you give us a number where we can reach you. One last thing, have you told this story to anyone?"

"Well, yes. I told Ernie and he insisted I tell you."

With McCoy driving, Street had a chance to look around as they headed to Logan Airport. Debbs' story about Piccard's Saturday morning visit was important. Piccard could either help fix the time of death or be evasive. Why he never mentioned the visit troubled Street. Was he hiding something? Sims wasn't hiding anything because she told Debbs, who was coming upstairs. That probably eliminated the chance that Piccard and Sims had a relationship. Did the investigators check the inventory of the kitchen and was there *prosciutto*? It is standard operating procedure to photograph everything on the premises.

"McCoy, when you get back, ask Santori for the pictures taken inside her apartment. Check out the refrigerator. If my memory's right, Dirk talked with Santori about finding fresh squeezed orange juice in the refrig. I think he said they never bought it. See if there's any fresh squeezed OJ that shows up in the photos. This is great. We're getting down to *prosciutto* and fresh squeezed OJ. That's a hell of a combination."

McCoy dropped Street off at the airport and headed back into the city. For the next hour, Street knew he would have a chance to think with no phone calls. He tossed his bag in the overhead bin. Then he walked to the cockpit and introduced himself to the First Officer. It was a brief courtesy call to let them know he was a cop and had a weapon with him. Street went back to his window seat, buckled in, and closed his eyes.

The plane lifted off and banked slightly as it climbed through white puffy clouds and headed south. Within five minutes they were just west of Cape Cod. Street closed his eyes again and found himself at the foot of Sankaty Head Lighthouse on Nantucket Island. For nine glorious days in July he roamed the

Island in his black Land Rover. Each summer the Island's mystique drew him back to the cobblestone streets lined on each side with weathered gray houses. There is an attitude on Nantucket that fits Street. For those persons truly ensconced in the Island it is a calling to be creative. It doesn't matter what one creates, so long as one creates.

Just before returning to the police force, Street bought a small cottage not far from Dionis Beach on the north coast of the Island. That cottage and his home on Beacon Hill were reality check points during difficult times. He imagined the winding narrow streets of Nantucket. Passageways he had walked a hundred times after midnight. At the start of each walk he expected to mastermind solutions for all the world's problems. At the end, all he had to show was a burnt out cigar and sea salt scattered across his face. Failure never felt so good. His midnight walks crossed streets with names like Mulberry, India, York, Silver, Salem, Liberty and Starbuck. There was even an Orange Street, although after this case with the Charles Hospital he might give that one a pass. By daylight he ran a course crossing beaches whose names ring clear in his mind each day of the year. Running west to east on the south coast, he would start at Madaket then Cisco, Miacomet, Surfside and Nobadeer. He'd run from beach to adjoining road and back again to the beach. The distance was about ten miles. He wished it was ten thousand miles.

Several times, when stumped on a case, Street would get an overnight bag and catch the ferry to Nantucket. It didn't matter whether it was June or January. The Island's magical dose of mind-cleansing worked year round.

The Island food was scrumptious. While he couldn't cook more than pasta with any reliability, he loved to eat great food. His Nantucket favorites were Norwegian salmon, grilled shrimp with curry, and Nantucket sole steamed in lobster saffron consommé. Dessert would be chocolate yogurt, a cup of *espresso* and then his cigar. The smallest detail of Nantucket was never more than a split hair from his mind.

"Ladies and Gentlemen, this is the Captain and I've turned off the seat belt sign. However, when seated we recommend you always keep it buckled like we do up front. We've reached our cruising altitude of 27,000 feet. At the present time we're passing over Long Island. The weather at Washington's National Airport is the same as Boston, partly cloudy. We expect to land ahead of schedule at 3:15."

So much for Nantucket dreams.

Chapter Nineteen: Washington

Kate Beecher looked great. He never got a chance to say anything as she planted her lips on his and slid her tongue inside his. Her arms wrapped tightly around his shoulders and then she moved them up and down his back. Maybe this was payback time after yesterday.

"Street, you don't look like someone shot you."

"Kate, trust me; this is how I like to look after being shot."

"We're going over to the Mayflower to meet with Tom and someone else. Then I'll take you over to the Willard and we'll have dinner. How's that sound?"

When it sounds that good there's no reason to say anything. Sit back, relax and enjoy it all.

The Mayflower was on Connecticut Avenue, only a few blocks from the White House. Kate gently guided Street through the long tubular corridor to the elevator banks and up to the 10th floor. She opened the door to Room 1030. Street made a mental note of the number. That was easy since it was the same number as a well known Boston radio station. Seated inside was Tom Adler and an unidentified man.

"Street, I'd like you to meet the Director of the OSI, General Irwin Korbee."

"Sir."

"Detective Street, why don't you sit down and we'll chat a bit."

Street had a hunch it was going to be less of a chat and more of a speech by the general.

Korbee looked like the local librarian, not the head of a super secret counter intelligence force. Street guessed he was about 65 years old and about five and half feet tall. Maybe he was a college professor on loan to the OSI. His black hair was spotted with gray. Street understood that climbing to the top of the OSI was a feat akin to reaching the summit of Mount Everest. This was a man of undeniable strength and accomplishment. He never heard of General Korbee and this was not the place to ask for his biography.

"Street, this is going to stay focused. First, we've done a security check on you with the assistance of the Boston Police. We know how you could afford to own two homes and a wine collection on the salary of a detective. Maybe you should have stayed with those law firms. Second, your path and that of Agent Beecher's have intersected at the Charles Hospital."

Street looked at Kate. If only he knew how completely they had intersected. Or maybe he did know.

"And, thirdly, you have not discovered the New World. You ain't Christopher Columbus! Agent Beecher has been working under cover at the hospital for some time. You know we use the hospital as a testing ground for experimental treatments. Our liaison office monitors all the procedures on the 7th Floor. It's an extremely important resource for us. Although it has been reported in the papers that VARIOLA virus has been destroyed, we have a small supply arriving at the 7th Floor for testing later. That's not the only lethal virus we store there.

"Even, you Detective, don't know about the vault we built below the basement. We call it the bunker. You couldn't get in if your life depended on it. Or, you couldn't get out if we didn't let you. Only Beecher, Marks, and Dr. Shiri have full knowledge of the storage facility. It's guarded around the clock. ID for entrance is by retina scan and fingerprints. There's a decontamination shower. And a six foot thick cement wall around the storage facility. It's basically a missile silo except no missiles. That's not the problem.

"Over a year ago, Gene World started testing a new drug, XM2 for the treatment of some cancers. It's used in combination with other drugs. So far that sounds unspectacular. Then about a year ago, small amounts of the XM2 started to vanish from audit reports. The first person to notice was Beecher. Now, why would someone steal this XM2. It has no monetary value and its medical use was unknown. And if someone connected with the 7th Floor was stealing XM2, then what about the integrity of our military programs? Do we shut the whole thing down and toss away close to 100 million dollars?"

"Excuse me sir, but I thought the Air Force liaison office was a free ride. I thought you exchanged transport and other general services in return for access to the research."

"Street, that's how it started. But you know how things go. Several years ago, we needed a storage location near a large medical community. Boston was ideal and the Charles seemed a perfect choice. So, during a hospital renovation, we built this secure underground facility. Your Governor knows about all this.

Then, last Spring, one of the doctors up there, Sims was her name, fouled up some dosages and gave a mega dose of this XM2 to her patient. It should have killed him. Instead, we think it cured him. We never bought into the misdiagnosis story. If someone stumbled on a cure for pancreatic cancer with this drug, our scientists tell us this XM2 has a high probability of success with other cancers and viruses. It definitely would have a military use. We just don't know all the details. XM2 is proprietary to Gene World. We've asked them for more information and they have not provided it. We can't get too pushy about all this stuff since we've got a very sensitive viral and bacteria storage facility right in the middle of Boston's medical center. Starting to get the picture?

"This fellow Dory has not been cooperative. We asked Dr. Shiri to apply pressure and she's started. In the meantime, it's a Mexican standoff. We know Dory didn't steal the XM2 because he already has access to it. That doctor who may have cured her dying patient lit a fuse.

So, Agent Beecher here is working a parallel investigation. She has to do it quietly. That's why one of your surveillance teams spotted her driving around Ernie Green's place. Everyone is a suspect. She was just following up on a lead.

"That's all there is. Questions, Detective Street?"

Street wished he had timed that speech.

"Two for starters. First, what do you want from me?"

"The answer is simple. We need your cooperation. We want you to share information with Agent Beecher. She'll do the same with you."

"Here's another question. Do you have more than one agent working inside the Charles Hospital?"

"Why do you ask?"

"I've got a hunch. This whole thing seems too big."

"The answer is...we can't give you an answer. That's for the protection of Agent Beecher and the other agent, if there is one. It's safer to leave all this information in a big mud pool. Visibility isn't great in mud pools."

"I've got other questions General."

"Ask Beecher and Adler; they'll help you as much as possible."

General Korbee got up and walked towards the door. For a second, Street smiled as he imagined the General slogging through one of those *mud pools* in his spit shined black tie shoes. Korbee shook hands with Street.

"Street, I expect we'll never see each other again. Your contact is Beecher and Tom Adler. Good luck on your investigation. By the way, and this is just my personal instinct, but I think those doctors were murdered."

Adler followed Korbee out the door. Beecher got up and walked over to Street.

"Next stop is the Willard and some dinner. That didn't take long, did it?"

It had not taken long. It also left an empty feeling inside Street. He had listened to every word from Korbee. His gut told him he had not heard everything from Korbee.

The ride across town to the Willard was quick. Beecher was full of questions and seemed genuinely concerned about Street. She asked about his wound. Was it a gun or a rifle? When would the ballistics report be back? What about the girl in the car? Did they have any suspects? Beecher left the car with valet parking and guided Street inside.

"Street, we already checked you in. Here's the key. Want some company?"

"Kate, that's the easiest question of the day. Let's go."

Seeing a familiar and intimate face was a relaxing tonic after the last two days. Beecher seemed very soft and maternal. Without even asking, she started to undo his shirt to look at the wound. Street fell back on the king sized bed and closed his eyes as she moved her hands across his right shoulder.

"Street, you'll survive. Has this affected your fingers. I remember them so well."

Beecher walked to the windows and drew the shades closed. She moved over to the stereo and flipped it on. It was pre set on classical music. The room had a basket of fruit and a small refrigerator stocked with beverages. Beecher's hands moved across his chest and started to loosen his belt buckle. She pulled off his shoes and socks. By now, Street didn't care what time it was, where he was, or how all the pieces in the 7th Floor puzzle fit together.

"Kate, did they teach you all this at nursing school or at OSI? Either way, it feels so good."

So often the aggressor or initiator, Street was delightfully immobile as Beecher undressed him first and then herself. Beecher pulled the blue gray covers down and guided him into a sandwich of fresh cleaned sheets. She moved next to him, taking one of her legs and sliding it underneath him. She put her lips near his wound and started to circle the bandage in sweeping wet trails. Her hands were moving across his body. One reached and lifted Streets' left hand to her face and she took two of his fingers and wrapped her lips around them. They exchanged no words.

Lying on his back Street watched as Beecher mounted him with her legs opened and his fingers still in her mouth. She was smiling broadly. He withdrew his fingers and moved both hands around her back, rolling them up through her hair. Street loved the smell and touch of her hair. It was thick and silky and his fingers disappeared inside. She moved from side to side as his hands played through her hair. Slowly her eyes closed as the rhythm of their bodies touching accelerated. She had put some oils on her skin and glided quickly across his body like a downhill skier. There was no friction as the oils spilled off her body and onto Street. He felt like she could slip down his body and off the bed. The room filled with an overpowering scent of lilacs.

"Your fingers Street, they're driving me crazy. Put them behind my ears. Now, behind my knees," as she lifted her legs almost straight to the ceiling. Street did exactly as she commanded.

Beecher awoke first. It was 7:30 PM. "Street, my wounded little baby, open your eyes."

It was at that moment, with his eyes still closed, that Street realized he had been in Washington 16 hours and still had questions to ask.

Beecher reached for the telephone and called room service. "Street, what do you want?"

"Kate, ask me another question."

"Street, I'll do the ordering. We'd like a couple orders of toast, no butter. Some bananas. A pot of coffee. And, two large glasses of fresh squeezed orange juice."

"So Street, what did you think of our meeting yesterday? Now you know why I was driving around Green's apartment. We're on the same team. In fact, maybe there's another person on the team. You've got to keep all this secret. If there is another agent, both of us are a lot safer in Korbee's so called mud pool. Go ahead, my detective hero, do you think there's another agent? Who do you think it might be?"

With his boyish grin, Street answered, "Kate, maybe it's me."

At nine AM, Beecher and Street were driving to National Airport. It was cloudy and rain was predicted. The drive from the Willard to the airport is about 15 minutes. It certainly was not long enough for Street. His foul mood was a perfect match for a cloudy farewell from Washington.

"Kate, you're not coming back with me? What about your safety? Aren't you worried? It'd be shame to get that pretty hair all messed up at the wrong time."

"Very cute Street. I'm returning late tonight. There's an eight PM flight. I called the Charles and they think I'm in Washington at an Air Force briefing. They obviously don't know about our meeting here. Adler's going to take me back to National tonight. Don't worry about me. This goes with the territory. And I'm probably better trained to take care of myself than you." Beecher dropped him off at curbside with a non-chalant *see ya later* and vanished into airport traffic. Street had the sick feeling he had been used. Instinctively, he looked down to see if there was any mud on his feet. He knew it was on his face, not his feet.

"Mickey, my flight leaves in about ten minutes. Did you reach Green? He might be calling about something I asked him to do."

"Street, no luck yet. Tell you what, I'll stop by the hospital on the way to the airport. So, how was Washington? What did you learn?"

"It's what I didn't learn that bugs me. It feels weird. I'll tell you more in Boston. I've got to make a few quick calls before my flight."

"Charles Hospital, may I help you?"

"This is Detective Street, Boston Police. Would you please connect me to Dr. Gaetano Piccard?"

"One moment, we'll ring upstairs."

Street fidgeted in his pockets looking for a ring of keys. He had them last night. Now where are they? Tracing his steps back, he could not remember where they were.

"This is Dr. Piccard, may I help you Detective?"

"Dr. Piccard, as a matter of fact, you can. I'll be at the hospital this afternoon around three PM for a meeting. How about we take a 15 minute walk before, at, say, 2:45 PM? Any problems with the time?"

"Sir, I'll make the time. Is the front entrance OK? Everyone's kind of jumpy up here."

"That's fine. Could you switch me back to the hospital operator?"

"This is Detective Street. Please connect me to Dr. Shiri's office."

This time, the wait was less than ten seconds.

"This is Detective Street. Would you tell Dr. Shiri that I'll see her at three PM. She's expecting me."

Street grabbed his bag and hustled down to Gate 5A. Other than losing his keys and listening to General Korbee deliver a speech in a hotel room, the Washington trip was a dud. Even the time with Beecher felt strange. Street looked for a gate agent.

"Excuse me, how much time do we have before departure?"

"About five minutes, maximum."

"Mickey, listen carefully. I forgot something. Check with the Mayflower Hotel and see who paid for room 1030. And see who paid for the room I stayed in last night at the Willard. I forget the number. Oh yeah, my keys, I can't..."

"Street, one mystery is solved. Kate Beecher just called from Washington. She found your keys and forgot to give them to you in the car. She'll have them at the hospital for you tomorrow."

Street hung up and dashed for the plane. He moved down the gateway and into his seat towards the front. This was Street's quiet time. This time, he couldn't manage to transport his thoughts to Nantucket Island. Whatever island he was on, it was lonely. At sea and out of sight of land, the water had no beginning and no end. He was at sea. Each time he pulled out his compass, the needle spun like a clock. It was less than 24 hours since he stared into a real clock and watched it move. That was in the emergency room at the Charles. How did he manage to get shot at in Cambridge? Was he the target or was it Karen Ferris? No matter who it was, why last night? And why in a car on a busy street? That shooter was in a big hurry.

As the plane accelerated down the runway and climbed away from the city, Street looked back and could see the Washington Monument. Maybe that's where he should have gone. At least he'd have a clear view. There are no mud pools up there.

Street's plane landed in Boston at 11 AM. McCoy was waiting at the gate and full of information.

"Mickey, you know I kept seeing the name United States over and over in Washington. Then it hit me. That's why we're all over the place. We aren't united. I found a dictionary on the plane. I'm probably the only one that ever asked for one. *Unity* is about singleness of purpose. It means everything is together. There's a common bond between Simsy, Dirk, the shooting, and everything else. We're going to find the *unity* in all this. And don't tell me it's the Charles. Even the village idiot could figure that one. We're so close we can't see it."

"Street, I talked with Ernie. He called Simsy's parents just like you asked. He said they were upset about the request to exhume. But they calmed down and want you to explain. Ernie thinks they might say yes if you call."

"Hey Street, how come Beecher has your keys. Did you do a little sight seeing in Washington, you know what I mean?"

"Mickey, figure it out for yourself. Don't let me leave the office without my extra keys or I'll send you back for them."

"Street, do you want me to come with you to the hospital this afternoon?"

"No, what I want you to do is get all those pictures that were taken at Simsy's place when they found her body."

"Street, you asked me for those. They're on your desk."

"McCoy, how do you remember all that stuff? It must be that college degree. Let's stop at headquarters and get those pictures. Then we'll eat. After that I'm going to the hospital, alone. I'll have more things for you to do."

"Street, does 1030 sound familiar. How about 310?"

"The first one is the room number at the Mayflower Hotel in Washington. The second number beats me."

"I don't know how much sleep you got last night, but 310 was your hotel room number. I checked them out and they were both paid for by CRM, Inc. That's CRM, as in Charles River Medical. The rooms were paid for by the hospital, not the OSI or any government agency. Why would they pay for those rooms?" Add one more question to the list.

Street was a student of running and often tried to fit his life's experiences into a giant running metaphor. He knew the history and culture of the long distance runner. His town house had an entire shelf devoted to marathons. He knew about Pheidippides, the Greek who collapsed while running from the battlefield of Marathon to Athens with news of the Greek victory over the Persians. He thought about the starting gun in this race. It was fired with a police call about a break-in at Dr. Judith Sims' apartment. The finish line was not in sight, but Street knew this race was picking up speed.

Chapter Twenty:
Danger Zones

S treet's desk was littered with papers. He took the photos from Sims' apartment. Street and his partner went into a small room and spread the pictures on a table. There were 24 color pictures. Of those, half showed Sims' body and the others her apartment. There was one picture of the refrigerator with the door opened.

"Blow that one up, Mickey. That's the picture we want. Can they do it, now, while we wait?"

The photo lab at police headquarters was in the dingiest corner of the basement. The Boston Police employed one photo technician and several interns from local colleges. This was intern day. Street and McCoy stood in the room as it glowed in red. The room was bathed in red. That red was the culture-color of photo labs and submarines. Down in the corner basement room with squeaking pipes overhead, it looked and sounded like a scene from a grade B World War II submarine movie.

Within ten minutes, Street had a 15 x 11 enlargement. Then, red light turned to white.

"Mickey, what do you see?"

"I see a refrigerator full of stuff. Nothing special."

"Well, buddy, here's what I see. Over there on the first shelf that looks like it could be *prosciutto*. Remember our friend, Dr. Gaetano Piccard? And below it is a container of orange juice. Give me the glasses, I want to see the label on the juice. It says *West Farms*. Damn, they're all over the place. But look at that! See the expiration date around the mouth. It reads 10/12/94. Bingo. You know what that means?"

"Street, if Simsy's body was found on September 11th, all it means is she had fresh orange juice. Big deal."

"Sometimes McCoy, you amaze me. Maybe you're in the mud pool."

"What the hell are you rambling on about? Mud pools? Did they give you some drugs down there in Washington?"

"Mickey, listen carefully. Call that *West Farms* and ask them how far they predate their orange juice. You know, what's the maximum usage date. I'll bet that orange juice was purchased on the way over to her apartment. According to Dirk, he and Simsy never spent the money for fresh squeezed juice. Maybe our friend Dr. Piccard has a taste for it."

"Street, even if he does, so what?"

Street explained one theory about Simsy's death. He was unsure. Maybe her death was an accident. Street's instincts kept pulling further away from any accident scenario. The medical examiner had not looked for puncture wounds or tested for drugs that could have knocked her out.

Street imagined Simsy at home alone that Saturday morning with Dirk on his way to New Hampshire. The doorbell rings just like Dr. Nancy Debbs reported, and it's Gaetano Piccard, a friend from the hospital with some *prosciutto*. She buzzes him up. He's got a pint of delicious fresh squeezed OJ with him. Who doesn't like that on a Saturday morning? The *prosciutto* is the key that unlocks her door. Then he pours some orange juice and adds a little *kicker* from the hospital pharmacy. Enough to get her sedated, but not knocked out completely. Maybe, this Piccard has some real sexual hang-ups and Sims is his dream come true. Maybe he's been watching her for a long time. Maybe he's exploding with rage. He's got her immobilized on the bed. Next thing he's pulled her clothes off and joins her on the bed. He rapes her; only, she doesn't know it because she's drugged. Her eyes are open but her mind is closed. Piccard concocted some *sleep now, forget later* cocktail. Everything's going great, except, while he's lying in bed feeling really good, she starts wheezing and can't breath. It's a one in a million thing. She's allergic to something in his seminal fluids. He's not going to call the 911 and have his voice recorded for posterity. So, he moves the telephone next to her right hand. Thanks to Piccard and his drugs, she can't call. He doesn't know she's left handed. Piccard puts the fresh squeezed OJ in the refrigerator. He doesn't know Sims was on the phone with Dr. Debbs when he buzzed upstairs. He figures no one knew he was in her apartment. He gets up and leaves. A real stand up kind of person--maybe, the next Mother Teresa.

Piccard never mentioned his visit to the apartment. Street was sure his fingerprints littered the apartment. Piccard might not enjoy his little walk with Street.

Street was ready to meet Piccard, but first he had to do something a lot more difficult.

"Mickey, I'm going to use this room and I don't want any interruptions. Leave me alone."

Talking was not easy for Street. Going back to his days in Queens after his dad was shot he closed up to friends. As his marriage shredded he could never find the words to reach out to Susan and express his feelings. He simply shut down. And when his partner died in his arms, again he failed to find words. Poetry was his escape into the verbal world. Poetry would not work now.

"Hello, Mrs. Sims, this is Detective Jimmy Street and I'm calling you from Boston."

Street wanted to keep going without interruption. He needed to say his words. For him, this was a chance unload his feelings.

"Mrs. Sims, I never met your daughter, but everyone who knew her thinks she was really terrific. I did get to know her boyfriend, Dirk, and he was destroyed by your daughter's death. They must have really been close. This is not easy for me, but we need your help. Ernie Green told me he talked with you."

"Detective, all we want is to let our daughter rest in peace and try and get on with our lives. We appreciate what you're doing, but I just couldn't do what you ask."

"Mrs. Sims, did you know I saw Dirk's body just after he was hit by a car? He was on his way over to see a patient your daughter was helping. He didn't believe your daughter died accidentally. Maybe, he was right. Yesterday, I was in a car in Cambridge with another doctor from the 7th Floor and shots were fired at us. I was nicked in the arm. Ernie Green is under police protection. Mrs. Sims, a lot of people are doing their best to get at the truth. Do you really think your daughter can rest in peace without the truth? Can you rest in peace knowing there may be a killer out there who got away with murder? Then, there's the question about your daughter's patient. She may have stumbled upon some great medical cure. And that's all lost right now. Mrs. Sims, if Judith were here, listening to us, we know what she'd want. This can be done quickly and in a dignified way. Please think it over."

There was no response. Street heard the phone click and Mrs. Sims was gone.

With McCoy driving and Street devouring his notes, they arrived at the hospital at 2:30 PM.

"Street, I forgot to tell you. They'll have a new car for you tonight. I'll work on that *West Farm* pre-dating question. So what do you think about this Piccard?"

"Good question. In 15 minutes, I'll know more. See you back at headquarters later."

Street didn't know, but 2:30 PM was a very special time for Atwood Dory. He flew down to New York that morning and was beginning the meeting of his life with the Gene World board and a legion of lawyers, accountants and PR types. Gene World's offices were located in mid Manhattan, within walking distance of Grand Central Station. Gene World started as a small entrepreneurial biotech firm outside Chicago and was now world class in size, profits, and power. Dory sat in front of a seven member board of directors. Only Dr. J. J. Muler, GW's founder, had a medical background. Other members on the board included Suzanne and Robert Summers, a husband and wife investment team. In the late 1980's, their venture capital firm had purchased the largest block of stock in GW. Also on the board were two attorneys, Jason Podesky and Walter Olio; both were senior partners in the New York firm of Olio, Podesky and Marberg. Professor Janice Rubin, a hospital administrator, and Darrell Sanders were the other members.

Dory kept his eyes focused on the founders, J.J. Muler and the Summers. That is where the voting power was. Everyone had a yellow lined pad of paper. Coffee, tea, soft drinks and cookies were spread across the center of the table. The drapes were drawn and the mood was a lot cooler than the November breezes outside.

Muler stood at the head of the table.

"Atwood, this memo you sent on the meeting with Dr. Shiri at the Charles puts a lot of our assumptions at risk."

One of the lawyers interrupted, "Sir, you must understand that even though Atwood only had a discussion with her, it is incumbent upon GW to report the possible adverse implications of that meeting to the stockholders. We should do it with a filing to the Securities and Exchange Commission."

Muler joined again, "Well, that's what I was worried about. Hell, even if we straighten it out, this news is going to hammer our stock."

Robert Summers, known for his curtness, looked at Dory from behind glasses so thick they had the density of plate glass windows.

"Atwood, did you listen or did you tell the bitch she's full of shit. She can't toss us out like some used condom. Who the fuck does she think she is. That little twit isn't going to destroy our investment. Now, I suggest you get in front of her face and tell her what's coming down. We'll sue their asses. We'll get our PR people to get everyone in Boston nervous about that viral storage facility in the basement. We'll go to her board of directors and get that little witch tossed out. Now if you haven't got the balls to do that, Suzanne and I will come up to Boston and do it for you. Get the picture?"

Dory stood and read from his notes.

"I'm going to speak with her again. Before then, I'll have a legal opinion to show her. A piece of paper from our firm that outlines what will happen if she doesn't pull back. Personally, I think she was grand standing and no more. I'll let you know within a couple of days."

The lawyers reminded Dory that time was a sensitive issue and the board needed a clarification within days.

"Street, how are you. I'm Dr. Gaetano Piccard. I really appreciate talking outside the 7th Floor."

Street liked him instantly. That's bad news for the kind of interrogation that was coming. They found a cement bench not far from the hospital entrance.

"Dr. Piccard, let's sit down here and talk for a few minutes. Is there anything you want to say before we get started?"

Street wanted Piccard to volunteer everything that happened the Saturday morning that Sims died. Street was not going to help.

"OK Dr. Piccard, I've got a few questions. Take all the time you want."

This was a critical moment for Street. The first question would come fast and Piccard's reaction would tell as much as his answer.

"Dr. Piccard, do you remember where you were on the morning of September 11th? That was a Saturday and it was the day Sims died?"

"Yes sir, I do. I went to her apartment and brought her some *prosciutto*. We had a cup of coffee and I left. She was fine."

Street's face was getting red. "Then, why the hell didn't you tell someone you saw her Saturday?"

"I did. I told Dirk. I assumed he told the police. It was no big deal. I'd come over a lot and leave off some *prosciutto*. Dirk and Simsy were my friends. So is Ernie."

"Not a lie!" Street knew he was telling the truth.

The trouble with being a detective so long is the portable polygraph you carry in your head. Street's was fine tuned and almost never failed him.

"You know, I can't verify what you said with Dirk."

"Sir, I know that; but I told you the truth."

"What time did you leave her apartment?"

"It was before 10 AM."

"And why are you so sure?"

"Simsy told me someone else was coming by for a few minutes."

"Who?"

"She never said."

"Dr. Piccard, we'll stay in touch. Write your name and address on this piece of paper. I've got a pen. It's one of our big fat police pens."

Piccard wrote the information and handed the pen to Street. He had another set of fingerprints to double check. He also had a dead end. Piccard turned his back and walked inside the hospital. Street sat on the bench, preparing himself for the meeting with Dr. Shiri.

"Detective Street! Dr. Shiri is expecting me."

"Oh yes, she'll be ready in a moment. Your office called a few minutes ago. Do you want to call them back now?"

"Yes, can I use that phone over there?"

"Sure, just dial 9 first and that'll give you an outside line."

"Mickey, what's up?"

"Street, Mrs. Sims called from Toledo. She said you just talked with her. She'd like you to call her back as soon as possible. And Ernie Green seems real anxious to reach you. Street, remember the social security checks we did at the hospital. Well, Ernie said the three nurses who went down to Martinique and stayed at the JASPER were all fired by Dr. Shiri. He also remembered something about Dirk and some of his friends in Washington who could fix any computer. Ernie wanted you to know that Dirk went to Washington a lot. He thought that information might help."

Street turned to Dr. Shiri's secretary and asked for an outside line to make a long distance call: Was it yes or no?"

"Mrs. Sims, I didn't expect to hear back from you so soon."

"Detective, I thought of something our daughter used to say. She said her research gained so much from patients after their deaths. She said that in death they were able to make contributions. Detective Street, that's what this is all about. It's about our daughter helping others to find the truth. You have our permission."

"Mrs. Sims, thank you. I know this wasn't easy. I'll call you later and work out the details. I promise we'll do everything to make this as quick and dignified as possible."

Street was shown into Dr. Shiri's office in the Charles Hospital. At first sight, he suffered an ungovernable urge to bow in respect. She was about a foot shorter than Street as she extended her hand outward and upward. As he reached to join hands, he felt skin as silky smooth as the emerald green, shoulder to floor dress, she wore. Japanese timber decorated the office in perfect harmony with the spacious floor to ceiling windows. It was as if he had taken passage across the Pacific for the interview.

"Detective Street, please sit down and be comfortable. We'll have some tea while we talk."

"Thank you, Dr. Shiri."

Shiri did not wait for Street to begin.

"You know, Detective, perhaps we could become more comfortable if I told you something about myself. I feel like I know so much about you. My family comes from Nagasaki. That's a seaport on Western Kyushu in southwest Japan. You know the name only because of the atomic bomb. Were it not for that event I surmise my life's course would have been much different. I was ten years old and our family lived outside the city. I still remember the terrible sights. I dedicated my life to medical research as a result."

Street was awed by the natural and undeniable elegance of the woman whose physical frame seemed so delicate. There was no doubt that she was a strong woman. Shiri's words soon evolved from talk to philosophy and Street was mesmerized by the eloquence of her words.

"Street, as I told you, medicine is my life. When we save just one soul we are really saving the world. Our world is made up of individual souls. If we accept the premise that saving one soul is saving the world, our days will be filled with much happiness. Coming from Nagasaki, we know much about life and death. My city is so beautiful with mountains that come down to the sea. You should see our botanical gardens.

"I'll tell you an interesting story about my city. Nagasaki has always been a stronghold of Christianity in Japan. It's ironic that when the US dropped the atomic bomb on my city, it fell almost directly on top of Urakami Catholic Church. That was built in the early 1900" and was the largest Catholic Church in the Far East."

"Dr. Shiri, I never knew that. Your outlook on life seems tranquil. If I had that attitude, a lot of my bad days would be OK."

Street laughed inside. "Shit, she'd make a great marriage counselor."

"You know, Street, life and death are in an eternal embrace and we are always feeble, living on the brink of death. Each of our days is like a flower that blooms in the warmth of summer and then dies from the ice of winter. That is our destiny and it cannot be denied. You and I are in combat each day with evil and death. All we can do is our best. We must ask, 'What is left after the dying is over?' and the answer will always be, life. That is our place. And coming from Nagasaki, well, that gives me a very different perspective on life. You should visit my city someday."

In two decades as a cop and detective, never had anyone issued words so powerful they tied Street motionless to his chair. He was now aware of the fact that the woman in the room was in a league of her own. Street felt stripped naked. All he could do was make a discreet effort to ask questions.

"Dr. Shiri, you've left me speechless. And that's a near fatal flaw in my line of work. I must ask you some questions although I'd much prefer to listen to your words. You speak with great wisdom."

"Street, perhaps some other time. I know you have a job to do and perhaps this time together may help."

"Let me start by giving you some information. I talked with the mother of Dr. Judith Sims today and she's agreed to permit the exhumation of Judith's body. My partner, Mike McCoy and one of our medical examiners, will fly to Toledo within the next few days. An FBI pathologist will join them and the Toledo police. The original investigation of her death was deficient in light of subsequent events such as the death of Dr. Eldridge. I was there moments after it happened, and it probably was murder."

Street saw the discomfort riding across Shiri's face as she listened and never took her eyes off his.

"Even before yesterday's shooting, we were developing a *prima facie* case that the deaths of your two doctors were connected. Our ME didn't do a good job in September. They're under-staffed, and, well, there are no excuses. He never looked for puncture marks. We think he might find one and maybe the residue of some substance used to anesthetize her. Once she was physically insensible, a killer could have inserted a vial of human semen in her vagina. Her killer would know how to trigger anaphylactic shock. Someone knew her medical records inside and out. Those records were kept here in the hospital. I've read the notes taken by the detective who was called when Dr. Eldridge found her body."

Shiri took notes as Street spoke.

"These tidbits may sound silly, but, combined, they add murder to the equation. First, we have proof that whoever entered her apartment came with fresh squeezed orange juice. Neither Dr. Sims nor Dr. Eldridge ever paid the extra money for fresh squeezed OJ. We have a photograph of the refrigerator and we also know the brand name. We're checking convenience stores in her neighborhood that sell fresh squeezed OJ. Maybe someone remembers a face. That may have been the way the killer got Sims to ingest a drug. Since there was no struggle or forced entry to the apartment, I think Sims knew her killer. Dr. Eldridge told the detective that Sims never ate peanuts at baseball games. We know she loved baseball games and drank beer, ate popcorn and ice cream. Why no peanuts? Everyone eats peanuts at baseball games."

"Dr. Shiri, have you ever gone to a baseball game?"

"Sure, I love baseball."

"Well, do you eat peanuts?"

"Yes: peanuts, popcorn, even those hot dogs. Eat a bunch of those and we hold a bed for you on the 7th Floor."

"You get my point. Why didn't Sims eat peanuts?"

"We've had trouble getting all her medical records, but I'll bet the exhumation will show Sims was allergic to peanuts. She never told Dr. Eldridge about her allergy. Her killer was very clever. He used seminal fluids that didn't match Dr. Eldridge's blood type. If it were the same, we would have been suspicious since she had no history of allergic reactions after sex with him. That would have created a contradiction of facts. Finally, a telephone was next to her right hand. What a stupid mistake. Whoever killed Sims researched her medical records and took extraordinary care to kill her and make it appear accidental. But he didn't know she was left handed. So, he placed the telephone next to her right hand. The smart ones always make the dumbest mistakes."

"Detective, that's an incredible story. Do you want to believe or do you believe it?"

"Dr. Shiri, my experience tells me the convergence of facts exceeds the probability of coincidence. That's a fancy way of saying, I believe. I believe all the way through. But since I can't prove it was murder, it could be accidental."

Street reached for a way to explain. "Are you a sailor by any chance? Does *celestiality* mean anything to you?"

"Detective, I'm no sailor, but I can tell you about something called cetyl alcohol. It's a chemical used in cosmetics and pharmaceuticals. The atomic number is $C16H33OH$. So what does your *celestiality* have to do with anything? Is that like a palm reader?"

"Funny, Dr. Shiri. *Celestiality* has nothing to do with palm reading. I flunked chemistry; but, thanks for that atomic number. *Celestiality* is a nautical phrase for navigation by the stars. The only problem is you need a clear sky to get it right. Things haven't been clear in this case most of the time. We take the few moments of clearing in the clouds and navigate. It's gotten us this far. I know we're in the right place. So, the answer to your question is that I think your two doctors were murdered."

Street leaned forward, "May I ask you a few more brief questions?"

"Proceed, Detective Street."

"Are you aware there is an agent in this hospital for the OSI, that's the Office of Special Investigations for the Air Force?"

"Well, with all the military presence here and the sensitive nature of our work. that fact would not surprise me. Especially with the bunker the Air Force built below the hospital to store viruses and bacterium in a secure location. I have not been specifically advised there is such an agent on hand, but, I could guess who it was."

"You think it's Captain Kate Beecher, right?"

"Absolutely not!"

Street's face hit a violent squall. It was a bit scared, a little sick, and empty. Dr. Shiri's remarks hit like a rolling night time storm that came fast and without warning. "How could she say it was not Beecher?" If Street's chair had a seat belt, he would have buckled in and ducked.

"Then, who do you think it is?"

"Detective, I'm pretty sure the OSI agent was Dirk Eldridge."

"No, my God, that's not possible."

"Street, have you seen a ghost? Eldridge came from a family with an Air Force background. His father flew during World War II and he had connections everywhere in the Air Force. After medical school, he worked on some special project for the Air Force. They gave him sterling recommendations. In fact, we have a letter on file from the Secretary of Defense. Eldridge flew a plane and gave rides to some of the doctors. Several times, Dr. Marks asked me about Eldridge's trips to Washington. Marks was the one who first suspected that he might be an agent."

"What about the three nurses that were fired."

"That's easy. Atwood Dory gave three nurses spending money for a trip to Martinique. We found out about the trip. Taking money for personal use from a drug company is strictly against the rules. I fired all three. You're welcome to see the file whenever you wish."

"Here's another question. I was in Washington for a meeting with the OSI in room 1030 at the Mayflower Hotel. That room was paid for by CRM, Inc. You know that's Charles River Medical. The same was true for my hotel room at the Willard. Can you explain?"

"Again, detective, an easy question to answer. The Air Force gives us a small security budget and asks that we spend it as they designate. It's simply for administrative things. A few days ago, our travel office received a request to rent two rooms in Washington. It required Marks' approval. He notified me. In fact, that's how Marks first became suspicious of Eldridge. It seems each time the Air Force requested a Washington hotel room out of our special budget, Eldridge was in Washington."

"Dr. Shiri, you've been a big help. In fact, you're the first person to shine lights instead of turning them off. I'm grateful."

"In that case, you'll be even more grateful in a moment. Street, you better see what we have in the basement."

With those words, Dr. Shiri buzzed her secretary.

"Detective Street and I are going down to the bunker. Please call security and advise them. Street doesn't have a retinal scan or fingerprints on file, so he'll have to get in on my signature. Call the chief of security and let him know. If there are any problems, call me on my portable phone."

Street stood up and walked towards the door. "Dr. Shiri, would you mind if I call my office first?"

"Fine. You know where the phones are outside. Please close my door and I'll meet you at the elevator." Street dialed headquarters.

"Mickey, it's Street. Find that son-of-a-bitch Adler in Washington at the OSI and tell him to call me before seven PM or he's going to read about himself in tomorrow's papers. Tell him that's the same for his boss, General Korbee. Are you sitting down Mickey? It looks like the other OSI agent was Dirk."

The mahogany doors to Dr. Shiri's office were tightly closed as Street waited at the elevator. Dr. Shiri sat and looked outside at the panoramic views of gardens beneath her.

"So, Timothy, was the reception clear in your office? Did you hear everything the detective had to say. What do you think?"

Shiri emerged from her office and guided Street to the elevator.

"Say, detective, are you going to be able to see ok?"

Street looked puzzled.

"It's your eyes. I can tell you've got heterochromia iridis. I saw a fatal condition of atomic poisoning in Japan where one of the symptoms was different colored eyes like you have. Back home it was a signature of death."

"How'd you know?"

"Street, I see into eyes. I looked into yours. It was not difficult. You'll live; so, relax. Or, try to relax until we get to the bunker."

Chapter Twenty One:
The Bunker

The *Book of Genesis* reveals that the sun, moon and stars are for mankind. Creation is for humanity. Despite such a generous endowment, ingenuity and genius accumulated since classical Athens cannot block the invasion of parasitic forms of life. Infectious disease survived before humanity first gazed towards the stars and it will last until the end of our stay on earth. Indeed, it could be the end of our stay on this planet.

Instead of pressing L, Dr. Shiri inserted a key and tapped B. Street and Shiri descended to the basement. They walked a long and narrow path that took them the entire sideways length of the Charles Hospital. The walkway had a yellow florescent line painted in the middle. It looked much like the lines that divide highways. Yellow arrows on the right side were positioned atop a single word, CONTAINMENT, painted in red. On the left side, yellow arrows were near the word EXIT painted in green. The corridor narrowed as they reached the outer wall of the hospital's main structure. Another elevator waited. Inside was a TV monitor and key control. This elevator only went down.

"Street, we're going down another 30 feet. There's a stairwell next to the elevator but this is cleaner. We have about 20 yards to walk after we get down."

When the elevator door opened, Street thought he was in some sort of a military bunker. An armed guard stationed at the elevator was dressed in Air Force blues. Dr. Shiri walked over to the rentinal scan unit and Street watched as she pressed her eye against a glass cover. Then, a sweeping light illuminated her face.

She placed her hand flat on a glass table and again a light swept across. With that second sweep a red light mounted atop a large windowless metal door turned green. Dr. Shiri inserted a key and prepared to enter with Street.

A three foot by three foot white cardboard sign was mounted on the wall. It was called the ENFORCER. One inch circular tags hung on nails inserted through the cardboard. Each tag was red on one side and green on the other. There were about 50 names and tags. This was the status board.

RED TAG-IN CONTAINMENT
GREEN TAG-OUT OF CONTAINMENT

With one quick glance it was easy to see who was in and who was out of the containment section. All the tags were flipped to green. Shiri lifted the tag above her name and turned it over to red. She then took Dr. Marks' tag and did the same. In an emergency it would be clear that two persons were inside.

There were two rooms inside, both with squeaky clean, white linoleum floors. Shiri and Street entered the *outer* room. Street guessed it was about the size of a swimming pool in length and width and eerily had a chlorine smell. This so called *outer room* looked more like an office with desks, chairs, computers and even a candy machine. But that's where the similarity ended. One of its walls was made entirely of glass. Looking through, Street saw the laboratory. It looked empty, motionless and very quiet. Inside, he saw fire extinguishers. He also saw what looked like eyewash fountains and all sorts of buttons. It was filled with lab equipment most of which Street did not recognize. There were two digital clocks and several TV monitors. Opposite the glass wall was a row of metal lockers. A large sign confronted everyone who entered the outer room.

WARNING!
-No Food or Beverages Allowed Inside
-Never Any Horseplay
-Never Work Alone
-Never Work More Than 1 Hour

-All Conversations Taped and Monitored
-Use Biohazard Checklist

"Street, behind that window is the laboratory. It's the bunker. We've got redundancy for every activity. There's generator power for this containment area that is separate from the hospital's generator. If that failed, we have battery power. Before going inside, we put on space suits and take a bleach decontamination shower. If you weren't wearing a spacesuit, your skin would come off in that shower. Leaving the bunker requires another shower. These space suits are totally self supporting, including a main and backup breathing apparatus. Each space suit has its own implanted cellular communications device and we have a relay antenna down here. These spacesuits provide constant read outs of heart rate, blood pressure and body temperature. If anything went wrong with the main oxygen, you'd only have a few minutes to get inside the shower room, get decontaminated, and exit. That shower has a fail-safe mechanism like in our missile silos. In fact, the actual keyboard and electrical circuits for the shower's *in-out* mechanism were brought in by the Air Force from a missile silo. Two buttons must be pushed simultaneously to permit exit from the shower. That's why no one is allowed to enter the laboratory alone. If someone got sick and couldn't hit the EXIT button, they'd be stuck in there.

"To protect us outside no one can leave without someone in this room hitting the button. That protects us against saboteurs. The laboratory is bullet and bombproof.

"Look inside, Street, and you'll see white duct work with a bunch of pressure gauges. The bunker's pressure inside is lower than the rest of the building. If there was a leak, air would flow into the room and never out. We've got a series of filters to trap viruses.

"See those phones on the wall? The green one connects to this room's speaker system. The red one goes to the hospital's main security area. Everything that goes on inside is recorded with video cameras. We even have what we call a *lockdown* button out here. With a *lockdown* there's no access to the viruses, bacterium and protozoa stored inside. That's another fail-safe.

"Inside, we have some virulent characters locked in vials and we like to keep our eye on them--even when they're alone! Street, think of it as death row. As long as these infectious agents are isolated and kept from living cells, they're harmless. It's the same as keeping serial killers under lock and key. But, let them come into contact with humans, and we'd join them on death row--death row without boundaries. None of them are on your WANTED posters in post offices, except they could easily kill everyone inside a big city ZIP CODE.

"Even if everything went wrong in the bunker, we can activate an *autoclave* system. *Autoclave* is an apparatus that sterilizes using steam under pressure. We could sterilize that whole lab in an emergency."

Street heard enough to send shivers up and down his spine and right to the ends of his fingertips. Not much made him feel queasy. This bunker did. They left the outer room of the containment building and Shiri flipped two tags on the ENFORC-ER from red to green. Then they walked to the elevator.

Street turned to Dr. Shiri and asked, "How long has this been here? I've never read about it in the papers."

"The Air Force and some other folks at the Department of Defense built it a few years ago. They brought in their own construction teams. The work was done during our hospital renovation. No more than 50 people have ever been inside the bunker. This obviously isn't part of our public relations program here at the Charles Hospital. That bunker is a remarkable piece of construction and technology. It's built like nuclear missile silos. The entire complex is like an egg, only this egg has a six foot thick cement shell. It's absolutely safe from sabotage, fire, and earthquakes. It'll be here a long time after the main building crumbles to the ground. But the public would never understand all the safety precautions. So, we don't even try to explain.

"Listen, if there was ever a nuclear attack, I'd head down to the containment building. It has food, medicine, a washer and dryer and microwave ovens. All the comforts of home. Except, it doesn't look much like an Ethan Allen showroom."

The elevator lifted them up to the long narrow passageway. Street remembered all the arrows. They followed the green arrows towards the exit. Then they entered the second elevator and moved up to the lobby. Street was glad to see the sunlight and familiar surroundings of the hospital lobby. If only these people knew what he had just seen. Even the hospital's orange color looked reassuring after the underground visit. He didn't expect a return visit and if he never saw it again in his life that'd be fine.

"Street, I know what you saw may be a little unsettling. But never forget, as I never will, that my roots come from Nagasaki. Life is very precious to us. That bunker holds the key to saving many lives in the future."

"Dr. Shiri, you've been very gracious and I appreciate the time we spent together. Here's my card, if you want to talk with me. I'd like your home address and telephone number. Use my Boston police pen."

"Street, the pen's so thick."

She wrote the information and handed the pen and card to Street. Once again, Street had another set of fingerprints.

"Street, perhaps we'll see each other again soon."

"That would be fine; but let's keep it upstairs on the 7th Floor, not down in your bunker."

It was almost six PM and Street was thinking of his gym. On the drive there, he could talk with Mickey about Dirk. He still could not believe what Dr. Shiri had told him about Dirk. Or was it Agent Eldridge?

Street felt alone with only his instincts as companions. There are no books on instinct and the way that develops inside. The wrong instincts have killed cops. Street wondered if his dad was working on instinct in the split seconds between life and death in that store in Queens. Every time Street was alone he went exploring. He relied on his instincts. He did so without joy. So many of Street's mind trips were in the middle of the night when he was alone.

Should he have taken a chance and tried to jump the druggies who had Street and his partner on their knees in a cold back alley? Would that have made a difference? Street never got to say good-bye to his partner that night. Were his instincts wrong?

Detective Jimmy Street felt lost inside. He was solid inside and outside. He was strong when it was required. Yet inside, he always sensed an emptiness. And he knew why. Street went through life without getting his chance to say good-bye.

He would have liked the chance to say good-bye to Dirk.

Chapter Twenty Two:
Psywar

Y ou know what our problem is Mickey? We're dancing to other people's psycho-babble. It's like going to a gas station and saying 'fill her up'. We're up in the front seat watching that fuel gauge move up to FULL while the guy in back is pumping us full of water. The gauge looks the same. But we don't go anywhere."

Vintage Street!

"Do you think Dr. Shiri was just yakking when she said Eldridge might be an agent?"

Street pulled out a folder with Detective Santori's original notes. It included Eldridge's home address and telephone in New Hampshire.

"Mr. Eldridge, I'm Detective Street with the Boston Police. I'm very sorry about what happened to Dirk. I only knew your son for a little while, but he was a very nice young man. And, he had a lot of moxie. He had a lot of friends around the hospital."

Street waited for some response but there was none.

"Anyway, Mr. Eldridge, I know your son liked to fly planes. And I also know he spent about a year or so in Washington after graduation from medical school.

"Do you know what he was doing down there?"

"Detective, is all this necessary now? What's the purpose?"

"Look sir, I saw what happened to your son. I'm good at what I do. And frankly, that sure didn't look like an accident. Could you please just answer my question."

"Detective, right after our son died, we got a phone call from a Tom Adler in Washington. He's with the Air Force. I know Dirk spent a year working on a special project with them after he

graduated. I think they recruited him while he was still in school.
Dirk almost went in the Air Force for a career as a flight
surgeon. He really loved his time down there. So this fellow calls
from Washington and tells us how sorry he was about Dirk. Then
he said that Dirk had been working for the Air Force all the way
through medical school. This guy Adler said there wasn't a lot
more he could tell us, except that we should be very proud of
him. He asked us to keep his words secret and that someday in
the future we'd get a letter from the Air Force that explained
everything. That was it."

"Sir, that's all I needed. I'm really sorry about what happened.
You've been more helpful than you can imagine."

"Mickey, take me to the gym in a few minutes. Have you got
the file on Adler in Washington?"

While McCoy was looking, Street called Kate Beecher's home.
That phone he knew from memory.

"Hi, this is Kate. I can't answer your call now so please leave
a brief message at the sound of the beep. Thanks."

"Kate, this is Street. I need to talk with you. It's about 6 PM.
In Washington you asked if I knew who the other OSI agent was.
I may have that answer. Be careful. See you soon."

"Street, here's Adler's beeper number. Shall I call it?"

Mickey didn't need to wait for Street's answer.

Fifteen minutes slid by and then the phone rang at headquarters.

"Street, this is Tom Adler in Washington. What's so important
you had to beep me. We told you to work with Kate."

Street was flushed with anger.

"Listen, you lying sack of shit. Try something, Adler. Over the
phone see if you can read my lips. I'll give you some words. The
first is the *Boston Daily Gazette*. The next is OSI. And the last
word is a name, Dr. Dirk Eldridge. Let's see if you or that
General can find me before I arrive at the *Gazette* with my story.
Adler, do you have a middle name?" SLAM.

Street rammed the phone down and stood.

"Mickey, take me over to the gym before I hit someone."

The gym is about five miles from police headquarters and takes
no more than ten minutes. Street wanted to stay in the police car

a little longer. "Mickey, let's kill a few minutes. Drive by Commonwealth and Fairfield. That's where Dirk was hit. There's nothing to see there. I just want to drive around for a few extra minutes."

"Mobile 37, this Zebra Team communications. Please stand by for a call on your cellular."

Street knew who'd be calling.

"Detective Street, this is General Korbee in Washington. Adler called me at home. I'm sorry we couldn't tell you about Dirk while you were in Washington. Even Kate didn't know. How did you find about Dirk?"

"General, you just told me, that's how. Someone put a little birdie in my ear and you just made it sing. You've got a really screwed up setup at the Charles. I wouldn't want to have the life insurance policy on Beecher."

"She knows there's risk. She's more capable than you may think."

"General, I'll be talking with you. And that means not with Adler. Stay in touch. For your sake, there better be no more surprises."

"Mickey, we've got some momentum. I'll skip the gym. Let's go back to headquarters and hit the blackboard. This circus act is over. All we've done is dance through hoops."

For Jimmy Street, his paper chase was over. Street would always be a hunter first. The hunter can track his prey for days through marsh lands and swamps and high grass. Great hunters have instinct and they know when it's time to stop tracking and start tempting. Street and Mickey went downstairs to the Zebra Command post.

"Hey folks, sorry to wake you up. We need a room with a blackboard and lots of those pretty colored chalks you always use. And we need every piece of paper. After that, you can go back to sleep."

One of the Zebra officers turned to Street, "You really missed your career. I could see you in the UN. You're so diplomatic. In one day you'd empty the place out and they could turn the UN into a theater. Go over there Street and we'll send everything inside. Any other requests your highness?"

"How about bringing in dinner? We're going to be here a while."

"Street, you can eat our leftovers, half price."

Street and Mickey sat next to each other and looked at the big empty blackboard.

"Mickey, we're going to fill that up, just like when we pull in for gas. Only this time it's not going to be water. We're going to use some psychology and make the action come to us. This part's going to be fun."

Street went to the blackboard and in red chalk starting writing names and headings in columns and rows:

Name	Role	Questions
Dr. Marks	Chief, 7th Floor	Relationship with Dr. Shiri Does he know about Beecher, OSI, Did he know about Dirk, OSI What does he want
Atwood Dory	Gene World	Interview 3 nurses he sent to Martinique Motive. Money. Dory-Marks? Does he know Beecher, OSI
Beecher	Air Force	How much does she know Did she know about Dirk, OSI
Dr. Sims	7th Floor	Did she find a cure? Who killed her and why?
Dr. Eldridge	7th Floor	Who killed him and why?
Dr. Ferris or	7th Floor	Were they shooting at her Street
Dr. Green	7th Floor	Wild card! Bait?
Dr. Debbs	7th Floor	Is there more there?
Dr. Feingold	7th Floor	The quiet one?
Questra Q	Marks' secretary	What's her secret?
Dr. Shiri	President, Charles	Too good to be true.
3 Nurses	Fired	Are they talkative?
Steven Hays	Teacher	We haven't talked yet

| OSI | Air Force | More half truths |
| The *Bunker* | Charles | Expensive little toy |

"Street, that's a nice list. So what? And what if the whole thing adds up to zero? What if Sims' and Eldridge's deaths were accidents? And suppose your shooting was just a random act of violence."

"See, Mickey, look at all those names as moveable objects. We're going to start moving them around. Take a Polaroid so we can carry it with us in the car. We're going to make phone calls. We're going to plant seeds. We're going to light a match and see what burns. Let me think for a few moments. And then we'll start. Maybe I'll get that workout after all."

This was a moment for teacher and student. The student, Mickey McCoy, was grounded in logic and detail. The teacher, Street, was guided by instinct. McCoy was making arrangements for the exhumation of Sims' body the following week. Before then, Street was going to shake things up a bit. Looking at the list on the blackboard, the two detectives pondered their options.

"Mickey, I think the killer's name is up there but I just can't figure out the angle or motive."

"Detective, there's a call for you on line two."

"Street here."

"Street, it's Kate. How are you? Would you like to get together?"

"Not tonight. Can I come by your office tomorrow. I'm probably going to be on the 7th Floor doing some follow-up work."

"Sure you can come by. I was hoping we might find a place a little more intimate than my office. I miss your fingers."

"Kate, I can't talk right now. I spoke with Adler on something and I'll tell you about it tomorrow. Be careful. If you need me, call."

"Mickey, let's get in touch with Dr. Marks. I need to freshen things up with him. Call his home and see if we can come by tomorrow morning. Then call Ernie and Karen Ferris that we're doing some follow-up. If we ask the right questions, maybe we'll catch a break. Let's meet that teacher, Steven Hays. You know what, can you track down those three nurses that Dr. Shiri fired for going down to Martinique? I'll bet they've got some interesting stories to tell about Dory and Gene World.

"How about a ride to the gym and we'll call it a day. And give me a polaroid of the blackboard. I'll look at it tonight. Mickey boy, we are in a groove and things are going to start happening."

Chapter Twenty Three:
It's Happening

Nine in the morning is not an uncertain hour. The first bell for classes at Copley High School rang 90 minutes ago. Now with one class digested, teachers huddled around home room for student conferences till 9:30 AM. Each day nine in the morning brought the certainty that each student could at least get a few words with their home room teacher. It's October and Steven Hays should not be alive according to medical textbooks. According to actuarial tables, his 27 year old physician should be alive and well.

"Mr. Hays, I'm Detective Street and this is Detective McCoy. We asked our office to call and let you know we were coming. Your name is very familiar to us."

Hays looked great. He was trim and neatly dressed. His eyes were bright and his complexion seemed normal. For a man fighting a medical death sentence, he looked great.

"Yeah, I'm the one who's supposed to be part of history, not teaching it. And poor Dr. Sims: she was fantastic. That night, when she gave me the overdose of the experimental drug, do you know she would not leave me and go home. She stayed all through the night. I remember, she kept talking about the Hippocratic Oath. I knew the Latin words, PRIMUM NON NOCERE. Dr. Sims explained how she may have betrayed those words. She recommended some drug treatments to reduce the effects of the overdose of that drug, XM2. I asked her what the downside was. She wasn't sure. I asked her what she'd do if it was her. She didn't know."

Street imagined the terror of that night with Sims and Hays struggling with both the cancer and a decision that had to be made. It was a life and death decision.

"You know detectives, that doctor was in tears. She seemed desperate for me to give her guidance. She didn't try and macho her way out of it."

"Did you know a Louis Berger or Dr. Karen Ferris?"

"Louis sounds familiar. Yeah, I remember now because everyone asked him about stocks. He was a celebrity of sorts. Even that guy, Dory, would come visit him with gifts and ask about stocks and so forth. I talked to him a few times in the cafeteria. Nice guy. I heard he lucked out also and went home."

"Mr. Hays, that other patient's luck ran out. He was hit and killed by a car, the same way Dr. Eldridge was."

"What a bad break that is. He walks out of a hospital and...boom. you can never tell, can you?"

"Mr. Hays, did you know Dr. Eldridge was riding his bike to your apartment when he was hit and killed by a car."

"No. I heard he died in an accident, and that's all. Why was he coming to see me?"

"For the same reason we're here this morning."

"Well, what's that?"

"Mr. Hays, is there anything you can recall about Dr. Sims or Dr. Eldridge that might help us figure out what happened. I don't care how silly it seems. I don't care whether it's nail polish, sunny shoes, anything at all that struck you as unusual."

"They both died in accidents. That's terrible."

"Mr. Hays, we're detectives. We're also in homicide. Do you understand now?"

"I do. Give me a few moments to think. How about if I just reel things off? You can stop me whenever you wish. I've got a class at in a few minutes."

McCoy put out his hands like a football referee telling the time keeper to start the clocks.

"Let's see. I remember Dr. Marks came around with Dr. Sims. I had never talked with him before. After the overdose, he came by many times. There was some doctor up there who made Italian food; I forget his name. A few times he stopped in my room and left off some *prosciutto*. Oh, there was another doctor, a woman, who seemed very friendly with Dr. Sims. She kept looking at my charts. And, the guy from Gene World, even he stopped in a few times. That's about it. One other thing, I heard Dr. Sims complaining to her boyfriend about that woman from the Air Force. Dr. Sims said she was always looking through her charts without asking. If I think of anything else, I'll call."

"You know, Mr. Hays, two doctors are dead on that 7th Floor. And we think they're dead, in part, because you're alive. There is something you could do for us. Would you make a phone call?"

"What kind of phone call?"

"Call the 7th Floor and ask for Atwood Dory. Leave a message that a magazine may be doing a story on your miraculous recovery. You wanted to check with him. And ask if he'd inform Dr. Marks. That's it. And, don't tell him about our visit."

"If this helps clear up what happened to my doctor, sure. When do you want me to call?"

"While we stand here and watch you."

Street and McCoy hustled to their car. There it was on the windshield, a bright orange Boston parking ticket.

"Mickey, I never did anything right in school. Figures I'd get a ticket here. And it's that rotten orange color."

"Street, you know that list we put together last night. Well, I stared at it last night. We haven't talked to the most important person."

"Mickey, I don't follow you."

"Street, do you remember that little sign on each patient's telephone?"

"Not really, why do you?"

"I wrote it down."

ALL TELEPHONE CALLS ARE MONITORED
CONVERSATIONS IN ROOMS ARE RECORDED

"Street, why don't we, well sort of, talk with Dr. Sims? If anyone on that 7th Floor was going to be recorded, it would be Sims with her patient."

"Mickey, it's a good thing I thought of that first, you little rascal!"

Street leaned over and gave his partner a slam dunk high five. Street zipped through Boston traffic en route to the Charles. On the way, he lit one more fuse for Dory.

"Atwood Dory's office please."

"Mr. Dory's office, may I help you?"

"This is Detective Street; is he there please?"

"No, he's in New York today. May I take a message?"

"That's OK; he'll call me. No message."

Street dialed the Zebra Team and requested a search warrant for Dory's office. Evidence in a criminal case may be destroyed. Street knew how to get a fast search warrant.

"Mickey, get the Joker in electronics. They have his number at MIT if he's not at headquarters. When that search warrant comes through I want Dory's office swept for listening devices. The warrant should come in while we're talking with Marks. Wonder how long it'll take for Dory to get his smart ass back to Boston when he finds out we're in his office?"

It was just before 10 AM as the two detectives arrived at the Charles. By now, Dory should have received a message from Steven Hays. By noon, his secretary will tell him about cops in his office. As importantly, others on the 7th Floor will also know.

Street walked down the hall and looked into Beecher's office. Her secretary said she would return in a few minutes. Street took a piece of paper and wrote a note.

Kate, you should know...we're executing search warrant this AM for Dory's office. Should be approved by noon. Meeting with Marks. Catch you later. Street

"Dr. Marks, I think you may have met my partner before, Mike McCoy."

"Detective, most importantly, how are you feeling? I heard what happened to you and Dr. Ferris. I've talked with her several times. She's still really shook up about the shooting. I put her in touch with one of the hospital's counselors. She needs to talk it out."

"I'm doing fine. Thanks for asking. Dr. Ferris was really terrific. It's not every day a cop gets shot and has his own personal physician riding with him. She spoiled me. We've got more questions. They may take some time, but they're important."

"Go ahead, gentlemen, I'm listening."

"Dr. Marks, are you aware that I met with Dr. Shiri?"

"Seems to me she mentioned some sort of meeting with a detective. She's a very impressive woman, isn't she?"

"That's one of the few things that is clear in this muddy mess."

"Detective, do you mind if I vent myself of some feelings in all this?"

In unison, Street and McCoy nodded with their approval.

"I know you're doing your job. And heaven knows, you do it with courage and skill. But don't you think everything that's happened may be a combination of coincidence and accident. I know your *reference* is crime; but mine is medicine. And in medicine, frankly, shit happens."

Street looked at McCoy as if both little kids hearing a parent swear for the first time. Marks acted so often as if he had exited Buckingham Palace with the Queen at his side. Even when saying *shit*, Marks seemed to do so with elegance. Neither detective said a word. This was not the time to interrupt him.

"So, the point is basic. This is a very large hospital with over 500 full-time employees. The Charles has been here a long time. So it was inevitable that at some time in our history, these terrible accidents could happen. And they did."

"Dr. Marks, I appreciate how you feel. But you don't have all the facts. If you knew more, you'd understand. Tell us, how well did you know Dr. Eldridge?"

"The same as the others. He was a terrific person with a great future in medicine."

"Dr. Marks, do you know what the OSI is?"

"Isn't that part of the Air Force?"

"It's the counterintelligence branch of the Air Force."

"Are you telling me Captain Beecher's a spy?"

"We never said that at all. We're talking about Dr. Eldridge. Did you know he was an OSI agent?"

Marks recoiled with those words. His doctors were not secret agents. They didn't do anything except devote their lives to the 7th Floor. Anything else would be disloyal. Marks shook his head side to side, "No, no. no."

"Dr. Marks, the answer is Yes."

Marks was firm but vulnerable. He was comfortable in his white lab coat. He was a creature of medicine. Taken outside that environment he was a little lost puppy. Street felt badly for him. With each question he was peeling away a layer of his world.

"There's more. You should know that we're waiting for a judge to issue a search warrant to get us into Dory's office. We're going to bring some additional people in to conduct the search. We'll try and do it without disturbing your patients and doctors."

"God, what's going on here? Can't you do that at night or over the weekend. What are people in the hospital going to say?"

"Sorry, but we have to do it now. Time is a commodity in short supply. We've got one final question, Dr. Marks. We know conversations are taped in patient rooms. You have little warning signs on the telephones. We need the tapes from Dr. Sims' conversations with her patient from the night she administered the overdose."

"Not in this lifetime. We have continuous running tapes that go for 168 hours; that's one week. The old tapes are erased and replaced. So I can give you the last seven days, but not the days you want."

"How about the tapes that directly preceded her death. That would be in early September."

"Once again, detective, they're erased."

"Dr. Marks, didn't it ever cross your mind that these tapes might be useful?"

"Never. Because your own medical examiner reported Sims' death was an accident."

"And what about tapes from Dr. Ferris and Dr. Eldridge. Same thing I assume?"

"Detective, you assume correctly."

"Dr. Marks, somehow I thought you'd ask more questions. Especially about Dr. Eldridge and the OSI. Where's your curiosity?"

"Detective, I AM trying to help in the midst of crisis after crisis. You may have forgotten but I have not. We have almost 50 patients up here on the 7th Floor and our mission is to fight for their lives. On top of that I'm trying to hire two replacement doctors for Sims and Eldridge. Keep those facts in your mind. Detective, what'd you think of the Bunker?"

"Dr. Marks, that visit was done in secrecy. How'd you know?"

"Ah, well, someone mentioned seeing you heading down there. I don't remember who it was."

Street and McCoy got up and left. Just outside the door, Street whispered in McCoy's ear, "He screwed up big time and he knows it. How could he know I went down in the Bunker with Dr. Shiri. He could have said she told him, but he didn't. Let's see how the search warrant is doing. We'll use a phone in the lobby."

Assassination of the truth and corruption of the soul are not *wake up* calls for a detective like Jimmy Street. Rookie cops often recoil in horror at the easy way people lie. The lies are no more discomforting than a sneeze. Experience on the force erases those childlike fantasies of lollipops and Santa Claus. Truth is a currency that is spent with the same torment suffered when choosing a soft drink.

"Street, I talked with the office. The search warrant was signed a few minutes ago by Judge Horace. It's coming over with two members from Zebra and the Joker."

"They're sending Joker here. He's hot stuff. That kid is good."

Jack Tanner was a detective on the Zebra Team. The Joker was the police department's electronics guru. He was not a cop. Joker worked part time for the police force and was an electronics student at MIT. No one doubted his genius with electronics. The Joker owned a wide open mouth that seemed incapable of silence except when sleeping. That is, if he ever slept.

"Hi, I'm Detective Street and this is my partner, Mike McCoy."

They were standing in front of Atwood Dory's secretary. And they were trying to read her messages upside down. McCoy was practiced in the art.

"We're waiting for something. We know he's not in right now."

McCoy nudged Street's arm with a little smile. Steven Hays had called and left a message. In the next couple of minutes, Street's second surprise of the day would ignite.

"High, not so wide and handsome: why, it's my favorite Saturday night special--Detective Jimmy Street."

"Oh shit. Joker can you give it a rest, please."

"Street, I'm here for your hootenanny search. Now, what magical electronic gizmos are we looking for? These giz hunts are a blast. Street, this other cop: you know, he never said a word to me all the way over. What a glop!"

"His loss, right Joker."

Jack Tanner from the Zebra Team pulled out an executed search warrant. The warrant, issued quickly, was necktie tight in its detail. Street knew that if he made one mistake the entire search was illegal. The search warrant was limited to Dory's office and papers and documents contained within that office. Even his secretary's area was excluded. Any materials that were removed or copied must be directly related to the investigation of the deaths of Dr. Sims and Eldridge. Other materials, whether business or private, that were not on the premises of his office, were protected. The search was limited to one visit. There could be no follow-up without application for another search warrant.

"Jack, this is kind of tight, isn't it?"

"Street, it's better than nothing. Plus you get Joker to entertain."

"Jack, tell Dory's secretary to call him in New York and advise him we're going to execute this search warrant. And, where the hell is Joker?"

It was never hard to find him. His full beard and uncombed hair fit perfectly with his naturally faded jeans and worn out sneakers. His pockets were lined side to side with pens, pencils, and little probing sticks he used to reach inside electronic equipment.

Joker designed the big fat blue and white pens that Street carried everywhere. At headquarters was an electronic control panel set over a map of the metropolitan Boston area. Green lights moved across the map. Each light represented one of Joker's pens and had a number and name assigned to it. If a pen went to red, that meant transmission ceased. The red light started to flash and a beep sound started. If the cop assigned to that pen failed to call in fast, a police car was dispatched to the scene. Joker's war room of moving pens was his pride and glory.

"Dr. Feelgood, I presume? Hi, I'm the Joker. I saw your gadget here; man, what's this all about?"

"It's simple: just one of our high tech thermometers."

"What's your name?"

"Dr. Feingold."

"Excuse me, Dr. Feingold, I'm Detective Street and our fellow here seems to have wandered the wrong way. I'll take him from you."

Joker, this is a murder investigation, not a class reunion. Take all your stuff and get in Dory's office and do your magic. Time's wasting away."

Street, McCoy, Jack Tanner from Zebra and the Joker moved into Dory's office while his secretary frantically tried to reach him in New York.

"Mr. Dory, there are a bunch of police in here and they gave me some papers that say *Search Warrant*. They're in your office now. I couldn't stop them. What should I do?"

His secretary continued, "Mr. Dory, I already called the law firm. I did that first. They're sending some one here. Mr. Dory..."

Dory was on his way to the airport and back to Boston. Street planned to be finished long before he returned.

Street divided the room into four areas. The first were Dory's papers and files. The second was his computer. Tanner was a computer expert and had brought along disks to make copies. He had already secured the unlock pass word from Dory's secretary as specified in the search warrant. McCoy was searching for physical kinds of evidence such as clothes, tools, receipts, and match books. He had a checklist used in quick searches along with his ever present pocket camera.

Then there was the Joker. Despite the antics, Joker was brilliant during searches. Like Street, he too was a hunter; and, if there was anything electronically amiss, Joker could find it or feel it.

Street began looking on Dory's desk and inside. He looked at the calendar pages when Sims and Eldridge died. They were like the other pages, filled with meetings and appointments with lawyers and bankers. The shelves were lined with books, many on Hitler. Street opened a few and, as he knew, none were autographed. That line served it's purpose while interviewing Dory, but Street never believed it.   Then Street saw the same two letters, ED that he saw on Beecher's desk calendar. Kate said they were initials for her eye doctor. Dory must have the same eye problems.

Street was rummaging through Dory's filing cabinets behind his desk. He did not know what to look for. When he saw it, whatever it was, he'd know. It only took a couple of minutes. It was a folder with the name, *Ana*. Street had heard those first two syllables many times and he reached for it. Street opened the folder and saw papers on anaphylactic shock. The reports came from a midwestern hospital. Then he turned as Joker started to yell.

"I've got the groceries!"

"Damn it, Joker, can't you speak any English. This isn't a supermarket. Keep looking."

"Street, you *kvetch*. Get on board man. I've got the groceries, the goods, the doggy bag. Don't you get it?"

Street, McCoy and Tanner moved towards Joker. He had found something. "Joker reached his fingers to his lips and moved them across mimicking a zipper closing. The detectives went dead silent. Joker pointed to a piece of paper and started writing.

AUXILIARY AUDIO INPUT, IMPEDANCE 25,000 ohms
INPUT VOLTAGE 13.6 VDC NOMINAL, NEG. GROUND
REMOTE SPEAKERS (8-OHMS IMPEDANCE)

Street grabbed Joker's hand and took his pen. Then he wrote:

JOKER, SAY IT IN FUCKIN' ENGLISH, UNDERSTAND?

The Joker looked around and no one was smiling. Joker understood what Street was saying. And he wrote:

DORY'S OFFICE IS BUGGED. TELEPHONE ALSO BUGGED.

The surprises keep on coming. Street motioned for everyone to get out of the office and walk towards the elevator. They were like a walking football huddle.

"Are you sure, Joker?"

"I'm certain. You ought to give me an extra onion for finding those babies. Don't get all hot and bothered Street, I've got a handle on it. Someone's listening to everything he says and he doesn't know it. He'll be surprised!"

"Joker, how do you know he didn't place the bugs and is recording for himself?"

"Street, there's no ON-OFF switch. If he were doing it, there'd be a control button so he wouldn't record the bad stuff."

"So, who's listening?"

"I don't know. But, they're in the building. There's a mini radio transmitter in the office; so I'd bet it's being recorded inside the building."

"Mickey, Tanner: let's leave this in place. In fact, why tell Dory he's being bugged. We can use that when we talk with him. I'm sure he's on his way back from New York. We'll wrap it up inside. Mickey, you and Tanner finish up. I'm taking our portable loudspeaker here for a little tour."

Street turned to Joker and asked, "Can that thing you've got in your pocket tell if other rooms are bugged?"

"Probably can do, man. If there's a radio signal coming out, it'll go from green to red. It can even tell if one's coming in. I put this baby together myself in the lab."

"Tell you what, Joker, let's take a walk. Each time we go in and the color goes to red, give me a tug."

Street walked to Kate Beecher's office. "Is she in, now?"

"Sure, say you're the detective, right?"

"Yup, just tell her I want to see her for a second."

Street didn't wait for the answer; and, as her door swung open, he walked inside. Joker tugged hard on his arm as they entered.

"Captain Beecher, how special to see you. This is Joker; he's part time with the police. We can't stay; I just wanted to say hi."

"Street, call me please. You know what I mean."

Next stop was Dr. Marks' office. Marks was upstairs in conference with Dr. Shiri. Street worked around that one. "I want to leave this special pen for your boss. I'll just put it on his desk." He was only a few feet inside when Joker started tugging again. That's three for three: Dory, Beecher, Marks. All with little radio transmitters tucked inside their offices. The 7th Floor was turning into Radio City.

"Joker, we're going to one other place inside the hospital."

"Is Dr. Shiri available please? I'm Detective Street. Perhaps you remember me from before."

"She's meeting at this moment. Is it important?"

"Well, yes and no. Could you ask if I could see her for just a moment."

Street followed Shiri's secretary through the door and into the office. Sitting there was Dr. Marks and Dr. Karen Ferris.

Trying to contain some of his surprise at seeing Dr. Ferris there, Street managed, "Hi folks, sorry to interrupt. Dr. Shiri, I wanted to give you a pen as a small token of my appreciation for your help."

"Detective, don't look so worried. We're discussing candidates for the openings on the 7th Floor. Dr. Ferris is this year's resident on the selection committee. Is there anything else I can do?"

"When you've finished, I'd like a few more words with you."

Street approached the elevator with Joker. You forgot to give me a tug in there."

"Street, no tug because her office is not bugged. Well, it's different than the other offices. She's got both receivers and a powerful transmitter. That office is powered up like a small radio station. I'd sure like to dance around there for an hour. Street, maybe you better call the *Black Maria* for her?"

"Joker, what the fuck is a *Black Maria*? Where do you come up with these names. Don't you sleep?"

"Street, look at our time together as an education--for you. A *Black Maria*? You've never heard of one? Shame on you, detective. That was the nickname of police wagons in the 1800's. Street, time for you to hit the books."

"Not your books, Joker".

Street sent Joker back to headquarters and he went to the hospital's main cafeteria to get a sandwich. Dr. Shiri would see him at 12:30 PM.

Alone at a table, Street played with his plastic straw, trying to puncture the top of his cola with his eyes closed. Now, any diversion from the Charles Hospital, was welcome. Why would someone bug those three offices upstairs--especially Dory's office. And what about Dr. Shiri's office and it's receivers?

Street was still in awe of Dr. Shiri and could not be confrontational with her as they spoke.

"Dr. Shiri, this is an inconvenience and I apologize. We have some new information and perhaps you can help again. When you guessed that Dr. Eldridge was an OSI agent, you were right. So here's our next problem."

"First, Detective, I understand from security that you and some other officers got a search warrant and went through Dory's office."

"Yes, that's true. He hasn't been cooperative and is a suspect. That's about all I can say at this time. While we were searching his office, we found that it was bugged. You know what that means?"

"Indeed, I do."

"We have reason to believe Captain Beecher and Dr. Marks' offices are in the same condition."

"Why?"

"Dr. Shiri, I have a lot of respect for you, so much so that I bought a book on Japan after we talked."

"Well, detective, I'm impressed and honored."

Street retrieved some notes from his pocket.

"The book says Japanese simultaneously maintain two ways as they deal with the outside world. Excuse me when I mispronounce these words. The first way is called *Tatemae* and that means, kind of, *skin deep behavior*. The other way is much deeper and important. It's called *honne*. That's what Japanese really think. The book goes on to say Japanese prefer to keep harmony and rarely expose the *honne* or *inside feelings*."

"I underestimated you, detective. You have a curious side. That will certainly serve you well in the future."

"It's helping right now, Dr. Shiri."

"Obviously, something is bothering you and perhaps you're hesitant to ask questions that might be offensive. Please, I want you to ask. I want to help you understand what's happening here at the Charles. I want to know!"

"Then, Dr. Shiri, as difficult as this is for me to ask, tell me why you have electronic listening devices planted on the 7th Floor. We believe the eavesdropping system originates here in your office."

Dr. Shiri swiveled her chair around, turning her back on Street. Looking outside, not at Street, she answered.

"Detective, you are correct. This is wrong and I know it. When I joined the Charles Hospital as its President, the 7th Floor was this mystical, off limits place. Dr. Marks was very protective and shared almost nothing with me. And I AM his superior. Over the last couple of years, we have formed a close and trusting relationship. He knows about the listening devices. Sometimes I want his advice and so I ask him to listen to meetings in my office. I know that is not ethical."

"Dr. Shiri, did he listen when we met before?"

"I'm afraid so."

"Is he listening now?"

"No, he had a speech to deliver. He left immediately after the meeting you interrupted."

"Dr. Shiri, what you're doing is illegal. Neither Dory nor Beecher is aware you have listening devices in their offices. I suspect they would not be pleased."

"Detective, there's no doubt you are correct. So, what should I do?"

"I suggest you immediately disable the system. Whether you tell Dory and Beecher is your responsibility. Mine is to get answers before someone else gets killed."

"Street, I AM very ashamed."

"Dr. Shiri, your hospital needs you. And I do, too. Save the recriminations until this case is solved."

"And, when do you think that will be?"

"Sooner than the killer expects."

Chapter Twenty Four:
Good-Byes

Days of quiet drifted through autumn in Boston. There were no more discoveries. There were no calls in the middle of the night. The days coincided with the coming of Autumn and the falling leaves. Temperatures were averaging 55 degrees mid day and the days were getting much shorter. Thanksgiving was only four weeks away and Christmas shopping had begun. Thanksgiving, Christmas and the New Year were all dates in Street's calendar that evoked mixed and often sad feelings. In 25 weeks, another Boston Marathon would begin. Street's training never started and never ended. The Marathon was Street's New Year.

With shorter days, Street stepped up his runs. He ran for hours, soaking up sunshine and cold gray clouds. Running in November was Street's favorite month, except for the Marathon in April. Only in November could he speed through the fallen leaves.

Street was training for the next Boston Marathon with two unseen and always present companions. When he crossed the finish line, Sims and Dirk were coming with him.

On Monday morning, Street and Mickey headed to Logan Airport. This was Mickey's trip.

"Mickey, when you get out there, please give this note to the Sims family. And make sure everything is handled quickly and quietly. After the botched job McCann did, I feel a lot better using an FBI medical examiner. He'll meet you at the airport. His name is Sam Stevenson. The Toledo police will handle transportation and everything else. Call me as soon as you know anything."

Mike McCoy boarded his flight for Toledo with mixed feelings. He had been a detective for five years and before that a beat cop for another five. In all that time, he had never seen an exhumation. Many cops go through their entire careers and never fire a gun or see an exhumation. It's one of those reality checks that puts a face back on a police folder. For McCoy, it was a reminder that Sims was a young girl from Toledo with a family that loved and missed her.

McCoy's flight landed on schedule and several people were at the gate waiting for him. Three uniformed Toledo police greeted him. A woman stood with them.

"I'm waiting for Sam Stevenson from the FBI. He's the medical examiner. My boss said his flight should be here by now."

The police looked to their left. The woman in a blue blazer smiled.

"Detective McCoy, the man you referred to couldn't make it. I'm here instead. My name is Samantha Stevenson. Call me *Sam*."

"Sorry, really I AM. I thought you'd look different. You know..."

"You mean facial hair, pot belly stomach, no earrings or panty hose."

"Something like that."

They all had a good laugh. It would certainly be the only one of the day. The four drove 20 miles directly to Morning Gardens Cemetery. There was a small green tent and some chairs assembled. McCoy was told there would be a board of health representative present along with a minister and the family. After a brief ceremony at the grave site, the casket would be transported to Parks General Hospital where Sam Stevenson would conduct the second autopsy.

McCoy spotted Sims' parents instantly.

"Mr. and Mrs. Sims, I'm sorry we have to meet this way. My name is Detective McCoy from the Boston Police Department.

Detective Street asked that I give you this envelope. I have not read it."

The parents walked away and McCoy watched them open the envelope and read.

Dear Mr. and Mrs. Sims,

You are very brave to help. I know it is not easy. I write poetry and dedicate this poem, 'Will I Dream?' to your daughter. I hope these words bring you some comfort, along with the fact that your daughter is helping us today. In fact, your contribution might very well save another life as we try and find those responsible.

Please call me if there is anything I can do.

Thank you,

Jimmy Street

Rain started to fall as Dr. Judith Sims' casket was placed in a hearse and removed to Parks General Hospital. McCoy rode in a police car with Sam Stevenson.

"Sam, here's everything we have in Boston. You know what our ME thinks happened. He did a rush job and we think he missed big time. We want to know if there are puncture marks. We want to know if she was drugged. And we need to know specifically what she was allergic to."

"I understand another doctor in this same hospital died."

"Yeah, not only was he in the same hospital, he was her boyfriend. And our ME says the seminal fluid doesn't match the blood type of her boyfriend. How long will all this take?"

"I'll have your answers later tonight. Then you'll get a complete written report within a few days. Mickey, you will leave here knowing what happened. That's a promise."

McCoy checked into his hotel and reached Street on his cellular phone in Boston.

"Street, she's at it right now."

"What do you mean, she?"

"Street, Sam is short for Samantha. She's at the hospital now. Her parents got your letter. They read it, but didn't say anything. I think they liked it. Today wasn't the time to talk. Damn, this is tough stuff."

"Mickey, just hang in there."

While McCoy was in Toledo waiting, Street was in Atwood Dory's office. There were two lawyers present.

"You realize Dory, that we probably should do all this at headquarters. You also know that you don't have to say anything. You've been advised of your rights and I have a tape recorder in use. You are not charged with anything at this time. Do you understand?"

"Street, I wanted to see you. This is getting real crazy. I don't know where those papers on anaphylactic shock came from. The label that said *Ana* was typed. That was planted. You've got to believe me."

There's no chance Street would interview a suspect in his office unless it served his purpose. Street was aware that, as they spoke, others probably were listening. He did not think Dr. Shiri was going to turn off her listening devices. Tuning into conversations is addictive. Two persons were listening.

"Timothy, that detective knows about the recording devises. I have no idea how he found them. I also told him they would be disconnected. So this is it. After this, it's over. Dory and GW have outlived their usefulness. He is out of control. He could destroy you and the 7th Floor. He is a danger to the hospital and probably to himself."

Downstairs, Street continued to listen as Dory talked.

"Street, look, I've made some mistakes including shooting my mouth off. I don't know if Dr. Shiri told you, but she's not going to renew our contract when it expires in a couple of years. She's been through a lot with all the publicity about the two doctors. And she's got a board of directors to handle. Our strategy at GW is to make ourselves indispensable before contract renewal time. Street, we don't want trouble or bad publicity. All we want is to maximize our investment here. That includes our new drug, XM2."

"Dory, that's the one Dr. Sims used with her patient, isn't it?"

"It sure is."

"Do you think she stumbled onto something with the overdose? Do you think Hays was cured or was it a misdiagnosis?"

"I'm no doctor, and our scientists tried a mega overdose on some animals. The animals died. So we don't know what happened. Maybe someone altered the XM2 formula. We just don't know. But I'll tell you this much: I never bought into the misdiagnosis garbage. They tried to sell it twice. No way."

Now Street had his chance. The next remark was not for Dory but for those listening somewhere else in the hospital.

"Dory, we're getting close on this case. My partner Mickey is out in Toledo and we have permission to exhume the body of Dr. Sims. We have some pretty good ideas about how she was killed. In fact, we have a few people in mind as suspects."

"Street, AM I one of them?"

"Dory, I can't tell you. There'd be no fun if I did."

"You call this fun?"

"Dory, let me tell you something. This hospital stinks from the Bunker all the way to the top. I see money floating around everywhere. Three nurses got fired because they were stupid enough to take your money and go down to Martinique. But you're not the only one. I've been lied to, patronized, shot at, and used. When this is all over, someone ought to take a bulldozer and turn this whole fuckin' place into a parking lot. Does that give you an idea how I feel?"

It was nine PM as Street stood talking to Joey at the gym's sign out table. Then the call came.

"Street, it's Mickey. Here's the scoop. Dr. Sims was murdered. No doubt about it. The ME is here with me. She'll have a report in my hands before I leave in the morning. Listen to this."

Mickey's voice was rising with excitement.

"She was drugged. They found traces of valium in fat tissue. I couldn't even pronounce the name of the other drug. There are no puncture marks. The drug was ingested. That means she probably drank it. It's a bad choice of words, Street, but someone slipped a *mickey* in her drink. It gets a lot worse. The ME painted a picture for me. Now I can't erase it from my mind.

"Street, it's like you thought. The killer talks to her while the drug takes effect. Sims is paralyzed, but conscious. Then the killer moves her onto the bed and opens her legs. She's helpless to fight back. It's horrible. She knows what's happening. Shit, the killer might have even given a play by play. Semen is injected into her vagina. No needle would be necessary. The killer has mixed a sperm cocktail. It includes peanuts dissolved in the sperm. Street, I'm reading from my notes. The sperm is absorbed by the mucous membrane in her vagina and she goes into shock. Then, whoever did this, puts Dr. Sims on the floor and moves her right hand next to a telephone. They didn't know she was left handed. The ME found tiny abrasion marks inside her vagina which make her think a syringe was used. The killer knew we'd check things like sperm. So they made sure it was not Dirk's blood type. If it were, that wouldn't make sense. They lived together. She would have had an allergic reaction earlier."

Street listened silently.

"Street, Dr. Sims suffered. The ME says her eyes were open and she knew what was happening. She just couldn't move, talk, even twitch a finger. Then she died. The ME also says our killer is a doctor or someone with a lot of medical expertise. Street, I think we've already met our killer; we just don't know who it is. Whoever it is, they're ice cold. How could they stand over Sims and watch her die?"

"Mickey, don't get worked up any more. This monster is ours. Take that to the bank! Say, Mickey, tell her folks she died quickly. Lie. Do it."

"I already did."

Chapter Twenty Five:
Read All About It!

Three months after the death of Dr. Judith Sims, the Boston Police officially reclassified her cause of death to murder. Whoever broke into her apartment in September started a chain reaction. Sims' remains offered direct testimony about the horrific way in which she died. Dirk Eldridge never lived to see his hunch vindicated or his girlfriend's fidelity to him exonerated. Two accidental deaths had moved into the murder column. Now the media would shine its spotlight on two unsolved murders.

What started as a break-in was now a story that devoured front page newspaper space.

DOCS DYING AT THE CHARLES
Boston, Ma (10/30): Boston Police have officially reclassified the deaths of two Charles River doctors from accidental to murder. On Sept. 11th the body of Dr. Judith Sims was discovered in her Brookline apartment. The medical examiner ruled her cause of death as an "allergic reaction" and called it accidental. After exhumation of her body in Toledo, Ohio and review by the FBI medical examiner, the cause of death has been changed to murder. After Sims' death her live-in boyfriend, Dr. Dirk Eldridge, also from the Charles, died in what was then called a hit and run accident in the Back Bay. The cause of his death has now been changed to murder. Both doctors worked on the 7th Floor at the hospital in a special unit that offers experimental treatments for terminally ill patients.

Officials at the Charles refused all comments and referred any questions to the Boston Police.

Detective in charge of the investigation, Jimmy Street, submitted a brief written statement:

We have been developing facts in this case for several months and there is an active, ongoing investigation. At this time, no arrests are imminent. We have many excellent leads and are confident that the perpetrators will be caught and punished. We welcome any help from the public. Detective Street was in a car that was shot at in Cambridge a few weeks ago. He was slightly injured.

In a development, the police say is unrelated, longtime Boston medical examiner, Dr. Jim McCann has asked for early retirement.

The President of the Hospital, Dr. Irizome Shiri, has been unavailable for comment. Dr. Timothy Marks, a familiar face in medical circles, has also refused all comment. The hospital pioneered with experimental research, funded by Gene World. The Department of Defense maintains a liaison office at the Hospital.

It did not take long for the newspaper story to send shock waves rolling through the Charles Hospital. The first phone call came from a secretary at Gene World in New York.

"Dory, GW stock is going to take a big hit today. Our traders say there's already a SELL imbalance and the opening may be delayed. That story up in Boston was picked up by the financial wires. Our lawyers are getting a filing ready for the SEC. This is going to be a three valium day." Dory hung the phone up without a word.

Dory was still unsettled from his interrogation by Street and the sight of Gene World's name in the morning paper.

Kate Beecher was the next person to get a call.

"Kate, this is Tom. I talked with the General this morning. That story up in Boston wasn't so bad. It looks contained as of now. Did Street talk to you about Eldridge? Seems he guessed that Eldridge was our other OSI person."

"Yeah, I knew he figured that out. Why didn't you tell me about Eldridge? I could have worked with him. You show a lot of confidence in me. Hell, even after he's dead you can't tell me. Street's right, you guys don't have your act together. Tom, there's another thing Street is right about."

"What's that?"

"You are a certifiable asshole. Got any more surprises for me up here? Maybe it's time you put another sucker in this job."

"Cool off! I know you're pissed. You're doing a great job. Stay with it. And keep us informed. Kate, watch your back."

While Dory and Beecher were juggling phone calls and saying *no* to reporters, Dr. Shiri was closeted in her office with several members of her board of trustees. Dr. Shiri was joined by three of the seven members. Peter Samson was Director of Development for a Cambridge software company and large benefactor of the Charles. Ellen Shaefer was the owner of a chain of hotels and chaired the hospital's most important fund raising committee. Dr. Emmet Giraldi, Jr. was Professor Emeritus at Harvard. The other board members were unavailable. Dr. Giraldi spoke for the board members.

"Dr. Shiri, we've all read the papers. This is a tragedy for the good name of the Charles Hospital. We're here to help and not to criticize. You enjoy the unqualified support of the board and we thought this was a good time to emphasize that fact."

Shiri rose to speak. What she said was more than the board expected.

"I AM deeply embarrassed by what has happened. We have lost two fine members of our family here at the Charles. Our name has been dragged on the ground as if we had some complicity in all this. I've met with the police, and the hospital is doing everything it can to be cooperative. I will do anything to protect the reputation of our hospital. Perhaps my resignation might help. If so, I AM prepared to tender it right now."

Shiri held a piece of paper in her hand. The board members were stunned. This was the woman who had won the hearts of Boston and raised millions of dollars through sheer willpower. She could pick up the phone and call the President of the United States.

Giraldi stood and asked to see the resignation. He took it and ripped it apart, tossing the pieces in the air. The other two board members stood and applauded. Dr. Shiri eased onto her seat and said, "Thank you."

Giraldi took the initiative and said, "This meeting is concluded."

While everyone emptied from Dr. Shiri's office, she called downstairs and asked Dr. Marks to visit. He answered the phone with a voice that sounded distant. Shiri feared the *daylight* of this story had impacted her friend very hard. She knew he was a strong person. He was also a very delicate human being. He did not have the capacity to keep life in balance when it came to the 7th Floor. The Floor was a living and breathing entity for him. She imagined how the news story must have impacted his psyche. When it came to the 7th Floor, Marks was brittle and easily rattled. She needed to handle him with care.

"Timothy, please come in. Three members from the board were just here. We had a nice chat about the story in today's paper."

"How could it be nice? It's a disaster for the 7th Floor. I don't know what to do."

"Timothy, I thought you'd react this way. First, the board was very supportive. We did nothing wrong. We are not the masters of evil. We are not even the servants of our patients. We are only human. We are not God. Put this whole thing in perspective and you'll feel better."

"I've had calls from reporters. Sally has called in tears. She said there was a TV station camera crew at our house. It's a zoo."

"Timothy, calm down. You have a responsibility to your patients and doctors and staff and not to those reporters. The 7th Floor is the crown jewel in this hospital. We're going to protect it. You've devoted your whole life to it. Let Detective Street do his job and we'll be done with it."

Dr. Shiri was indulging in wishful thinking.

Street was collecting on I-O-U's from his friends in the media. No, they would never alter the facts of any story to pay back favors. But they were willing to listen, off the record, and then report what they were told. Street was consistently reliable and accurate. Most reporters with a byline were willing to affix their names to a story that Street offered. The alternative was to be out in left field with an angry editor on their back. Street's currency were his I-O-U's and he was spending them quickly.

Street needed a specific follow-up story. Marcus Carr was his favorite reporter in Boston. It was impossible to decipher who owed whom more. This afternoon, Carr was writing so fast he never touched his tuna sandwich. Street and Carr met downtown at the Newbury Grille. At the end of lunch, Carr's only question was, "Street, you wouldn't put your buddy here out to dry?"

"Marcus, I've told you the truth. The chronology may be wacky, but the facts are there. You won't regret it."

Tomorrow's lead story would be the bowling ball. Now Street was getting the pins lined up to fall. Back at police headquarters his first phone call went to Ernie Green.

"Ernie, this is when we start to take charge. Remember when we talked at the gym? I said I needed a favor. And you remember what it was?"

"Yeah, you wanted me to submit my resignation."

"Do it now, today, as soon as we hang up. Write it yourself if there's no word processor around. Then make copies. Give one to Dr. Shiri and another copy to Dr. Marks. Then tell everyone. Make it short and sweet. Just say you need a change."

"Why is today so important?"

"Ernie, trust me on this. It's tomorrow that's key. I've still got you under protective surveillance. You'll be safe. Just think of Dirk and Sims. This will all work out, I think."

"You think!"

Street's next call went to Karen Ferris. She was out of the hospital and Street had her beeped.

"Street, this is Karen. Wow, I saw that story in the paper. I wish Dirk and Simsy could see what you're doing for them."

"Karen, it's not for them. It's for justice. God that sounds sanctimonious. How about...it's my job?"

"Don't be modest. Street, what can I do?"

"You can come down to headquarters as fast as possible. I'll wait here. Don't tell anyone where you're going. Trust me on this."

"Street, nothing's ever easy with you, is it?"

"So, I'll see you in 30 minutes?"

"I'll be there."

There were two more calls to make. Street reached Kate and told her there would be another newspaper story tomorrow. He told her about facts in the medical examiner's report that were withheld from the media. Street also asked her to reach General Korbee in Washington. Then Street made the call he did not want to make.

"Dr. Shiri, this is Detective Street."

"Detective, I was going to call you. I turned the taping devices off."

"I didn't call about them. It's bad news."

Street, now what's wrong?"

"I know who the killer is. And you know the killer. You just don't know that you know."

"Detective, what should I do?"

"You can't do anything. It's too late."

Against all his instincts of politeness, Street hung the phone up without hearing her response.

Mickey McCoy was sitting next to Street during the phone calls. He looked as Street spun his magic web.

"Street, I'm your partner. Who is the killer?"

"Mickey, beats me. I have no idea."

"Well, Street, that's charming. What are you doing?"

"Oh, I'm cooking up a broth for tomorrow. Wait till you see the papers. When Dr. Ferris gets here I'm going to ask her to call in sick tomorrow. That adds another wild card. Mickey, maybe you'd better get the boss and tell him the Charles Hospital case is coming to an end."

"Yeah, either it's coming to an end or you are. Man, what a cocky son-of-a-bitch. This whole thing could blow up in your face."

"Sure it could, Mickey. Look on the bright side: you'll get a promotion. And you'll get all of Joker's pens."

Thursday morning at five AM in early November is dark.

Street was up and dressed in his jogging outfit. He had 50 cents for the Dartmouth Street newsstand. From Beacon Hill, he ran down to the Charles River and across the Mass Avenue bridge to Cambridge. Then he turned and ran back along the Boston side of the Charles River. When he got to the Arthur Fiedler Bridge, he turned south and ran along the Boston Gardens past the Ritz and down Newbury Street. Sixty minutes after he started, Street arrived at the newsstand. There still wasn't much light, but there was enough to see that Marcus Carr earned himself a giant favor from Street.

EXCLUSIVE
"DR DEATH AT THE
CHARLES HOSPITAL

(Boston, MA 11/10) by Marcus Carr: Reliable sources have confirmed that a killer is loose inside the Charles River Medical Center, one of the world's most prestigious hospitals. It is believed the killer has an association with the Hospital's famed 7th Floor. That Floor was founded by its present Chief of Medicine, Dr. Timothy Marks.

There are approximately 50 patients on the 7th Floor and another 300 in the Hospital.

Since September, two doctors who worked on the 7th Floor have been murdered. Police report the first victim, Dr. Judith Sims, died of an allergic reaction that was caused by the killer. Her live-in boyfriend, Dr. Dirk Eldridge was killed in an accident intended to appear as a hit and run.

Sources tell the GAZETTE that the FBI and the counter-intelligence unit of the Air Force, the OSI, are investigating the murders in cooperation with Boston Police. One of the physicians on the 7th Floor, Dr. Ernie Green of Brooklyn, New York is receiving police protection. Several other physicians on the 7th floor have been questioned. Mr. Atwood Dory, who works on the 7th Floor and represents Gene World, was questioned at police headquarters and released. Gene

World is one of the largest pharmaceutical manufacturers in the world.

When contacted, the Mayor of Boston expressed his full confidence in the Charles Hospital. She called the Hospital safe. The Mayor received a personal guarantee for all patients' safety from the President of the Charles Hospital, Dr. Irizome Shiri.

Detective Jimmy Street said he expects the killer will be in custody shortly. When asked if he had a suspect, the answer was "Yes".

Note: see related stories: The History of the Charles, Famous Patients at the Charles, and a Photographic Tour of the Charles.

Street arrived at police headquarters by 7:30 AM. Mickey was already there reading the *Gazette*. There were calls from national news wires, cable news services, one network, and a host of local radio and TV stations.

"OK Street, now what happens?"

"Mickey, we wait. Time out. We'll let the action come to us. Have you talked to the surveillance team watching Ernie?"

"Nope."

"Call and make sure we know where he is. And get a hold of Ferris. Another thing: get our contact at the airport. Here's a list. I want to know if any of these folks leave town today."

"Anything else?"

"Tell me when you're finished and we'll get some breakfast."

Chapter Twenty Six: Kamikaze?

J apan has often suffered at the hands of invaders. In 1281 the Mongols sent 100,000 men in a great swarming armada. In preparation for the invasion, Buddhist priests sought help from the gods. Then, as the armada approached, a giant typhoon engulfed the armada, sending most to their stormy deaths. The Japanese named this intervention by the heavens, Kamikaze or Divine Wind. In World War II, Japanese suicide pilots cloaked themselves in the mystique of Kamikaze as they flew to certain death in order to save others.

Dr. Irizone Shiri walked solemnly into police headquarters. The iron woman who ruled the Charles Hospital was dazed and lost.

"Please, Detective Street, where may I find him?"

The desk officer asked her to wait as he phoned upstairs. Street asked that she be escorted to a third floor meeting room.

"Mickey, Dr. Shiri's on her way up. I didn't expect her. What does she want?"

"Street, this is your show."

Street saw her walking slowly from the elevator banks towards him. As usual she was wearing a beautiful floor length dress with painted white orchids from toe to shoulder. The beauty of the dress spot lighted the agony on her face. She barely made eye contact with Street.

"Detective Street, you have seen this morning's paper?"

"I have."

"Let me explain what you have done. We had ten patients check out of the Charles by ambulance this morning. The halls are flooded with family and friends of our patients. Fifteen nurses have called in sick so far. Dr. Green has resigned and Dr. Ferris called in sick. It is chaos. We are a place of refuge for those who are sick. It is our mission to cure those who are ill and comfort those who cannot be cured. We are a place of gentleness. You have crossed the boundary of decency."

Street sat as his hands moved across his face. His eyes were closed. For the first time he could measure the impact of today's story. He was after a killer. Had he lost perspective? Whatever he planned, there was never any intention of causing pain to the innocent in order to catch the guilty. As high as he was, while jogging this morning, he was that low as he looked into Shiri's eyes. They were red and worn. His partner grabbed Street's arm in support.

"Dr. Shiri, what can I say? We're trying to catch a killer. Everything in that story is true. I see your pain. But what about Dr. Sims and Dr. Eldridge? What about Dr. Ferris and myself? You weren't in the car when someone tried to kill us."

Street did not think Shiri heard a word he said. Her body stood before him but her mind was back inside the Charles. McCoy asked her to sit down. As she did, tears rolled down her cheeks. How could someone so exquisite be so sad. There was nothing Street or McCoy could do. For 20 minutes, Street, McCoy and Shiri sat and looked and never spoke a word. Street glanced at the clock. It was exactly 10:30 AM. When blanketed in silence a telephone can scream with noise. Street picked up the telephone. As the words came across, his body started to quiver.

"Street, this is the Chief. You better sit down. Communications just rang and said someone called from the Charles Hospital. They said someone is down in their bunker, whatever that is. He went in and won't come out. That's all I know. You better get over there fast."

Dr. Shiri knew instinctively something horrible had happened.

"Detective Street, what's wrong?"

"Dr. Shiri, come with us. I'll tell you on the way over to the hospital."

It took five minutes to race from headquarters to the Charles Hospital. McCoy drove as Street was on the radio. Three other cruisers were dispatched. By the time they neared the front entrance of the Charles, two of the cruisers had arrived. A small crowd had gathered. Street and McCoy jumped out with Dr. Shiri close behind. They ran through the lobby as a security guard cleared the way. Beecher shot through the lobby and jumped into the elevator with them.

"Kate, what's going on down there?"

"Street, I don't know. Someone got into the outer containment room. Our guard called upstairs. Whoever it is killed the power. We've got power in the rest of the building. We don't have our backup lighting on yet. All we've got are flashlights."

The elevator whisked them down to the basement. The long corridor was black. Using flashlights, they moved quickly towards the second elevator at the end of the corridor. Beecher led the way with Street and McCoy close behind. Shiri walked as fast as she could and still couldn't keep the pace. There were still no lights. The elevator was open and dead."

"Street, the stairs. Fast!"

Beecher lead the way down with Dr. Shiri still at the rear. It was only 20 yards to the outer containment building. Standing outside the containment room with a flashlight in one hand and a gun in the other was the Air Force security guard.

"He must have killed the lights. He told me there was a power failure so I went to switch on the generator. It was disabled. The security locks on the door were all disabled. That's supposed to be impossible. When I came back, he was gone."

The door to the outer containment room was open. Street could smell the chlorine. Beecher lead the way inside. It was empty.

"Street, whoever got in is gone. The room's empty."

The outer room was empty. Shiri then screamed.

"Oh God, no it can't be!"

Inside the laboratory, a flashlight moved around in the dark. Peering through the glass, they saw him lift the flashlight and spotlight his face.

It was Dr. Marks.

Fifteen minutes ago, Street and Shiri were locked in silence at police headquarters contemplating events swirling around them. She seemed to welcome the sound of silence. So many ugly sounds were marching across their lives. Maybe she had come over to headquarters for no reason. It might have been her call for help. Whatever it was, it was 15 minutes and a lifetime past. For a split second, Street wished he could rewind the last 48 hours. He knew that life doesn't come with a rewind button. The time was 10:45 AM.

Beecher took command of events in the bunker.

"He's in there. Seal the area starting in the lobby. See if we can get power on. No one gets down here without my permission. Pick up your phone. See that number written underneath it. Call it. Ask for General Korbee. When you get him, get me."

Beecher went over to Shiri and touched her hand. Through the glass windows they saw Marks moving randomly around the lab with his flashlight bouncing beams across the room.

"Dr. Shiri, listen very carefully. You've got to tell me. Can we put the space suits on and go inside? Should we wait for the lights? Is Marks in any danger? Without power can we talk with him?"

Street turned a flashlight on his face and called to Beecher.

"Kate, come here."

Street and McCoy stood near the doorway that leads into the containment shower.

"Kate, I'll call headquarters. Is there danger of an explosion down here? Maybe we should call the fire department. They've got all sorts of gear. No, I can't do that. This is a hospital. That's automatically a general alarm. It's panic city then. We don't even know why he's in there."

"Street, there's no danger of an explosion. Worry about the viruses and bacterium in there. I know this containment facility. But, I don't know exactly what viruses and stuff are inside the lab. We rotate them. Let's see who's upstairs on the 7th Floor. You should get Dory down. He'll know what GW has in there. Tell police headquarters we don't know. And for God's sake, don't send the marines in yet."

THUD. BANG. Marks was hitting the glass with his left hand. Beecher yelled at Street.

"Fuckin unbelievable; he's in there without a space suit. Look at the floor. There's newspaper everywhere. He's wearing some kind of medal with a blue ribbon. Get me some paper and a pen."

She took one of Street's fat blue police pens and wrote a note which she pushed against the window.

"Dr. Marks, are you OK? Can you get out? The power's off. Are you in any danger? Stay calm. The intercom went off with the power.

Marks pressed his face into the glass. His face was pushed so hard against the glass that his nose was flat with his face. His eye balls looked weird. They were moving in circles. His face was twitching between a smile and frown. He put his thumb inside his mouth like a baby sucking on a lollipop. His bow tie and striped blue shirt were perfectly in order. The contrast was sickening.

"Kate, I'm no shrink, but he doesn't look like all his oars are in the water. He looks drugged. I've seen that look before. Shit, I've seen it on my knees with a gun at my head. He's unwinding. He's having a meltdown."

Street sat next to Shiri and held both her hands in his. He tried to comfort her as she watched her friend Marks move around in the lab. She could not bear to look at Marks. Maybe this was all a terrible nightmare and she could awake in peace.

"Dr. Shiri, I think Dr. Marks isn't feeling well. Can you bring a psychiatrist down here. Who has Marks' home phone number? We better call. Once we get power, maybe they can talk. Please get someone now. You can make outside calls with the phones down here."

WHACK. WHACK. WHACK.

Marks was slamming his hands against the glass. His flashlight fell to the floor. He threw something at the glass. Street thought it was a chair. Marks' flashlight lit up a message scribbled on a piece of lab paper.

"Turn the lights on. Why aren't you at work? Hi Iri, What are you doing down here? Street, do you have more questions. You all go. I'm staying here for a while. I'm talking to some of my friends in the jars. They're sleeping now. Maybe I should wake them up. Please just turn the lights on when you leave."

McCoy asked Street, "What does he mean about his friends in the jar?"

"Kate, are you thinking what I'm thinking?"

"Yup. He's delusional. He's drowning in a pool of deceit. And God only knows what's in those jars. We should be able to lock down all the viruses. Street, hit the switch on your right. It'll jam all the drawers inside the lab. Do it now."

The switch moved up and down. But, like the power, it was disabled. Street flashed his light inside the lab. Some of the drawers were already open. As his light pierced the darkened lab, the beam hit Marks in the face. He was sitting on the floor with his legs crossed.

"OK Beecher, we better do something. This isn't a good. We can't just wait around in the dark."

As Street spoke, the lights came on.

Street looked around the room and counted heads. He saw McCoy, Beecher, Shiri and two new faces. There was another Air Force guard and a man about 40 years old.

"Who's this guy?"

Dr. Shiri answered, "Detective, you asked for someone to talk with Dr. Marks. This is Dr. Gold from psychiatric services."

"I'm Dr. Gold, what the hell's going on here?"

"Look, doc, I don't have the time to explain. Do you know Marks?"

"I've seen him around. That's it."

"Talk to him. Maybe you can give us a clue what's going on inside there. And inside his head."

Beecher grabbed Gold by the hand, "And think of that room he's in as Chernobyl...as in nuclear meltdown. This isn't just some guy locked in any old room. Got it?"

Gold approached the window and surveyed the lab. The lights were working and so was the intercom. Street showed him which button to press.

"Dr. Marks, I'm Dr. Gold. Could we talk for a few moments in private."

Gold motioned to Street and the others to move outside the room. They huddled on both sides of the entrance to the outer containment room and out of sight. They listened as Gold talked.

Street and the others heard every word. It was Marks' voice, but it sounded stretched thin like a rubber band. Gold walked outside and joined Street, Beecher, McCoy, and Shiri.

"Dr. Shiri, I can give you a quick feel for this. It's my best effort."

Street pointed at the clock, "Gold it's 12 noon. Time is not working with us on this one. I've got a bad feeling. Get to the facts."

"Dr. Shiri, it's my opinion that Dr. Marks has suffered a reactive psychosis."

"Damn, can't you doctors talk in fuckin' English just once?"

"Detective, he reacted to an event. His balloon burst. The newspaper story pushed him over the cliff. He's in a downward spiral. What I hear and see is a combination of things. First he's acutely psychotic; he's not in touch with reality. He's delusional. He's hallucinating. He's hearing voices inside his head. He's paranoid. He's suspicious. And he's delirious. Do you understand, detective?"

"Well, shit Doctor, what doesn't he have?"

"Detective, he's in a fluid state now. He's in and out of touch with reality. If we could get him when he's in touch, maybe we could get him to come out of there."

Beecher interrupted, "No one's coming out of that Bunker without taking a decontamination shower. He doesn't even have a space suit on. Who knows what he's breathing. He may be dead already."

Dr. Shiri spoke so quietly it was difficult to hear.

"We're forgetting that's my friend in there. We must find his wife Sally and bring her to see him. Maybe his children, too."

'Excuse me, Dr. Shiri, but it's my opinion that if you overload him with his family, like his kids, it could embarrass him. He seems to be a very proud man. Flooding him with family might backfire. My suggestion is to get some food inside and let him calm down. Let him initiate the next conversation. And let's try and find out what he wants."

Street listened and then said, "That sounds good to me. And it was in English, too."

Street took Beecher and McCoy upstairs. Parked at the entrance of the hospital was a mobile command unit. Inside the unit was Joker.

"Street, you are the Godfather. This is the grand daddy of trouble. And did you hear all that psychobabble from that psych-jockey Gold down there?"

"Joker, how'd you hear what he was saying?"

"Street, while you're down there on the skids, I installed a little microphone. One of those testing one-two-three."

"Captain Beecher and Dr. Shiri, this is the Joker, a necessary evil in our business. He works part time for the force and helps with electronics. He's very good. You might remember his face. He's easy to understand. Think of him as a portable radio station."

"Street's jealous 'cause he doesn't have my vocabulary. Think of him as a museum piece with muscles. So, what's the deal?"

"Joker, we've got a doctor who's locked himself up in something they call the bunker. It's like a warehouse for viruses. Our shrink thinks the doctor inside is crashing. Can we introduce any monitoring equipment in that room?"

Beecher jumped towards Street, "That place was built by the Air Force like a missile silo. I don't care how smart this kid is, he's wasting his time. He can't help you. Send him home for cookies."

"Hey, sweetie, did you know your office was bugged and yours truly found it?"

"What?"

Street confirmed that Joker was right.

"And who did that?"

"Kate, we've got bigger problems now."

"Miss pin-up, I'll find a way to get TV monitor into that Bunker. If the government built that bunker, it's probably easier to open than a can of peas."

"Street, if your obnoxious little twit here is right, we've got major league troubles."

"Street, we're wasting time. I need the blueprints. I'll snake a probe through the plumbing and bring it in through the faucet in the lab. Do you want color or black and white?"

"Joker, just do it."

Street sat down at a computer in the mobile unit and typed out a brief message to headquarters. Then he faxed it to headquarters:

Boston Police
URGENT:YOUR EYES ONLY

TO: Chief of Police
FR: Detective J. Street
RE: Mobile Unit 9, Charles River Medical Center
DT: 11/11/94

Situation is that Chief of Medicine on 7th Floor, Dr. Timothy Marks, barricaded inside the bunker, a below ground storage facility for viruses. Many are dangerous, contagious, and deadly. Advise CDC in Atlanta. Air Force OSI agent on scene. She has advised superiors in Washington. Notify Zebra and Governor.

Try to contain media coverage. Risk of panic. Trying to locate Marks' wife. Bring her to this location.

Doctor is irrational and dangerous. May be killer of two doctors. Psychiatrist says he is 'crashing'. Risk assessment in progress.

Joker attempting to get TV monitor into bunker.

Contact other hospitals in re: possible evacuation of Charles.   Keep request quiet.

Will advise.

It was 1:30 PM. Police headquarters was bombarded with media inquiries. Communications said a *situation* was in progress with a sick employee and that he posed no immediate danger to the hospital's patients or staff.

"Detective, I'm Sally Marks. I heard on the radio that there was a problem at the Charles and then I called Tim's office. His secretary told me what's happening. Damn you all, is it any wonder? Tim's life is wrapped up in this place. We saw the newspaper story. You're destroying his reputation. I hold you all responsible. I want to see my husband."

"Mrs. Marks, I feel badly for you and your husband. But we've got a situation here. Come on, we'll take you downstairs."

Street and Beecher lead Mrs. Marks into the lobby. Dr. Shiri was near the elevator with three uniformed guards. She and Mrs. Marks embraced.

"Iri, what have they done to my husband? Is he OK?"

"Sally, let's go talk with him. Maybe you can help."

Street, McCoy, Beecher and the others squeezed into the elevator. When the doors opened, Street was greeted by the Joker.

"Almost done, Detective. I see you brought along the Air Force. We're below the surface; shouldn't that be the Navy?"

With that remark, Beecher looked over at Street, "When he's done his job, get his ass out of here. Maybe one of my guards will shoot him by mistake, if I'm lucky."

The walk to the second elevator took a few seconds. McCoy lead the group towards the stairs. "We're not all going to fit inside the elevator. Let's walk."

Dr. Gold stood outside the door leading into the containment room.

Street spoke, "Mrs. Marks, this is Dr. Gold. He's a psychiatrist in the hospital. You should talk with him before going inside."

"Mrs. Marks, I'm Dr. Gold. Please listen carefully. I never met your husband before today. He's got a terrific reputation. Here's what happened and I'll tell you what you can do. Simply put, your husband is sick. We call it reactive psychosis."

"I know what that means."

That caught Street's attention. "Excuse me, Mrs. Marks, are you a psychiatrist?"

"No."

"Then, how do you know what it means?"

"Tim had a problem back in school. I thought it was common knowledge."

Dr. Shiri joined the conversation. "Sally, I've worked with Tim very closely. We're good friends. I never heard of a problem."

"In medical school, Tim's best friend and roommate committed suicide. He set fire to their apartment. Tim needed psychiatric help. The word psychosis sounds familiar. It was so long ago."

Street looked at McCoy and Beecher and no words were necessary.

"Mrs. Marks, when your husband saw the newspaper story he snapped. He seems to be delusional. He's paranoid. Your husband thinks there are people trying to stop him and his research with a drug called XM2. He thinks he killed those two doctors. When we go in, it's very important that you don't act scared or upset. That could cause problems. I suggest you try and get him talking. Talking about anything. Ready?"

Sally Marks walked alone into the outer containment room. She looked through the glass and could not see her husband.

"Tim, are you in there; it's Sally. Are you OK?"

Marks approached the window. Instantly, she was horrified to see him in there without a space suit.

"Tim, where's your space suit?"

"Sally, these are my friends. I don't need one of those silly space suits. They won't hurt me. They're sleeping in the jars. Speak softly; I don't want to wake them up. Why are you here?"

She looked back to Gold and he motioned for her to keep talking.

"The kids are fine. I wanted you to know that. We're going out to dinner tonight. What time will you be home?"

"Sally, I may have to sleep here tonight. Someone's trying to stop the research and I've got to protect the viruses. I found a cure for pancreatic cancer. Dr. Sims knew that. I killed them all."

"Timothy, you couldn't step on a fly."

"Sally, keep the doors locked at home. Change the phone number. Ask that detective for protection. I'm sorry about you and the kids. Whoever's after me may try to hurt you."

"Timothy, who's after you?"

"Sally, you saw the paper this morning. They're all after me. They'll do anything to stop the research. You better leave now. Say good-bye to my friends in here."

Sally left the room and burst into tears. She had talked to a complete stranger. Joker came by with a little TV monitor.

"Street, here it is. TV pictures from inside. The probe is in the water faucet. As long as he doesn't have water coming out, you've got a clear wide angle picture from inside the room. Where's your honey-bee who said I couldn't do this? The Air Force thinks their little toy down here is the cat's meow. Well, no way."

Street looked at the monitor. Marks was on his knees cleaning the floor.

"Now, what's he doing? Dr. Gold, could you go back and ask him."

"I can try."

Gold walked into the outer room. There was Marks, on his hands and knees, polishing the floor.

"Dr. Marks, it's Dr. Gold. How's it going in there?"

"Just fine, Dr. Gold. It's almost two PM and some of my friends in the jars are getting up now. I'm going to let them get some exercise. They're always locked up in these jars. So, when I let them out, I want the lab to be spotless. Could you do me a favor? Ask my secretary to check my mail and calls. I'll return calls tomorrow."

"Dr. Marks, when do you think you'll let your friends out?"

"As soon as I finish cleaning up. Probably in about half an hour. Come on by; they're lots of fun."

Gold left the room. Street and Beecher were ashen faced. Dr. Shiri heard Marks' words and went upstairs with his wife.

Street barked to the guard, "Call upstairs and see if Ernie Green's around."

In less than a minute, he was on the phone.

"Ernie, get down here fast. I need some answers. Do you know what's inside the bunker?"

"Street, I've got a pretty good idea. I'll be right down. We've got a mad house up here."

"Down here, we've got worse."

Street ran upstairs to the mobile unit. There were two TV station remote crews on the scene. Street ran past them without a word. Beecher waited for Green outside the containment room. McCoy waited with her. It was 2:10 PM.

Boston Police

<u>URGENT: FOR YOUR EYES ONLY</u>
TO: Chief of Police
FR: Detective Jimmy Street
RE: Status Report, Charles River Hospital
DT: 11/11/94

Latest developments. Marks' wife is here and she's talked with him. Nothing favorable.

Marks threatening to open *jars* and let his friends out to get some exercise. That's how far gone he is. He's hallucinating. Marks cleaning floor in preparation for letting viruses out.

Risk assessment has changed. Recommend a careful evacuation of patients and staff.

Governor should ask President for assistance. We may have another Chernobyl.

Joker put a TV probe into bunker. He looped it through the faucet. Air Force said room was impenetrable. They were wrong. What else are they wrong about?

Please advise.

Ernie Green walked into the containment building at 2:30 PM.

"This is weird, no retinal scan, no fingerprints, it's like going into a 7-11. So this is the Air Force definition of security."

Street was waiting for him. Was Marks serious about letting his *friends* in the jars out for some exercise? Beecher had talked with General Korbee in Washington and the OSI sent three agents trained in germ warfare. The agents were scheduled to land at Hanscom Field outside Boston at 2:45 PM and fly by helicopter directly to the Charles. Their estimated time of arrival was 3:15 PM. No one was trained for a possible suicide mission into the Bunker.

Now Street and Beecher peppered Green with a series of questions.

"Ernie, we need short answers. Pull no punches. When in doubt, give us the worst case scenario."

"Street, I can't believe Marks is the killer. They say upstairs he admitted killing all the doctors."

"Ernie, that's not the issue now. We'll straighten that out later. Here's a list of questions." Street, Beecher and McCoy handed a short list to Green. A couple of the questions came from headquarters.

Questions For Green:
1) What viruses/bacteria are known to be inside the bunker?
2) Are they airborne?
3) How can we tell if Marks has opened any jars?
4) Will the bunker keep exposure inside? *** 'HQ' question
5) Is there any risk to outside population? *** 'HQ' question
6) Can viruses/bacteria be destroyed?
7) What happens to Marks if exposed?
8) Can we go inside bunker and remove Marks?

"Wow guys, this is a lot to ask? Say, how's Dr. Marks?"

"We're asking; now tell us. Answer these questions, now!"

Ernie took the list and started to answer. Everyone's eyes were riveted on Green. This was center stage with spotlights and no cue cards. Street noticed Ernie's beat up white-now-brown tennis sneakers. in that split second, his thoughts slipped back to Sims and Dirk.

"OK, here goes. Gene World has some stuff in there. I know XM2--the anti-cancer drug that Simsy used--is in there. We've also got some VARIOLA, smallpox. There's Sabia, Ebola and something the Air Force brought out of Peru. That's all I know about. I'm sure there are more. Dory may know more. There should be an inventory list in that computer with back up files at the security desk."

"Ernie, we're one step ahead. The computer files are erased. Same with the computer disk."

"Well, that's not good. Assume all the viruses, bacterium and tubercle bactillus are..."

"Wait, what's tubercle?"

"Street, that's the bacterium that causes tuberculosis. You know there's lots of stuff down there. We keep samples of the AID's virus. It goes on and on. That's why that inventory list was so important. To be safe, assume everything is airborne. That's not the case; but you better figure it that way.

"Street, if Marks took everything out of there and walked around Boston, he could easily infect and kill most of the population. BOOM! DEAD! Understand?"

"What about the jars?"

"You can look inside and see if they've been opened. He could have opened some and re-sealed them. To be safe, figure they're all open. Of course, you could ask him."

"Ernie, that's so simple, but not a bad idea. We'll do that."

"Street, ask Beecher if the bunker will keep its integrity. It's supposed to. If it does, there's no risk to anyone outside."

Beecher jumped in with some answers.

"Street, that bunker will hold. The only thing that worries me is that your joker got a TV probe in the bunker. We can destroy everything in there with an autoclave system."

"What's that?"

"We sterilize everything with steam heat. Actually, we can bring the temperature up to 2,000 degrees. That'll sterilize and melt everything."

"What about Marks?"

"If he's inside, he melts."

"Ernie, what if Marks has been exposed, what can we do?"

"You'd have to get him out of there. Then put him in a space suit and transport him upstairs to the Zipper on the 7th Floor. It depends on what he's exposed to and how long he's in there."

"And can we go inside and get him?"

"That's risky. You'd have to get a space suit on. A lot would depend on his mental state."

"Ernie, you're good with computers. Maybe there's a way we can recover the inventory. Even an old list might help. Will you check through Marks' office. Ask his secretary. Ask Dr. Shiri. She's with his wife. Maybe he has a computer at home."

"Street, I submitted my resignation yesterday like you asked."

"Ernie, I wish I'd submitted mine too."

"Street, they're in! I just got word our team landed at Hansom. They'll be here as advertised at 2:45 PM."

Street looked at his watch and it was 2:31 PM.

"Dr. Gold, how about we go in talk with Marks. He's been quiet for a while. He turned the light off in the bunker. Maybe he's sleeping."

"Street, he's using a lot of nervous energy. Chances are he's tired. And he could be getting irritable on top of everything else. Let's go easy."

Street, Beecher, McCoy and Dr. Gold walked into the outer room. The bunker was dark.

"Before we go in with the cavalry, I need Joker... Joker, this is Street, do you copy?"

"Hey, you're the man. I've been listening. They don't have anything like this at Disneyworld."

"Joker, does your TV monitor have night vision?"

"Street, you're talking to the man. Of course it does."

"What's Marks doing?"

"I'll adjust the probe. It's not easy looking outside a water pipe. Hold on. Yup, I got him. Man you ought to see this sight. He's taking a siesta. He's lying on the floor with his arms and legs spread out like a big star. Looks like he's got buttons all over his chest and on the floor."

"Buttons! Are you crazy?"

"They're bigger than buttons. I got it. They're jars. This cowboy has taken a hard fall. He's got hundreds of jars all over the place. Street, this is a weird site."

"Are they open or closed?"

"I can't tell. They look as if they're in one piece. I've got it on videotape. I'll try and enhance the pictures."

"Joker, transmit the videotape to headquarters."

Beecher heard Joker's words and then sat on the floor. Her face was flushed.

"Street, he's on the brink. You better get this hospital emptied out fast. I'd clear a few blocks around here. And call one of the TV stations and find out about the weather. Especially winds. We better get some space suits on."

"Kate, you said the bunker is foolproof."

"On paper it is."

"Dr. Gold, I don't know your first name."

"Captain Beecher, it's Lenny."

Beecher took Street, McCoy and Gold over to a corner.

"Unless someone has a better idea, I think Lenny should get in a space suit and go into the outer room and start a dialogue."

"Beecher, I'll go in and talk with him, but not in a space suit. When he looks at me in that space suit it'll make him more anxious."

"Handle it your way."

Gold moved into the outer containment room and sat down. He wanted to calm Marks and persuade him to return the jars to the drawers, lock it all up and come out. Gold knew that getting Marks to calm down would be difficult.

"Dr. Marks, it's Dr. Gold. Can you hear me in there? Could you please turn a light on?"

Gold went to the window and saw Marks lying on the floor, exactly as Joker described him. Marks' eyes were open and transfixed on the ceiling. Glass jars were littered across the room and several were on Marks himself. Marks slowly and carefully moved the jars off his body and placed them on the floor. He got up, turned a light on, and pressed his face to the window.

"Dr. Gold, were you followed down here?"

"No, of course not. Your friends are down here. You know, Detective Street, Captain Beecher, Detective McCoy, and I think Ernie Green is also around here someplace. Your wife and Dr. Shiri went upstairs to get a drink. She can take you home tonight."

"No, she can't. I take the T. Only on symphony nights does she drive in town."

"Dr. Marks, I can't come in the bunker with you, but perhaps we could talk while you put the jars back."

"They're not going back. They're my friends. We've worked together for years. Want to know a secret? I killed Dr. Sims. Dr. Eldridge, too. I altered the XM2 she administered to her patient. No one knows how I did it. I've got the only samples. Imagine, a cure for pancreatic cancer. It sounds unbelievable. But so did a vaccine for polio or putting people on the moon. I'll bet this discovery is worth another Nobel Prize. Two doctors died for this cure. And you're looking at the killer."

"Dr. Marks, what would you like me to do?"

"Why don't you invite the other folks to join you. Could you get my wife and Dr. Shiri?"

Gold dashed outside. Street heard every word.

"Why does he want everyone?"

"He needs to vent a lot of feelings. To open himself up. To ask forgiveness. I don't see any harm. He's put the jars on the floor. He thinks they're his friends. As long as he feels that way, we're probably safe."

Street turned to Beecher, "What do you think?"

"I think there's not much else we can do. We do what he asks."

Within five minutes, everyone was assembled outside the containment room. They formed a tight circle. Gold spoke.

"Listen carefully. He wants us all in there. Let him carry the conversation. Under no circumstances argue or cry. You must remain calm. If you can't, get out. We have two goals. First, get Marks to put the jars back in the drawers so we can lock them down. The second is to get him out of there. He doesn't have a space suit in the bunker so here's the plan. We get him to come out through the containment shower. Beecher has already made arrangements to switch from a chlorine and bleach shower to water. He'll get wet; that's it. We'll put our space suits on while he's showering, not before. When he's out, we'll put him in a space suit and get him into isolation. Some Air Force people will go into the bunker and make sure everything is locked down. That's it."

Street had a question. "Dr. Gold, do you think he killed the two doctors?"

"Based on the condition he's in, it's impossible to know. Marks doesn't know himself. And he doesn't know who killed the doctors. You'll have to figure that out yourself."

Beecher asked a question.

"Dr. Gold, what's the downside on all this?"

"Captain, I don't know the upside or downside. What other alternatives do we have?"

At 2:45 PM, the group walked into the outer contamination room. Sally Marks was closest to the window. Street and McCoy stood at the rear with Beecher. Ernie walked in and stood next to Street. Dr. Shiri was holding Sally Marks' hand. Atwood Dory was in a darkened corner. Dr. Gold approached the window and smiled at Marks.

"We've talked a lot today, Dr. Marks, and I've heard so much about you. May I call you Timothy?"

"Of course, and when I finish talking with the jars, I'll give you their names, too."

McCoy nudged Street and Beecher, "That's a bad sign."

Street heard Joker's voice through a radio receiver in his ear. He couldn't talk back, but Joker was yelling, "I'm watching in the TV monitor and that sucker almost stepped on a jar. Better tell him to watch it."

Street walked up to the window.

"Dr. Marks, hello again."

He whispered in Gold's ear as he retreated, "He almost crushed a jar with his foot."

"I remember you, Detective. Well, you've solved your case. I'm the man you're looking for."

Street said nothing. Gold continued to talk.

"Timothy, we've put together a plan to get you out of there safe. We'll have you home soon. Would you like to talk about it?"

"Dr. Gold, I'm safe with my friends. They're in these jars. We lock them up and keep them down here. You work in the hospital and I'll bet you didn't even know they were down here alone."

"Well, I didn't know. But I do now, and I'm sure your friends are very grateful."

"Doctor, you're beginning to sound like Dory. He thinks a few well chosen words and, POOF, all's well. That's crap. You don't give a damn about my friends. For you, these jars are nothing. These jars hold ancestors from the beginning of mankind. They've hung around to try and save humanity. And what do we do? We lock them away down here. Is that fair?"

"Timothy, the way you explain it: no it's not fair."

Gold turned and looked at Beecher and Street and pointed his thumb down. He looked worried. Marks' state of agitation was severe. It was time to re-evaluate the situation.

"Timothy, we're going outside to talk and we'll be back in a few minutes. Is that OK?"

"No, it's not OK."

Marks picked a few jars up from the floor. He put one partly in his mouth while his eyes moved in circles. Gold realized that he and the others were captured by Marks.

"Timothy, if you want us to stay, of course we'll stay."

Street could only hope that Joker was hearing the downward spiral and doing something about it.

Boston Police

Hello at headquarters. This is Joker in the mobile unit. Street's getting egg all over his face down in this bunker. That doctor needs a chill pill. He's freaking out. I think it's gonna blow up. This is an *el foldo*. You better get folks out of here *pronto*. I don't know what's in those jars but that doctor's got one in his mouth. That's about it. JOKER

At police headquarters, Joker's message came across loud and clear. The Mayor of Boston ordered the hospital evacuated and the area cleared. The Governor reached the President's national security advisor. Whatever the Mayor wanted was his. A news blackout was ordered. Other hospitals in the area were instructed to shut down their outside ventilation systems and close all windows and doors.

"Street, I know you can't answer, but this is Joker. I've been tuned in. Sounds like your *pooh-bah* down there is cashing in his chips. I told headquarters to clear the area. Keep your head down, hunter."

Street wanted to give Joker a big kiss. He's one smart kid. Street whispered the news to Beecher and McCoy.

Gold had another idea. It was risky, but he'd take the chance.

"Timothy, I'd like you to invite me into the bunker. I'll be alone. Is that, OK?"

"Gold, I don't trust you. I don't know who you are. My friends in here don't know who you are. You're not coming in."

Instinctively, Sally Marks started to talk.

"Tim, think of me and the children. Please get out of there. It's not safe. These people out here care about you. We love you. We need you home. I love you. Please stop this."

"Get her out of here. You made her say that. You've threatened her. See, what I told you. There's nothing my enemies won't do to stop me. They'll even kidnap my wife. Get her out!"

Street walked to Sally Marks and gently took her hand and walked her out. She looked over her shoulder at her husband. He never looked up. An Air Force guard took her upstairs.

"Iri my friend, you're still here. I'm sorry. Everything is spinning. Our enemies are out there. They're closing in. That story in the newspaper. It's true. There is a killer on the loose in the hospital. I'm the killer. Do you know how many dead patients I have. Thousands since I started. I'll bet I've got 100,000 dead patients. And our enemies will destroy this cure I found. I had to keep it a secret. Iri, get out. This place is not for you."

Gold motioned for her to leave. Marks was spinning faster. He started to walk around the bunker moving between the jars. It was like playing Hop Scotch with spikes on your shoes and your best friend's face on the sidewalk.

Marks moved close to the window. Beecher looked in his eyes and knew this was it. She edged towards the door and found the yellow button. It was the doomsday switch. If she hit the button a loud klaxon would sound throughout the hospital. Every fire house in Boston would get an alarm. Police headquarters would get the same. She put her thumb on the button and waited. Was Marks going to crash. Would the alarm push him over? Beecher made her choice.

GONG! GONG! GONG! GONG!

Street and McCoy jumped at the sound. Gold looked at Beecher in horror. Red and green lights started flashing in the containment room and bunker.

Street yelled over, "What the fuck did you do?"

"Street, he's crashing! Everyone get out of here!"

Marks started to spin himself in circles. He was screaming. "They're coming in to get me. They're going to kill us all."

Marks held jars in his hands. He smashed them against the window. Then he sat on the floor and started throwing them into the air. An oozing goo slithered down the window as the viruses and bacterium were splattered. Marks was jumping up and down, smashing jars on the floor, walls and ceiling.

In less than two minutes, it was over. Every jar in the bunker was turned into a glass heap. There were more poisons concentrated inside the bunker than any place on the face of the earth. Chernobyl was Disneyland. Only air tight steel doors separated humanity from the deadliest viruses and bacterium that crawled across history.

But was it airtight if Joker was able to snake his TV probe inside through a water faucet?

Marks was screaming as everyone cleared out of the containment room. He was breathing in hellish viruses second by second.

"Kate, what about Marks?"

"Street, look at him. That's what the living dead look like. He's dead. The Air Force people should be here now. We must move quickly."

Beecher, Street and McCoy were the last to leave the containment room. Tears were flowing from Marks' eyes. He held broken bits of jars in his hands. Marks was crying, not for himself, but for his friends--his friends in the jars. His friends included the XM2 formula that Sims and Ferris used to save dying patients.

Chapter Twenty Seven:
Endings

S everal Air Force technicians dressed in yellow protective gear entered the outer containment room.

"Who's in charge here? Look at him. He looks OK.

Damn, the window is covered in crap. Was it war in there?"

Street didn't appreciate the cold military analysis.

Street added, "He's alive in there. We have to get him out. His wife's upstairs. He could survive, right?"

Beecher pulled a piece of paper from her pocket.

"Street, you better read this."

Agreement

Date:

The undersigned employee of the Charles River Medical Center 7th Floor hereby agrees to the following special terms as a condition of employment. This letter agreement shall be binding on all heirs and is signed without coercion.

I agree that, (1) in the event of any cure or treatment discovered while an employee, all rights to such shall accrue without condition to the Charles River Medical Foundation (CRM), (2) I shall never publish or report any findings from the 7th floor without the prior written consent of the Chief of Medicine, (3) in the event of my death or incapacitation, all I grant power of attorney to the Charles River Medical Center.

I sign the foregoing Amendment to my employment agreement of my own free will.

Signed: Witnessed:

"We have Marks' signed copy upstairs. He knew the risks. We all did. We have to do what we have to do."

"Kate, and tell me, what's that?"

One of the technicians explained as Beecher watched Street's face contort with anguish.

"Detective, that man is a walking bomb. If he even breathes in a room, people will be infected through airborne contamination. He's a doctor. He understands. Or he did before he lost it. We must decontaminate the entire room and everything in it. We have orders. After we clean it, we'll seal it. Forever! There's no choice."

"What do you mean, *clean it*?"

"You're better off leaving and we'll take care of things. Our mission is to protect the general population."

"I'm not going anywhere till you explain."

The technician looked at Beecher and she nodded *yes*.

"We're going to do an autoclave. That's a sterilization process. This bunker was built like an oven. We'll bring the temperature up to about 2,000 degrees."

"You can't do that."

"You asked; I'm telling. We'll heat it to 2,000 degrees and everything inside will come to a boil. That includes the guy in there. Then we're going to suck the air out and create a vacuum. The viruses and bacterium and whatever else is in there will cease to exist. And the rest of your city will be safe."

"You're going to execute him? You don't even know his name. You never asked. You're machines."

"Detective, he's already dead. Even he knows it."

"Kate, I need a few minutes with Marks. Can anyone find Green?"

One of the Air Force technicians asked, "Captain Beecher, is that OK?"

Beecher put her arm around Street and touched his left eye. She wiped a tear away with her finger. She reached for his hand and squeezed. Her lips touched his cheek. She could taste the salt from his tears. "Street, I'm here with you. Don't suffer this alone." She answered the Air Force technician.

"Let the detective talk with him. What about Marks' wife?"

"Kate, call upstairs and tell Dr. Shiri what's happening. I think his wife will want to come down and say good-bye. Maybe you can find his kids. I've got to get Ernie down here." As he spoke, Green ran into the room. Someone had found him.

There's no death penalty in Massachusetts. Street never saw a criminal execution. The death of his partner was the only execution he ever saw. He never said good-bye to his partner. Sometimes he wakes at night in a cold sweat. One night, he found himself on the floor of his bedroom, on his knees, with his hands behind his head. Street needed the time with Marks to square things. Maybe this time he could say good-bye. Street never said good-bye to his dad. There were things he needed to say and questions to be asked. Even if Marks couldn't understand, Street had to try.

Beecher and the Air Force technicians were talking as Street phoned upstairs to the Joker.

"You did good, Joker. You better remove the TV probe. You know what they're going to do?"

"Street, sorry about the way things happened. You gave it your best shot."

"Street, the technicians overheard you talking with Joker upstairs. One of them has a question."

"Detective, did your man loop a TV probe into the bunker?"

"He did. It's in the faucet."

"Well, how did he do that? That bunker was sealed. The water system is self contained. There's no access to the pipes."

"Wait, I'll ask him."

Joker's explanation was simple: he worked from a set of blueprints. When the bunker was built, the Air Force plumbers used a valve to draw water from the hospital's back up water system.

Whatever bravado the Air Force technicians brought with them washed away.

"Beecher, Street: that guy installed a TV probe through the hospital's main piping. That means the bunker isn't sealed. This hospital is at risk. We're going to melt the room now. Street, leave the guy in there. You're out of here. The good-byes are cancelled."

"Like hell! I'm out of here."

Street drew his revolver and pointed it at the technician. McCoy pulled his gun for back up. Marks watched from inside the bunker.

Then, Street exploded, venting all the frustrations boiling inside him.

"You people make me sick. Who gave you the right to build this crazy thing? You just went and did it. You're sicker than anyone in this hospital. This is your underground chamber of horrors. Well, assholes, the whole fuckin' mess blew up in your face. You couldn't even build it safe. My guy upstairs spent ten minutes looking at blueprints and found a way inside your mega-millions hell hole. Damn, I should toss you in there with Marks. He's the victim."

Street paced across the floor.

"I'm talking with Marks. McCoy get them all out of this room. Kate, I want you out of here, too."

Beecher and the technicians moved outside. Street saw one of the Air Force men pick up a phone. He knew they were calling for help.

"Dr. Marks, this is Detective Street. You remember me."

"Speak. Look what I've done to my friends. The jars are broken. They can't kill us now."

"Dr. Marks, I'm no psychiatrist or anything; so, I don't know the right words. I think you understand me. The newspaper story was true, but I helped a reporter write it. I meant you no harm."

"Street, I don't care. I've killed them all. It makes no difference. We're all dead. We'll join my dead patients and dead doctors. Sims and Eldridge, I killed them both."

"Marks, you didn't kill them. I don't believe it and no one else does."

"Sure I killed them. Street, you brought Ernie down here. Well, get out, Ernie; it's dangerous down here. Street, get him out."

"Street, I'm not going anywhere till I talk with Dr. Marks. I don't give a shit."

Marks' face lightened when he saw Ernie.

"Ernie, are you OK? You should get out of here."

Marks was coherent. The sight of one of his residents dragged him back to some sense of who he was and where he was. Street saw the chemistry between the two and let it flow.

"Dr. Marks, we're all with you. Everyone upstairs is worried. You can get out of this. We'll come down here and take care of you. Simsy and Dirk were my friends. I know you didn't kill them."

"Ernie, I've killed everyone on the 7th Floor. I've killed the hospital. My reputation is dead. I've killed my next Nobel Prize. I altered the XM2 and it saved two patients. The altered formula was experimental. It worked. We had the cure. Now it's on the floor. There are no notes. It's in my head. Everything's gone."

"Dr. Marks, you made the sun shine for Simsy's patient. You saved his life with XM2 and whatever you did to it. You can save other lives. Come on out."

"It's too late, Ernie. They're going to melt everything. They're going to melt me. It's true. Ask Street."

"Street, that's not true is it?"

"Ernie, it is."

"Street, you can't let them do it. He didn't kill anyone. He found a way to enhance the XM2 drug. That could save thousands of lives. You're a cop; call other cops. That's murder. Stop them. If he dies, the cure for pancreatic cancer dies. Now that's murder!"

Street let Marks and Green talk. He picked up a phone and called headquarters.

"Get me Zebra. This is Street. It's an emergency."

"Zebra Command."

"This is Detective Street. I'm at the Charles. Get the chief. Find him. It's life or death. I'll wait."

The wait was 90 seconds. The chief came on the line.

"Street, you've done a hell of a job. Are you safe? Don't take any chances."

"Sir, you know there's a man trapped in this bunker below the hospital. Some of the viruses and stuff are loose. The Air Force wants to heat this up and melt everything in it. That'll kill the doctor inside. That's murder. Please sir. Send me more backup. Stop them."

"Street, about five minutes ago I received a call from the Governor. He had a call from the President. Street, I'll repeat, the President. Those Air Force technicians are under direct Presidential order to destroy all the contents of the bunker. Emphasis on the word *all*. The Governor said he'll send in national guard troops to replace us if we don't obey."

"Street, this is a direct order. Let the Air Force do what they have to. Leave that hell hole and go upstairs. We've got a near riot on our hands. Help us get things controlled. Talk with the media. You're great with that stuff. Tell them everything's OK."

"Sir, everything's OK if you're not the guy inside the bunker. Please."

"Street, no more. You've got your order. Do it."

The phone went dead. Everything was going dead. Then, it rang again.

"Sir, is that you?"

"Street, it's Joker upstairs. I heard what came down. Street, the chief means business. You're my hero. You got guts. Get yourself out of there fast *amigo*. The Air Force has some mean looking guys walking around this place. And not all of them are in uniform. I can monitor their two way radios. They're coming back down."

Joker, thanks. I really screwed this up. I need to talk with Marks."

"Street, I heard Green talking about some drug XM2 and jazz about a cure. Ask Marks to write down what he did and put it in front of my TV probe in the faucet. I'll videotape it. At least that way the cure is saved."

Joker, that's a great idea."

DOWN ON THE FLOOR! KISS THE FLOOR!

Street knew the feel of cold steel against his face. What he saw were some guys standing over him and McCoy. These must be the people Joker mentioned. They had guns pushing against his face. They pushed so hard he started to bleed. One of the men had his knee rammed in Street's back. Another kicked McCoy.

Street watched as they barked commands back and forth. They knew exactly what they were doing. A lot of the words were technical. Street knew what was happening. The temperature was going up in the Bunker. He saw Marks yelling. Street knew he was trying to tell someone what he did to the XM2 that Sims used.

They disconnected the sound. Marks was grasping for air. He took his shirt off. Sweat rolled down his face. Then his eyes closed and he fell to the floor. Street saw him lying there. He hoped he was dead and would not feel the soaring heat.

In ten minutes, the liquids in the jars were boiling. Marks' skin was turning dark. His hair was on fire. Then his skin. Street turned away and vomited.

Street looked back at the Bunker. There was nothing to see.

He walked up the stairs, down the corridor, and then took the elevator to the lobby. Three Boston police stood outside. He saw Kate, Dr. Shiri, Marks' wife, Dory, and the doctors from the 7th Floor.

"It's all over."

Beecher put her arms around Street while Karen Ferris helped McCoy to the Emergency Room.

"Street, I don't know where those OSI agents came from. I never saw them before. They flew in with the technicians. They wouldn't let me downstairs."

"They're goonies. Kate, they didn't want you to see how they play. I'd love to nail their asses. I wish the Air Force knew about them. They'd be history."

"Street, Joker is on the air. Can you hear me? Your wish is my command. Man, I saw it all come down. I saw them whack you and McCoy around. My TV probe got it all. I've got it on tape. When they melted the bunker they zapped my camera."

"Joker, give that tape to the Chief."

"Street, the chief saw it all. I connected headquarters with the TV probe."

Ernie looked at Street. "I'll get you down to the ER. You need some fixing up."

Street broke free from Ernie's gentle tug.

"Mrs. Marks, I did the best I could. Your husband didn't suffer."

McCoy heard that remark and said to himself, mimicking Street, "Lie."

"Dr. Shiri, is everyone OK up here?"

"No, look around. Our hospital is disgraced. We've caused such terrible pain. How could this happen? I should have been in there with Tim."

"Dr. Shiri, he died before going in there. That wasn't Dr. Marks in there. The Dr. Marks you know is always going to be alive on the 7th Floor. He was a hero. At the end, he tried to give us the information on XM2. He altered it. Those jerks down there turned the sound off. They killed the cure when they killed Marks."

"Why did Marks kill Sims and Dirk? He said he did."

"Dr. Shiri, like I said, that wasn't Dr. Marks down there. He's no more a killer than you are. I'm not done. The killer's not done. There's no hell anywhere that's too deep or hot for me to climb into and suck up the person that killed Sims and Dirk."

* * *

SCARE AT CHARLES False Alarm at Charles Hospital Causes Evacuation
(Boston, Ma 11/12) EXCLUSIVE by Marcus Carr: Boston hospitals, schools and all emergency state agencies had a scare yesterday when a special research laboratory at the Charles River Medical Center was damaged in a small fire.

The hospital was evacuated for a few hours. In a daring attempt to save the laboratory, the Chief of Medicine at the hospital's famed 7th Floor died of smoke inhalation. Dr. Timothy Marks founded the 7th Floor and was a Nobel Prize winning doctor.

The Governor of the Commonwealth of Massachusetts ordered all flags flown at half staff in his memory. The President of the United States issued a statement that paid tribute to Marks' contributions in medicine and his service in the military.

Dr. Irizome Shiri, President of the Charles Hospital, announced, in a tearful press conference, that the 7th Floor will be re-dedicated and named the Marks Pavilion.

The Charles Hospital has been plagued recently by the murders of two physicians, Dr. Judith Sims and Dr. Dirk Eldridge. Detective Jimmy Street told this reporter that investigation continues. Yesterday's fire was totally unrelated to the murders.

Street received an on-site decoration for personal bravery. Street tried to rescue Marks from the fire. Boston Fire Department officials had no comment and referred all inquiries to the Boston Police.

There was no structural damage to the Charles Hospital. All departments at the hospital are working on a normal schedule.

Chapter Twenty Eight:
Happy Holidays

T hanksgiving was difficult for Street.

The days were getting short in late November. He added two miles to his morning jog in an effort to clear his head. He dedicated each day's run to someone from the Charles.

Mondays were for Sims and Dirk. More than ever he wished he had a chance to know Dr. Judith Sims. Tuesdays were for Dr. Shiri and Dr. Marks. He always paired them. Neither was perfect but both dedicated their lives to healing. Wednesdays were dedicated to all the doctors from the 7th Floor, especially Ernie and Karen Ferris. Ernie had withdrawn his resignation from the Charles. They touched him in different ways. Thursdays were for Kate. Street saw her more frequently. They went to Nantucket in mid November for a glorious weekend. Kate was thinking of leaving the Air Force and returning to nursing.

Fridays were for the evil Street confronted. A great runner sometimes needs to hate. Street always remembered that evil spelled backwards was...live. Joker's tape cost the Air Force bullies their commissions. Saturdays he ran for his dead partner. He always ran for him on Saturdays. They used to run together on Saturdays. Sundays, Street ran for himself. That was the hardest distance of all. Street was unhappy with himself. He never got the chance to say good-bye to Marks. He never got to say good-bye to his dad. He never got to say good-bye to his dead partner. He never got to say good-bye to his ex-wife. It seemed his whole life was swamped with endings without good-byes.

As usual, Street planned to spend Thanksgiving with his sister and her kids. Street always brought the pumpkin pies. He'd plunk down at his sister's house and gobble food through the football games. She lived 30 minutes west of Boston in horse country. Street had no other family nearby. This year he thought of Kate. She flew back to California to spend the long weekend with her parents. Street imagined how awful Thanksgiving was for the Sims, Eldridge, and Marks' families. Street looked forward to January 2nd when all the holidays and parties were over. This was not the happiest time of year for him.

Wednesday, the day before Thanksgiving, Street and McCoy found a sealed envelope on their desks. Both envelops were imprinted with the logo of the Boston Police. And both messages were the same.

Detectives Street and McCoy:

I wish you both a Happy Thanksgiving.

We've given you carte blanche on the Charles Hospital investigation since September. You have displayed courage and skill in pursuing the investigation.

However, we have limited resources. Effective this date, we are moving the Charles Hospital investigation into the *inactive* file. As you know, that means it can no longer take priority over other cases.

The deaths of Dr. Sims and Eldridge are officially classified as MURDER:UNSOLVED.

Have a nice holiday.

The Chief

"Mickey, did your note say what mine did?"
"Yup, it sure did."
"Well, Chief, have a nice holiday yourself...you turkey!"

Street figured it was about 20 weeks to the Boston Marathon. There's no way he was crossing the finish line without Sims and Dirk at his side and the killer locked away. Whoever killed the doctors was probably having a better holiday than Street. That could change, too.

"Mickey, did we ever find those three nurses that Dory sent down to Martinique?"

"Sure, I talked to one of them on the phone. I forget her last name. The first name was Cindy. You told me to call her."

"And..."

"And it was a big fat zero. We checked her out. And the two friends that went along. All three had alibis when Sims and Eldridge were killed. We even know what they were doing the night someone shot at you and Ferris in Cambridge."

"What about Dory and Gene World?"

"He's been mending fences since the bunker. What I hear is that Dr. Shiri is in no mood to rock any boats now. They're going to renew GW's contract. Dory is a happy camper."

"It figures that low life comes out smiling. Mickey, why don't I like that guy? You know me. I like most people."

Street continued, "Say, Mickey, here's one for that computer mind of yours. Whatever happened to the car that hit Dirk? We know the crime lab released it. Where do you think it is?"

"Beats me."

"Make a call on it."

Street just kept popping questions. When you're lost, the right way out of the woods is one of 360 points on a compass. If you try long enough, you'll get it.

"Street, that white Monte Carlo is still around. They're going to auction it off with other lost property after the first of the year."

"Mickey, what the hell. Let's take another look at it."

"Come on Street, you're going nowhere on it. That car has been cut open more than any patient at the Charles."

"Mickey, that's funny. For you anyway, let's go."

The Monte Carlo was sitting in a garage in Boston's Dorchester section--in space number 547. Street got the keys and drove it outside.

"OK Street, this is really exciting. Tell me what we're looking for."

"If I knew, I'd look for it."

"Street, this is a waste."

Street and McCoy got on their knees and touched everything in the car. Police stickers indicated what had been removed.

"So, Mickey, where's the radio?"

"Good thinking Street: the radio drove the car. You are really on top of things. Let's go."

"Mickey, I'm serious. Where's the radio?"

"Street, they're usually removed and kept separately. Same for tape decks and special speakers. They even keep the radar detectors."

"Mickey, let's get the radio."

Street tracked down Joker at his apartment in Cambridge.

Joker, this is Street. I thought you'd be gone for Thanksgiving."

"Soon, man. I'm folding my tent here and leaving tonight. Did you call, turkey to turkey?"

"Joker, do me a favor. Mickey and I are over at the impound garage in Dorchester. Do you know where that it?"

"I've done some work there."

"Can you come down now for a few minutes?"

"For a high muckety-muck like you, sure."

"Thanks."

When Joker arrived, Street had the car radio and stereo from the Monte Carlo in his hands.

"Joker, can you hook this thing up. I've got an idea."

"Street, if I can get a TV probe into a faucet in a sealed underground bunker, what do you think?"

Ten minutes later, Joker had rigged the radio and stereo to Street's police car.

"OK Street, now what?"

Mickey's face mirrored the same question. Now what?

"Guys, I want to listen to the radio."

Joker threw his hands in the air.

"Good move, wise one. You brought me down her so you could listen to the radio. Next week, want me downtown so you can try out your telephone? Street, you need a nice long vacation."

Street flipped the radio on. The station was playing classical music.

"Joker, I want to see what stations are pre-selected. Hit the other buttons."

Two other stations were set to classical music.

"Joker, is there a cassette tape in the stereo?"

"Yeah, it's Vivaldi's Four Seasons. So, now you know. Whoever drove this car likes classical music. That means if you check out about one million people in Boston you might get the driver. Congratulations. Have a nice Thanksgiving. This bird's airborne."

McCoy joined in, "Street, this doesn't do us any good. One of the guards in the garage may have switched to a classical station."

"Do you think they also bought a classical music tape and left it in the car. Our killer likes classical music."

On the way back to headquarters Street received a call.

"Street, it's Kate. I'm home in California. You should come out here. The weather's great. I'll be back December 6th. How about dinner that night. This time I'll cook at my place. All you have to do is show up. And maybe bring a great bottle of wine."

"Kate, I'll do you one better. When does your flight arrive?"

"About five PM. It's Flight #233, non stop from LA."

"See you then. Thanks for calling."

Chapter Twenty Nine:
Home Cooking

Dr. Shiri, this is Detective Street. How was Thanksgiving?"

"This has not been a great year. It was sad."

"I know what you mean."

"So, any progress?"

"Not really. I'd like to come by and just talk things out. Maybe I'm missing something. What about tomorrow?"

"Street, late today is better."

"No can do. I'm picking someone up at the airport around five PM."

"OK, tomorrow at two PM."

"See you then."

Street called Mickey to his side.

"I'm seeing Dr. Shiri tomorrow. Can you get Joker to join me?"

"I'll call him. Why are you seeing Dr. Shiri?"

"Remember that car radio? The one tuned to classical music? I remember Dr. Shiri likes classical music."

"Street, that's great. After you interrogate her, why don't you interrogate my sister. And don't forget the Chief. He likes it too. After that, let's go down to Symphony Hall. We'll find lots of suspects there."

"Mickey, ease up a bit, OK?"

Street left for the airport to pick up Kate. She could help him in many ways.

"Welcome back, stranger."

Kate came off the plane wearing a California look. She wore a short yellow skirt with white dots and a white silk blouse. Her sneakers were brand new and her white bobby socks made her look not much more than 17.

"Kate, how do you cross your legs in that thing. It's so short. You're just too hot to be an agent."

"Street, I'm your agent of love. The calls weren't enough. Street, think of the word lust. Then multiply it a few times. Get the picture?"

If those words did not, the kiss did. She pushed her toes up and wrapped her hands around Street's shoulders. Then she took her hands and moved them through his hair as she pushed her tongue into his mouth and rolled it.

"Kate, we could get arrested for this."

"Fine. Make sure you book me overnight."

"So, we're going to your place and you're cooking?"

"And you brought the wine?"

"Deal's a deal."

Street's car was parked at the exit door from the terminal. His OFFICIAL BUSINESS: BOSTON POLICE tag was on the windshield. Street drove through the tunnel to Boston. Then they moved west on Ted Williams Highway, Route 9 for most. Kate's apartment was in Cleveland Circle. That part of Brookline was a mix of apartments with college students and medical employees and beautiful brick estates. Kate rented a carriage house with its own garage.

Street had been there before, but never for dinner. This moment was long overdue.

"Relax, Street. Did you bring a change of clothes?"

"I've got them. Let's get this wine open to breathe a little."

"Street, then you'll tell me about its legs and bouquet and we'll never eat dinner."

"Kate, switch subjects for a second?"

"Sure."

"Dr. Shiri. I'm going to see her tomorrow."

"Good. Tell her I said hi."

"No, listen. I've put some pieces together. I told you Shiri installed a listening system that monitored conversations and telephone calls in many of the 7th Floor offices, yours included."

"I know; she's nosy."

"You know, she likes classical music."

"I didn't know, but that's not a crime. Wait, Street, let me look that one up."

"Smart ass. I get a lot of hassling on that. The car that hit and killed Dirk had a radio that was tuned to classical music."

"Street, that's big. You really need to relax."

Kate flashed a smile, walked over and pinched Street's ear. Her look said *"Silly boy."*

"You're like Mickey. It's not that silly. The killer liked classical music."

"Well, that narrows it down."

"Kate, stop. Would Shiri have any possible motive for killing Sims and Dirk? She's a doctor; so, she could handle the medical part. She could get a syringe with semen and with peanut extract that triggered Sims anaphylactic shock. She had access to Sims' medical records any time she wanted. I just can't get a motive."

"Money. If Sims cured her patient with XM2, it'd cost Gene World a fortune. We checked that possibility out--the money angle. But we looked at Dory. Those words on my calendar, ED, stood for Dory. That's his middle name. You nailed me on the eye doctor thing.

"See, GW couldn't collect on cures, only on treatments. That's in their agreement. In fact, I personally verified that with Dr. Shiri. And they were making a fortune on treatments for pancreatic cancer. A cure would have been ironic. Here they are underwriting the 7th Floor and some doctor stumbles on a cure that would make their treatment almost worthless. Dory had a big-time motive."

"As far as Dr. Shiri goes, that's a dead end. I'd take another look at Dory. Maybe you'll do better than me. Street, I didn't fly three thousand miles to talk about this stuff. Give it a rest."

"You're right. Next time I bring it up, put me out of my misery. You've got my permission."

"That's a deal."

Kate prepared pasta in olive oil with baked whole shrimp spread throughout. Appetizers were juicy red tomatoes on a bed of lettuce with a honey mustard sauce. Dessert was vanilla ice cream balls wrapped in melted chocolate with raspberries on top. There was no coffee.

Street brought two bottles of wine. One was a *Lafite* '76 and the other was a *Mouton* '82. They drank the *Mouton* with dinner and savored the *Lafite* after. Kate had a fire going. Street played a classical CD as they cuddled in front of the fire.

"Street, if I quit the Air Force, would you leave the police? California's a real fun place. You could get a job out there working for law firms. Street, you could make bigger money. I could go back to nursing. No more Boston winters."

"That's a big question. I need time to think. We're talking about some really serious stuff here. I'd still have to come back and run the Marathon in April."

"Street, how fast do you think you could run from here to the bedroom? And how fast could you take my clothes off? And how slow could you make love with me?"

Street lowered Kate into her bed. They were naked. Their clothes left a trail from the kitchen to the bedroom. Kate's bedroom was full of the smell of lilacs. Street remembered that was her favorite. Her skin was soft and oily. Street felt safe and comfortable as he wrapped his legs around her. Kate was talking while they made love. She loved to talk while in bed. She was giving directions just like a traffic cop. Every time she'd talk, it'd drive Street crazy.

"Street, I'm going to lick each of your ten fingers and ten toes. Then I'll move up. You relax and I'll do the driving. Street, take your contacts out. I want to see those wild eyes of yours."

"Kate, you're already driving me nuts."

It was a glorious night of love making. They alternated between love making and sleep through the night. Street's watch alarm sounded exactly at seven AM. He cuddled next to Kate.

"Babe, it's that time. I've got to get up. What about you?"

"I'll wait till you get up and shower."

"Kate, what about something to drink?"

"Look in the *frig*. I think there's some left over juice. It's still OK to drink."

"Kate, I'll bring you some."

"No. I'll stay in bed and sleep a few more minutes. Whatever's there, take it."

Street put on shorts and a T Shirt and lumbered into the kitchen. He put some water on to boil for coffee. That much he could do in a kitchen without causing trouble. Street picked up the phone and dialed home to retrieve his messages. He found his Boston police pen on the kitchen counter and grabbed the back of a laundry slip to write down his messages. His clothes were scattered across the kitchen. Then Street opened the *frig* with his eyes still half closed.

"That looks like juice. Where are the glasses? This coffee cup will do."

Street poured himself a big glass of OJ.

"Damn, this tastes great. It's fresh squeezed. Street drank it all and poured a second cup. Where'd this come from?"

"*WEST FARMS*"

"I've heard that name before. Where? Sims' place. Sims *frig* had fresh squeezed OJ from *West Farms*."

He heard Kate walk in. She moved slowly behind him. Why isn't she sleeping?

"Street, did you drink the OJ? How'd it taste? I forgot about the leftover fresh squeezed in the frig."

"Kate, there was fresh squeezed OJ in Sims *frig*. It also came from *WEST FARMS*".

Kate flashed an ugly look. It was a look Street had never seen before. Her tender smile and warm eyes evaporated. Kate's face reddened and she gritted her teeth. Blood vessels popped out from the sides of her head.

At that instant, Street knew she was with the killer of Sims and Dirk. "Street, your water is boiling. Just like down in the bunker when Marks came to a boil. You remember that, don't you?"

Street looked at Kate. She was smiling in an evil way.

"God, Kate, please tell me it's not you. Was there anything in the OJ?"

Street, who always imagined himself as the hunter, knew he was trapped. The hunter came to a drinking hole and this time it was a glass of OJ. He made a rookie's mistake. He should have read the label first. Curiosity should have prompted him to look. But he never suspected Kate. Who reads labels at 7 AM? Like so many poisoned African watering holes, Street read about in his travel books, this place was quiet and serene and appeared safe.

"So, I'm going to die like Sims. Hell of a way to solve the case."

"But you had a lot more fun." Kate stood twenty feet from Street and ran her hands between her legs in an ugly way. "You'd better say good-bye, quickly.

"Damn you, Street, we had it all. What kind of detective are you? I'm pissed!"

Street's eyes rolled to the ceiling.

"You're pissed? Fuck you. I've got that juice gurgling around inside, and you're 'pissed?'"

"You still don't get it, do you! You and your damn weird eyes. Maybe you're blind. There were millions at stake. Money for both of us. Vacations. Clothes. Cars. A new life. We had it all! I assumed you'd unwrap everything and come running to me. What do you make as a cop? $50,000, tops!

Street's mind was in overdrive. Where was his revolver. Maybe he could grab it and make it outside and get help. Then he saw the bulge under Kate's bathrobe. That was a gun. His or hers--no longer mattered.

Kate looked down and smiled at Street.

"Even you can figure out what's in my pocket. And I know how to use it.

"I've got some of your sperm inside me. What a charming little reminder. And how appropriate. Sort of a reminder about the way I *did* Simsy. Semen! bodily fluids."

Kate saw Street's eyes starting to move in circles.

"You weren't supposed to drink that OJ. Don't you read labels? **West Farms**. Hot shot detective, my ass. Now we're history. Change that! You're history. What waste.

"Street I'll let you die with the answers. You're entitled. Since you didn't ask, I'll tell you. I did it for the money. Does that surprise you? That drug XM2 was my chance for freedom. And I earned a piece of that prize. I had arranged to sell the altered formula to a foreign drug company. Every month I covered up the stupid mistakes of Marks. If the Air Force knew how sloppy Marks was with security, they would have closed down the show on the 7th Floor. Like that money Marks gave Sims to continue experiments on XM2. Can you believe it? He opened a bank account with her. What a fool. And I told Marks. He never listened. He kept the altered formula for XM2 in his head. It was worth hundreds of millions. I just wanted my share. I almost had him convinced to share it with me and the Air Force. If I sold it to another company, people would still get the cure. Marks was so paranoid. He didn't trust anyone. Can you imagine not trusting people, Street?

"I saw Simsy the day after she over-dosed her patient Hays. She told me what happened. What she didn't know was Marks already told me he altered the XM2. It was going to be his next Nobel Prize. I knew Sims had stumbled on his cure. It was the higher dosage that made it work. It was a dosage so high that everyone figured it was lethal. So, it was never administered. But it wasn't lethal. I figured she told Dirk.

"I called her Saturday morning. Dirk told a bunch of people he was going home to do some flying. Sims never went flying with him. I saw Dirk's name on files in Adler's OSI office in Washington. It was easy to figure he was OSI with his family's Air Force background and his Washington trips.

"I cooked up the semen cocktail. Nice touch? All that bitch ever talked about was baseball. It was sickening. Money meant nothing to her. And Dirk, same thing. Sure it meant nothing to him. He was the rich kid from New Hampshire. If he grew up like I did, it'd mean plenty. He kept mentioning Sims wouldn't eat peanuts at ball games. I pulled Sims' records and there it was.

"ALLERGIES: PEANUTS

"I'm a nurse. It was easy to get into the hospital's sperm bank. All I did was mix in some peanut extract.

"Street, she took a long time to die. The bitch knew she was dying."

Street had to make his move. He was getting dizzy. Like a marathon runner, he hit a wall but had to keep going. Whatever was in the OJ made him feel like he was floating. Was this really Kate talking?

"God, this is how Sims felt before she died."

Kate was walking around the kitchen. She pulled Street's revolver from her bathrobe.

"Killing Dirk wasn't hard. I overheard him talking. I knew where he was going. And he always rode his bike to work. Dirk probably saved Hays' life. I was going to do him like I did Ferris' patient. I had an OSI car. They're invisible. Our no-trace mystery cars. I scraped it on the way out of the garage. No big deal. After I whacked him, I got into Adler's car. That was almost a mistake. I thought I'd catch Dirk sooner. I didn't intend to run him down so close to Adler's car. I called Adler just before leaving the hospital and asked him to meet me. When I called, he moved fast. I was lucky. Adler was in town for the week. I told him I thought someone was following me. Adler's a goof. He didn't see me do it. His car was two blocks away. When he saw the crowd, I told him someone was hurt and I tried to help."

Street knew his time was getting short.

"And you, my dear, don't blame me for the Cambridge shooting. I was aiming for Ferris. I caught a late flight back from DC and returned to Washington in the morning. You never imagined I snuck in a quick round trip.

"One more thing, Street. ED never stood for Dory. You couldn't figure that one. Reverse the letters. ED to DE...Dirk Eldridge. My fellow OSI agent. Even Sims and Ernie didn't know he was in the OSI.

"My valium cocktail works fast. Feel comfy, Street? Try yelling for help, Street, and the words won't come out. Don't trouble yourself about the OJ either. If you didn't drink it, I was going to put some in your coffee. You just couldn't say good-bye to this case. If you could have left it alone, who knows."

Beecher reached for Street's big blue and white Boston Police pen.

"Street, you're such a loser. You handed these dumb pens out collecting fingerprints. That's minor league stuff. I'm fuckin' sick of these ugly things. If only you could have let go of this case, things would have been different with us."

Beecher threw the pen to the floor, crushing it under her feet.

"That's the last I'll see of your pens. Street, it's kind of appropriate, isn't it. When we first met, you used one of these pens to get my fingerprints. Now, when we say farewell, there's another pen around. Maybe we were just pen pals?"

Street thought, "Dumb bitch, she just activated the transmitter in the pen. If it's working, that pen gave my location and it's now flashing red at headquarters. The smart ones make the stupid mistakes."

"Street, you're going to be electrocuted in the bathtub. I told you not to take the little TV in there. That's very dangerous. Street, they'll find your body in about two hours. I promise to wear black to your funeral. It should be a big crowd."

Beecher noticed Street was smiling.

"Street, what's so funny? You're going to die."

"Kate, how about a farewell toast of wine?"

Street, lying on the floor, reached up and grabbed an opened bottle of wine.

"I don't trust you, Street. Maybe you laced it with something. If you want a bon voyage toast, drink up!"

Now Street was seeing double. He was listening to a Kate he never knew. Street was relaxed and terrified at the same instant. He was losing control. He was hearing voices. He thought he heard Sims and Dirk.

"Street, you promised you'd run the Marathon with us."

Street thought he saw the finish line. Was he hallucinating like Marks? He took one last deep breath. Street lunged for the stove, grabbed the boiling water and threw it in Beecher's face. It was a direct hit. She screamed.

"You fucker, I can't see. My face. You bastard. My face! You're dead anyway. You're dead, Street."

Street grabbed the half emptied bottle of wine and took a drink. He then tossed it in the air and it smashed to the ground. If Joker's pen didn't work, he could imagine the headlines.

DETECTIVE JIMMY STREET FOUND DEAD IN BATHTUB. CITY MOURNS HERO COP

This was his twilight zone. Street was falling asleep; Beecher was screaming.

Chapter Thirty:
The Finish Line

T he finish line for the Boston Marathon is on Boylston
Street near Copley Square. The mid April day was crisp
and bright. Another long winter was gone and summer
was near. There, in Hopkington, buried in a field of
thousands of runners, was Jimmy Street.

It was a glorious run, his best ever. Street smiled all the way.

Detective Jimmy Street finished near the very end of the pack.
It was his slowest time. Street did not care because he was
running with two friends. He saw their faces and felt the warmth
of their hands with every step. He'd never run a race holding
hands the whole way. Sims was on one side and Dirk on the
other. He knew that somehow they were with him for the
marathon. He could feel their hands. Street made a promise to
himself and kept it.

As Street struggled for the finish line, he was saying good-bye
to two dead doctors. And maybe to his dad, his dead partner,
and to his ex-wife.

Street ran with rubber legs across the finish line. Or maybe
the finish line ran to him. McCoy came up and handed Street his
traditional victory cigar.

Joker was there, too.

"Joker, this is your race too. And I want a lifetime supply of
your big police pens."

"Street, you human dynamo. Check my new lighter out. I'm
testing it on your victory cigar."

Joker's lighter shot a flame two feet into the air. It lit Street's
cigar and McCoy's shirt.

FIC
Tan

Tanger, Woody.

The dead cure.

DATE			